M000032777

TOO NEAR THE DEAD

A NOVEL BY

Helen Grant

Too Near The Dead
Helen Grant

© Helen Grant 2021

The author asserts the moral right to be identified
as the author of the work in accordance with the
Copyright, Designs and Patents Act, 1988.

This is a work of fiction. Any resemblance to actual persons, living or
dead, or actual events is purely coincidental.

All rights reserved. No part of this publication may be reproduced,
stored in a retrieval system or transmitted in any form or by any means,
electronic, mechanical, photocopying, recording or otherwise, without
the prior permission of
Fledgling Press Ltd,
1 Milton Road West, Edinburgh, EH15 1LA

Published by Fledgling Press, 2021
Cover Design: Graeme Clarke
graeme@graemeclarke.co.uk

ISBN 9781912280407
www.fledglingpress.co.uk

Printed and bound by:
Print on Demand Worldwide, Peterborough

For my mother, Joan

Chapter One

First, sleep so profound that it is like Death: without the smallest spark of consciousness to light the darkness, without the dimmest sense of the passage of time. I am not myself; I am nothing.

Waking is ponderous and full of resistance, like struggling in a tar pit. I am dredged up from sleep; it wants to suck me back down into itself. My eyelids are heavy – so terribly heavy. I lie there, unmoving, thinking about opening my eyes but not doing it, while the minutes ooze past, slow as syrup.

The air is warm – perhaps a little too warm. There is a stale taste to it. My mouth is dry. Awareness is beginning to return to me, like bubbles rising to the surface of dark water.

It's normal for me to sleep on my back; I've always done it, ever since I was a child. But the posture I've been sleeping in is a strange one. I've been hugging myself, I think. Am I hurt in some way?

No. I'm not hugging myself, not exactly. My forearms are crossed over my sternum in an oddly formal way. My right hand is draped over the left. My fingers have a muffled feel to them, a lack of sensitivity. It takes me a few moments of rubbing my hands together to realise that I am wearing thin gloves.

Surprise finally forces my eyes open. I expect dim light. Instead there is blackness, a darkness so absolute that for an instant I think I have been struck blind. I squeeze my eyes shut, and see the tiny sparks produced by my own retinas, but when I open them again there is nothing but black.

I can feel the first stirrings of alarm. *Calm down,* I tell myself. *It's just very dark. There are no street lights here.*

There should be *something* though, shouldn't there? I open my eyes as wide as I can, straining to see some dim outline of the room, but I can't pick out a single thing. It's quiet, too. My own breathing, a little accelerated, is loud in my ears. There's an oddly resonant quality to it.

Switch on the bedside lamp. That's the obvious thing to do. I always sleep on the same side of the bed, and the lamp should be on my left. All I have to do is reach out and feel for the switch on the cord.

I start to unfold my arm to reach out, but almost immediately my elbow comes into contact with a hard surface. The bedside table and the lamp are not there. I try to make sense of this. Is it possible that I have moved around so much in my sleep that I am actually lying across the bed, pressed up against the wall? I try to stretch out with my right arm to feel the mattress beneath me. When my right elbow hits a hard surface too, I freeze.

Calm down, calm down. Just think about this.

Have I somehow rolled right off the bed during the night without waking myself up, so that I am lying jammed between the bed and the bedside cabinet? I try to wriggle in the space, to twist my shoulders, with no effect other than a crisp rustling sound. I turn my head from side to side and there is a crackle of fabric there too.

My tenuous grip on my own composure is fading fast. I can feel myself sliding towards a black pit of hysteria.

Unable to move my upper body, I kick out instead and almost immediately my foot hits something. In spite of the immediate impulse to flail like a trapped animal, at some level it registers that I have *shoes on*. I'm not barefoot, as I undoubtedly was when I got into bed. I can tell this from the hard little knocking sound my foot makes when it strikes whatever is above it, and from the way the impact travels through my toes without causing them any actual pain.

I have an image then in my head, of a doll carefully dressed up and wrapped in tissue paper, and placed in a box. I am not a doll, but there is only one other situation I can think of in which a fully-dressed figure could be enclosed in a space like this one, and I don't want to consider that; I am afraid I will lose all control.

Information, that is what I need. Assess the situation, like a paramedic at an accident scene. I start with my hands. The gloves are thin, and they are close-fitting. It will be difficult to draw them off in this enclosed space. I try anyway, because it is a relief to concentrate on this one small task. I have enough room to move my wrists, so eventually I manage to pull the glove off my right hand, although it turns completely inside out in the process, as though I'm skinning myself. With my bare fingers I explore the glove on my other hand. It is clearly designed for elegance rather than warmth. I can feel a little frill at the wrist, a froth of fine lace. There is a tiny button too, just to the side of the pulse point.

My bare hand creeps over my breast, exploring. I am not wearing a nightdress. Whatever I have on is far more structured than that. The fabric has a slight stiffness to it, and a satiny slipperiness, but I can also detect a very fine texture. I think it may be a heavy silk. I can feel rows of tiny pintucks running down the bodice, and over my sternum

9

there is a long line of dainty buttons. Experimentally, I breathe in deeply and expand my chest. I can feel the grip of the dress on my body; I think it is boned. There is very little room to move my legs, but I can feel heavy skirts around them; the fabric whispers with every movement.

This is not a garment that anyone would wear to sleep in. In fact, it's not something you would see anyone wearing nowadays except in very specific circumstances. A dress like this might pass in a costume drama, or at a very formal event – depending on the colour, perhaps a wedding.

My fingers pass over the neck of the dress and slide up my throat, snagging on a curl of hair that lies against it. Then they move up to my jaw, and then my ear, where I find a small drop earring fixed: a pearl, I think, judging from the glossy feel of it.

I can feel a crisp light fabric against the back of my hand. It's all around my head, as though I have been packed in it.

A veil, I think. I explore further, to see what is holding it on my head, and find a headpiece made of what feel like wax flowers and berries. There is no further doubt about it. I am dressed as a bride.

I slide my hand carefully down to my breast again and then I lie perfectly still for a while. I think the thing that has prevented me losing control so far is the sheer improbability of the situation. It has to be a mistake; there has to be something I'm failing to grasp.

There is one piece of the puzzle that I don't have yet. Still, I don't move straight away. If there is something unthinkable to face, I want to have those last few moments of ignorance before it bursts in on me. So I lie there and listen to the sound of my own breathing, and feel the gentle motion of my chest rising and falling. The air still has that stale taste, and it seems to me that it is less refreshing than before; I have to draw in a little harder to get enough of it.

At last I put up my hand hesitantly, and test the space in front of my face. In all the time I've been lying here, it hasn't got any easier to see. My eyes haven't adjusted because there is absolutely no light. The darkness above me tells me nothing: it might go on forever, like the vast reaches of outer space.

It doesn't, though. My fingertips meet a flat, hard surface. I let them skate over it, testing for edges, finding none. Then I put the palms of both hands against it and push as hard as I can, to no effect.

I'm breathing really hard now, sucking at what little air is left. I pound on the surface above me.

"Hey!" I shout as loudly as I can, almost deafening myself in the enclosed space. "Let me out! Let me out!"

I yell and yell until it isn't really words any more, nor even vaguely human-sounding: it's the sound of an animal dying in a trap. I struggle and fight but there isn't room for anything; I only succeed in bruising my forehead on the hard surface above me.

The air is running out. I am going to die. I have been buried alive.

Chapter Two

I wake hyperventilating and slick with perspiration, my hands clenched into fists and the echo of my own screams ringing in my ears. I gasp and cough and shiver, shaking my dark hair back from my face. Tears ooze from the corners of my eyes. It is a long, long time before I am calm enough to breathe without choking or even recognise where I am. The relief of being *out* is intense, but all I can think about is the horror of being *in*. Inside the coffin. Buried.

At this moment I don't ever want to close my eyes again. I roll onto my side and fumble for the light switch with clumsy fingers. A *click*, and the bedroom is illuminated with soft golden light. The room is cool and quiet. I almost wish there was some noise: traffic, music, distant sirens like I used to hear in London. But we're a long way from the main road here, and it's not like many cars go past at this time of night anyway.

My alarm clock shows me that it's 03:17. I stare at it for a while. In a little over four hours it will ring, but the time between now and then stretches out like an abyss. Weary as I am, I dare not go back to sleep. What just happened didn't feel like a dream, although I know that's what it must have been. It felt *real*. In every other dream I've had, I could see and hear things vividly, but I've never been able to *touch* things like that, and feel them under my fingers: the crisp fabric, the polished wood. The thought of it makes me queasy.

In the end I sit up, throwing back the duvet, and slide out of bed. My robe is lying over the back of a chair. While I am putting the sleeves the right way through and sliding my arms into it and tying the belt I look around me, reassuring myself that I am really here, in my own bedroom. In *our* own bedroom.

It's still too new to me to feel properly familiar. Other times, even when I haven't had some horrible nightmare that felt too intensely real to be pure imagination, I've been disorientated on waking. Part of me still expects to see my old bedroom in the flat come swimming into focus around me. The window there was on my right, so the morning light always came from that side. The building was old, and the window frames didn't fit very well, so even if there was no wind or rain to rattle them, the vibration of passing cars would do it. And of course the room was a lot smaller than this one, and crowded with shabby furniture.

This room doesn't look lived-in, not yet. There are removers' boxes stacked up against the walls, still sealed with tape. The walls are mirrorless and pictureless. The curtains, transferred from the flat, are too small for the big window: they barely stretch across it, and they are a couple of centimetres too short. With no rug beside the bed (I still haven't found the box with that inside), I have to put my bare feet straight onto cold floorboards. The quiet here, the absence of city sounds, make the place feel isolated, but the loneliest thing of all is the expanse of smooth, unwrinkled sheet on the other side of the double bed.

James is in Madrid, being lionised by his Spanish publisher. He's messaged me with photos of the reception he went to, and the chic restaurant they had dinner in, and his elegant room in the boutique hotel where they're putting him up. He's doing his best to make me feel included in everything, but I'm painfully aware of the fact that he's over there, and I'm here alone. We didn't plan it like that. A year ago, when the trip to Spain was organised, we didn't foresee what we'd be doing now, nor where we'd be. Everything has changed since then.

I pad downstairs to the kitchen, switching on all the lights as I go. The kitchen is cold. It even *smells* cold. There's a subtle but pervasive odour of something chemical – fresh paint or cleaning fluid. The expensive stainless steel range cooker has never been used, so there are no lingering smells of warm food and no residual warmth from it. There isn't even the aroma of freshly-made filter coffee that used to hang over the kitchen of the London flat, because it's James who is the coffee drinker, and James isn't here. I'm strictly a tea drinker. I like my tea the colour of teak oil, very sweet, and with hardly any milk. I'd never normally drink it if I woke up in the middle of the night, because it would probably stop me getting to sleep again, but right now sleep is the last thing I want. If I could stay awake forever, I would. So I find a mug and a teabag and stand there hugging myself against the cold air and waiting for the kettle to boil. The hissing sound as the element heats the water is comforting. It's too quiet here. Sometimes I'll be working on something during the day and there will be a gap in the birdsong outside and the silence will be so absolute that it makes my ears ring.

Peace is a good thing, I remind myself. There is too much noise pollution in the city, the same as there's too much light pollution. In London, I would look up at the night sky and it would be that strange opaque colour, somewhere between grey and yellow, that comes from too much artificial light. Here, you can look up and see hundreds, probably thousands, of stars, set into velvety

14

blackness. It's beautiful, and if it's also a little strange, that's just because I'm not used to it. That's why it makes me feel a little… unsettled. It would be easier if James was here – if he was moving about the house during the day, and breathing softly beside me during the night.

The kettle boils and I move to make the tea. I deliberately avoid raising my eyes to the cupboard above the work surface. The whole kitchen is done out in charcoal grey, the doors of the drawers and cupboards finished to a high gloss so that every movement is mirrored in their murky depths. To see my own face, leaden-hued as though dead, looming up at me, is more than my nerves can stand at this moment.

It was a dream, I say to myself. *Just a dream.* But my hands are starting to tremble and the teaspoon rattles against the side of the mug. I can feel it again, the rising panic, the nauseating horror of being tightly closed in on all sides. The impenetrable, terrible dark. The thickness of the air, the tightening in my throat and chest. The need to scream and scream but the knowledge that it will do no good at all, because no-one can hear me.

The mug slips from my fingers and explodes on the slate floor tiles, spattering my bare legs with hot tea. I shake and shake, until my teeth chatter. I look down at the broken shards of china and the streaks of tea bursting out from the impact point, but I don't trust myself to try clearing them up. My hands are trembling so much that I will surely cut myself to ribbons.

Instead, I step back, away from the whole mess, and then I turn my back on it and make my way tremulously across the kitchen, shoulders hunched, my legs feeling weak under me. I'm not even going to try to make more tea. There are a couple of bottles standing on the work surface – some of the first things unpacked from a box I opened at random, and not yet put away. The nearest one is a stubby brown bottle of brandy, which is not something I normally drink: I inherited it, literally. I don't bother looking for a glass; instead I find a tin mug, which won't break even if I drop it from a great height, and I pour a generous measure of the brandy into that. With the brandy burning a warm trail down my throat I start to feel a little better.

I don't want to go back to bed, nor even into the bedroom. I know that's something I'll have to do – it would be ridiculous not to – but I'd rather wait until the sun is up and light is streaming through the window. I go through into the living room, where shrouded furniture is reflected in the plate glass windows that run from floor to ceiling. Beyond their nebulous shapes there is nothing to be seen, because there are no lights out there; there are no other houses within view of this one. In daylight I am proud of this room, of its magnificent size, but now it feels comfortless and exposed. I keep going, out through the other door, and into James's study.

Here, there are at least curtains to draw and a high-backed armchair to curl up in, and enough of James's things lying around that I can imagine he might walk in at any moment.

I could call him, of course. He wouldn't be annoyed if I did, even though it must be half past three in the morning – half past four in Madrid. He keeps odd hours himself, especially when he's nearly at the end of a book; he's been known to get out of bed in the small hours because he can't bear not to keep writing. I could phone him at the hotel and he'd say, "What's up, Fen?" sounding sleepy or maybe not sleepy at all because he'd been sitting up jotting down thoughts for his next project, keeping himself awake with black coffee.

Yes, I could call him, but I'm not going to, not even for

the comfort of hearing his familiar voice. What would I tell him? That's the thing. Of all the people in the world, the last person I could tell about that horrible, claustrophobic dream, that nightmare of being closely imprisoned in my own wedding dress, is the man I am engaged to marry.

Chapter Three

I never expected to be rich. I guess I'm still not rich in the having-four-different-houses and travelling-by-private-jet and wearing-a-tiara-to-dinner sort of way. But I never thought I'd have enough money to give up my regular job for something far less secure. I never thought I'd be able to buy my own home, let alone somewhere like Barr Dubh House. I'd made my bed, and I was lying on it.

Truthfully, I didn't expect to be getting married, either. That's still a surprise, when I think about it.

I spent a lot of time inside James's imagination before I ever actually met him. Editors and publicists meet the authors; copyeditors less often. I was working on someone else's book when James's novel hit my desk. I remember the other book was a spy thriller, which wasn't my favourite genre to begin with, and it had had several rounds of structural edits, as a result of which the manuscript was riddled with little inconsistencies. It was also overdue, and as I worked my way through it I began to suspect that everyone involved had lost the will to do anything further with it. It was disheartening to be typing comments like "Didn't this character die on page 21?" when I was on page 237. The whole job was so consuming at the time that I didn't give a lot of thought to the next one until it was done.

I finished working on the spy thriller on a Friday and I downloaded James's manuscript to look at over the weekend. I liked to read a whole work through before looking at the fine detail – except, perhaps, in the case of the spy thriller, which I would rather not have read at all. I had no particular expectations of James's book. At that time, James Sinclair wasn't a well-known name. I hadn't read his debut novel, which had done tolerably well but wasn't a bestseller.

When I got back to the place where I lived, the couple on the ground floor were having another party. Even if I'd been stone deaf, I would have known from the vibrations that ran through the building. As it was, I was glad for once that I was on the top floor, in spite of all the stairs. On the second floor, Mrs. Khan was looking out through a crack in the door. She rolled her eyes, and I grimaced back at her. We both knew that it was pointless going downstairs to complain. The party throwers would probably have turned the music up, if it were possible to turn it up any higher. I toiled my way up the last flight of stairs, let myself into the flat and closed the door behind me.

I knew it was sad to be working on a Friday night. I held out for a bit, while I made myself a plate of pasta in an unappetising sauce and ate it in front of the news. Eventually, though, I gave in. It wasn't as though I had anything else planned, after all. I booted up my laptop and opened the file with James's book in it.

The Unrepentant Dead, by James Sinclair – that was the title. I had a glass of red wine at my elbow and I took a sip before going any further. The title was intriguing, even if it was a bit grim. I considered it for a moment, and then I scrolled down to the beginning of the text and began to read.

If this were a romantic film, I would have read the

entire book at one sitting and fallen in love with James on the spot because of his soulful prose. I didn't read the whole book that evening, and I didn't fall in love with James, either. But I read about a quarter of it, and when I stopped it was simply because it was too good to gorge upon. I've read a lot of books by anyone's standards, both as an ordinary reader, and professionally as a copyeditor. James's book was special. My copyeditor's brain noted that he made very few mistakes with grammar or spelling. Of course, everyone makes a few, however careful they are, but James was very correct, which was a great relief after the last job. That wasn't what made his book stand out though. It was such an original idea. It was based on a legend common in both Scotland and Ireland, of the *sluagh,* the restless dead – spirits who return to this world, flying out of the west like a flock of birds, to steal away the souls of those who are close to death. James hadn't simply made a ghost story out of this. He had made it into an allegory for the malign influences of the past, against which his heroine struggled to assert herself. The book was tender, tragic and occasionally horrific; it was weird and beautiful. It was also a book with *heart.* It's hard to explain what I mean by that. It didn't feel as though he had tried to write what he thought would sell, or written to impress. It felt as though the author had really written his own feelings into the book.

Was I curious about the person behind this amazing book? Yes. Did I rush off and look at his website, or look to see whether he was on Twitter or Instagram? No. The truth was, the more I read of his book, the more I loved it, the less I wanted to know about James Sinclair. I'd heard enough tales from my colleagues, of authors who wrote beautiful, sensitive novels and were narcissistic monsters in real life. If James Sinclair was like that, I didn't want to know. Nor did I want to know if he was old or hard-looking or avuncular. I had a sense of the shape of him, of his personality, through the way that he wrote, and I wanted to hang onto it, even if it was a mirage.

I read the rest of *The Unrepentant Dead* that weekend, finishing the bottle of wine as I did so, and on Monday morning I started again from the beginning, this time as a copyeditor. Amendments were highlighted, and any comments I added appeared to the right of the text, to remain in the file until the author had read and – hopefully – accepted the changes.

Most of the time I confined myself to the usual things: correcting typos and checking for inconsistencies. At the denouement of the story, however, I couldn't resist commenting. *This is amazing,* I typed in the comments. I really meant it.

When I'd finished working on James's book, I was straight onto the next manuscript – this time a historical romance. The author of that particular work had a persistent habit of using commas and semi-colons instead of full stops, so that reading her work was rather like listening to someone who never shut up, not even to draw breath. I didn't give *The Unrepentant Dead* much thought until a number of weeks later, when it turned up in my inbox again. James and his editor had agreed on some very last minute though minor changes – I forget why – and the editor wanted me to take a final look at the manuscript.

By that time, there was not much to look at. James had accepted most of my previous amendments, so the marks showing that there was a change had nearly all vanished. The changes he had made since then were uncontroversial. Then I came to the climax of the story, where my comment, *This is amazing,* still remained. Underneath it was a comment in a different colour. *Thank you Fen,* it said.

21

I was illogically pleased with this simple exchange. I spent most of my working life pointing out the errors in other people's work, so it was nice to express appreciation and be acknowledged in return. I was almost sorry to have to delete the comments and send the file off again.

The critics agreed with me about *The Unrepentant Dead.* It was reviewed enthusiastically, and then it won a major book prize. The prize didn't bring a lot of money with it, but it brought literary glory. That is not to say that it propelled the book onto the bestseller list either, but it made the publisher we both worked with very eager to hang onto James: prize-winning authors brought them a lot of cachet. Suddenly there were enormous reproductions of the book's cover all over the office. All of this meant that there was a certain amount of pressure on James to produce another book, and produce it quickly, before the momentum was lost. Never mind that it had taken him three years to write the last one.

All the same, he managed it. The next manuscript that eventually pinged into my inbox was shorter than the last one had been, and I thought that you could tell that it had been written under time pressure. There were more little inaccuracies for me to pick up. It was still brilliant, though. He had an intense, vivid style of writing – whether the scene was a cobbled city street or an expanse of moorland, he brought it to life, utterly – but he managed it deftly, without overdosing the reader with lengthy descriptions.

If, like me, you have worked for years correcting and polishing manuscripts, it's easy to become brusque about it. There is no use pussyfooting about, after all, especially not when the deadline is looming. With James's book, though, I did my very best to be diplomatic. I liked his writing too much to do otherwise. By the time I had finished going through the manuscript, it was bristling with red corrections and comments explaining them, but I'd added a few remarks of my own. *I love this*, I said of one moment of electrifying suspense, and of the redemptive scene at the end of the novel, simply: *Beautiful.*

I did see that manuscript again before it was published, and at first I thought all my comments had simply been removed, along with all the suggested amendments that had been accepted. The first ones certainly had. I was faintly disappointed, and then embarrassed. Perhaps I'd struck a wrong note, sounding pathetically starstruck, or perhaps my comments had simply come across as insincere, like those people whose favourite and indiscriminately-applied adjective is "incredible". But then I came to the final scene, and underneath my comment was another one from James Sinclair: *Thank you for your comments, Fen.* I looked at that for a moment. When I closed my laptop, I was smiling to myself.

Several months passed, and then one afternoon when I was deeply engrossed in my work, I heard voices outside the office door. I didn't look up. People quite often had tours around our offices – prospective interns or authors, and occasionally book bloggers. They tended to home in on the enormous shelf of free books, rather than lingering around the copyeditors' desks.

Then someone cleared their throat right in front of my desk and I nearly jumped out of my skin. I looked up into a face I didn't recognise, with dark intelligent eyes and sharp cheekbones. I was so flustered that when he said, "Are you Fen Munro?" I very nearly said, "No."

But I nodded, and he said, "I'm James Sinclair." He smiled at me, and his rather severe features were suddenly engaging. He said, "I had a meeting here and I wanted to drop in and thank you for your comments on the book. Well, both books. You were very diplomatic."

"I wasn't being diplomatic," I said. "I really liked them." I was doing my best not to stare at him. Then I winced inside; *liked* didn't sound enthusiastic enough. I should have said I *loved* them.

He didn't seem to mind. "Well, you were kinder than the copyeditor who worked on my first book, anyway."

"That was probably Gen–" I began to say, before stopping myself. "I mean, Suzanne Caan, right? She's a legend for her bluntness."

He looked at me for a moment and then he grinned. "You were going to say Genghis, weren't you?"

"Shhh," I said urgently. Then I lowered my voice and said, "Yes." There was something infectious about his amusement, but all the same, I really hoped he wouldn't repeat the name to anyone else. "She's alright – she's just a little..."

"Brutal?" he suggested.

I bit my lip, trying not to laugh. "A bit."

"I hope–" he started to say, but he was interrupted; someone put their head around the door and announced that his taxi had arrived.

"Got to go," he said. "It was good to meet you, Fen."

"It was nice to meet you too," I said, but I'm not sure he even heard me; he was halfway out of the door already. I didn't see him again for half a year.

Chapter Four

Sunlight is shining on my closed eyes. This time I wake from a true, deep and dreamless sleep to an orange glow behind my eyelids. I open my eyes and blink at the bright morning light.

I've been lying across the armchair in James's study, with my head pressed against one of the padded wings and my legs over the armrest, bare feet dangling. I strongly suspect I have been sleeping with my mouth open, drooling a bit. Worse, the moment I start to move, I can feel various bits of my body protesting: my neck, my lower back, my right arm. Everything feels stiff.

Uncoiling myself slowly and painfully from the chair, I see the tin mug lying on its side on the floorboards. There is a sticky residue of brandy at its lip, though seemingly I managed to drink nearly all of it before I fell asleep.

Everything in the room – the chair, the mug, the small stain on the boards – is very clearly delineated by the strong light streaming through the gap in the curtains. I rub my eyes. I thought I'd drawn the curtains right across, wanting to shut out the unfriendly night. Apparently I didn't. I drift over to the window, and pull them back, wincing at the sunshine.

Outside the window there is a strip of gravel path, a patch of earth that will eventually be a flower bed, and a fence. Beyond the fence is an expanse of rough pasture, stretching away to the treeline perhaps three hundred metres away. Now, at the very end of summer, the pasture is green and overgrown.

The land belongs to Barr Dubh House; it was one of the reasons we chose this place. We don't have any livestock to graze on it, but it will be a wonderful buffer of peace and solitude, a perfect environment for James's writing. It's also an unimaginable luxury: a house with actual *land*. In London, I didn't even have a window box. It's still very hard to take in – the change in our lives, and everything that goes with it.

As I stare out of the window, my eye is drawn to movement at the treeline. It's too far away for me to see clearly what it is. Not an animal, that's for sure, although the solicitor who handled the sale of Barr Dubh to us told us we might see deer: I see a patch of colour that clearly isn't fur.

Lilac, I think, and then: *No, lavender.* That's the right name for that shade of light purple.

I squint at it. It must be a person, but I can't quite work out what they're wearing. Whatever it is, it's voluminous: fabric seems to billow out from it, so that the movement seems to take the form of a series of surges. I briefly wonder if I'm seeing something other than a human figure – a piece of tarpaulin or tent fabric blowing in the wind? But there is no other movement; the trees and grass are unruffled.

A person then.

But whoever it is, it's not as though they are wandering right past the house staring in through the windows. I watch for a few moments longer and the patch of lavender dwindles and vanishes. Presumably the person has stepped into the shadows under the trees. I wait, but they don't reappear.

Maybe there's a path over there. I make a mental note to go and have a look later. Then I turn away from the window and head for the kitchen. What I need right now is very hot, very strong, very sweet tea.

An hour later, I'm in the car, heading for the town. It's not far in miles, but it takes longer than you'd think, because of all the twists and turns, not to mention the uneven road surface on the stretch between Barr Dubh House and the main road. There is also a triangular warning sign with a stag on it, galloping at full tilt. I have no idea how seriously to take this. Perhaps deer are as rare as yetis on the roads here, and the local council are just covering themselves. Or perhaps there is a real danger that I will come around a corner and find one charging across the road, tossing its antlered head at me. I go cautiously, just in case. I pass a few cars going the other way, to the town further up the valley. I also see a tractor with some terrifying-looking agricultural machinery attached to it. Mostly though, it's just me following the serpentine route of the road, like a leaf borne downstream on a current. On one side of me are fields and a distant hill, and on the other, a forested slope. We have very few neighbours. There is hardly anyone at all living between us and the town.

Even when I get to the edge of the town, the place does not immediately open itself up to me. The first houses I pass are large Victorian mansions, set well back from the road in mature gardens with tall shrubs and hedges discouraging the idle gaze. The park with its jolly-looking bandstand seems deserted; I suppose by now the schools have gone back.

I park in the square with its dried-up fountain, a monumental creation of polished granite. I suspect this town had a heyday, and quite a lot of time has passed since then. But it's still grand, in a faded sort of way. Most of

27

the buildings around the square look as though they date to the nineteenth century, and even if at least one of them has what looks like a small shrub growing from the top of it, the balconies and pediments and bay windows are impressive.

I get out of the car and stand for a moment on the pavement, looking around me. In a year's time, I suppose, this place will be as familiar to me as the London streets around my flat were. I will probably be on nodding terms with people I haven't even met yet. At this point in time, however, I don't know a single soul in the entire town. Even the solicitor was from Perth.

Anyway, pretty soon I'm going to have made my first introduction. I'm here on a mission. It takes me a minute to orient myself – I have no idea whether the High Street numbers run up or down the hill – but after that, it's not difficult to find what I'm looking for. This isn't a huge town, after all – there are two main streets and most of the shops are on one of them.

It's a smart little boutique with glossy white paintwork and shiny windows, incongrously chic between two shabby-looking shops. *McBryde's* says the fascia, and underneath in smaller letters: *everything for your wedding.* I wonder whether the name is really the proprietor's, or simply a truly terrible attempt at humour. At any rate the window display is beautiful, showcasing a gorgeous gown with a fitted bodice and full skirt made of ivory raw silk, with a tartan sash across it in soft shades of blue, green and grey. The bride's outfit is centre stage, but slightly behind it is a matching outfit for the groom, the kilt in the same tartan as the sash, and the sporran covered with silvery grey fur.

I look at these things, and for a moment I hesitate. James is the one with Scottish ancestry, after all; I feel like a bit of a fraud looking at tartan wedding gear.

The woman in the shop is reading a book when I come in. She puts it down before the door has even swung closed behind me, but with my bibliophile's eye I've already noted that it's a copy of *The Thirty-Nine Steps*, and an old one at that, with its orange and white cover design.

"I know," she says, seeing me looking at it. "I should probably be reading *Brides* magazine or something." She grins at me, her face freckled under a corona of russet curls. I warm to her already. "I'm Seonaid McBryde," she tells me.

"Oh. So the shop is really–"

"Named after me, yes. My friend said I should go the whole hog and call the shop McBride's with an i, but I thought that would be cheesy." She puts her head on one side. "And what can I do for you?"

"I'm getting married next year."

"Ooh, congratulations." She sounds as though she means it, even though she must hear this from every single customer who comes in. "Are you getting married locally, then?"

"Yes," I say, a little self-consciously. "We live here. Well, we do now. We've bought a house a couple of miles out of town."

I end up telling her probably a lot more than she really wants to know, about our plans for Barr Dubh House and our old life in London and the jobs we haven't entirely left behind but hope to carry on up here, with me freelancing rather than commuting to an office. James has only been away a few days and I've spoken to him, and to my best friend, Belle, on the phone, but I've missed having proper human contact.

"So your fiancé's a writer?" asks Seonaid. "What's his name? Maybe I've heard of him."

29

"James Sinclair," I say. "He wrote *The Unrepentant—*"

"*The Unrepentant Dead*?" Seonaid finishes for me. "Wow, so he's *that* James Sinclair? He's famous, then."

"Not really," I protest, but I'm quite pleased anyway on James's behalf.

"I loved that book," she says.

"Me too," I tell her. "I mean, not just because he's my fiancé. I worked on the book as a copyeditor before I even met him, and I thought it was amazing."

"Please tell me you're going to let me dress you *and* your bridesmaids," said Seonaid. She grins. "There's not another wedding dress supplier for twenty miles around, anyway."

I laugh a little at that. "I'm only having one bridesmaid," I tell her. "And we're not having a *huge* wedding. We wanted something..." I think for a moment. "Understated but tasteful."

It's almost comical the extent to which her face falls at this. She says. "At least tell me you're planning to wear a long white dress, and not a dove-grey trouser suit or something."

"Not a trouser suit," I say. "A dress. Maybe even a long dress. Only not white. White just makes me looked washed out. With my dark hair and eyes I just look like a vampire in it."

"Ivory?" Seonaid suggests hopefully, but I shake my head.

"I was thinking of a more definite colour than that."

She looks at me with a critical eye. "Blue? I could see you in blue. There are some styles that would look fabulous made up in cornflower blue." She considers. "But what about your fiancé? Is he going to wear a kilt? We should check what colours the Sinclair tartan has."

"Maybe," I say. "We haven't one hundred per cent decided about that."

30

"I can check for you just in case," she suggests. "You wouldn't want to clash, after all."

"Well actually," I say, "I did have an idea about the colour." It's true, I did, and I might have had to think for a moment before putting a name to it, if I hadn't seen something that exact shade already today. "I was thinking about lavender."

There is a silence.

"Lavender?" Seonaid says slowly.

"Yes," I say. "I love that colour. I guess it's my *favourite* colour." And I go rambling on about how it's a little bit warmer than blue somehow, and it reminds me of the flower, and I love the smell of that too. Gradually I realise that Seonaid isn't saying anything, and she isn't nodding or smiling either. She looks perplexed.

"What?" I say. I raise my eyebrows. "Don't you like lavender?" This surprises me, because I think any purple shade would look stunning on Seonaid herself, with her masses of Titian hair.

"No," she says, "It's not that."

"You think it's not my colour?" I can feel the warmth rising into my face.

"No, no," she says quickly. "I think you'd look good in any shade of purple, and anyway, I'd never try to tell a customer what she should or shouldn't choose. It's just..." Her voice tails off.

"It's just...?"

After another long pause, she says, "It's unlucky."

I stare at her. *Unlucky?*

Seonaid lets out a long sigh. "Look," she says, "I know it's totally illogical. It's just superstition, right? But nobody likes that colour – you know..."

"Lavender," I say flatly.

She nods. "I know it sounds completely nuts. And I

31

mean, I could make you a dress that colour. I don't keep fabric that colour here, but I could order it in. It's just... it might not be comfortable for you. If you get married anywhere around here, and people see you, they'll talk about it."

I shake my head. "I've never heard of any superstition about getting married in that colour."

"Well," she says reluctantly, "I guess it's kind of a local thing."

For a few moments I cannot think of anything to say to this. We look at each other and it passes through my head that perhaps she is having a bit of fun at my expense. I've never heard of any shade of purple being unlucky, for a bride or for anyone else. *Married in red, wish yourself dead*, I've heard that one, not that I'd take any notice of it, if I really wanted a red dress. And then there's *Married in black, wish yourself back*. But purple? I don't think there's even a rhyme for that one. Did she make it up, this local superstition?

Of course, I gave myself away as a newcomer the moment I opened my mouth, but then I went one better and told Seonaid all about my old life in London too. Maybe she thinks I'm just a daft townie with all sorts of romantic ideas about Scotland, ripe to believe any old nonsense.

"I guess I'll have to rethink this," I say awkwardly. "Thanks anyway."

"I've offended you," she says, looking stricken. "I'm sorry. I didn't mean to. Please don't leave."

I glance away, hesitating.

On the other side of the plate glass window, the autumnal sunshine is gilding the Victorian facade of the building opposite. A couple of older women are standing on the pavement chatting, in no particular hurry to go anywhere. One of them is accompanied by a black and white collie, which sits at her feet looking up hopefully. A red post van drifts past but otherwise the street is quiet.

This is a small town, where everyone knows everyone, where people look each other in the face and greet each other as they pass. That's one of the reasons we came here, after all: because London, with its great mass of anonymous people, was stifling me. I don't want to start off on the wrong foot here – the touchy incomer who can't take a joke. The city girl with an inflated idea of her own importance. No; that's not who I want to be.

Then my gaze falls on the battered copy of *The Thirty-Nine Steps* lying next to the till and that decides it for me.

"I'm not offended," I tell Seonaid. "I've just never heard of lavender being unlucky before." I do a good imitation of shrugging unconcernedly. "I could look at some other colours."

She's so pleased that any lingering feelings of pique melt away. Out come swatches of cloth in all different colours: oyster, champagne, eau-de-nil and other, stronger shades like raspberry and cornflower blue. She digs out a book of tartans too, and shows me two different Sinclair tartans: a red one and a blue 'hunting' one. I try and fail to imagine James in either of them, but it's fun looking.

I'm in the shop a long time, but at the end I still haven't come to any conclusions.

"I like the blue, and that very light green," I tell Seonaid. "But I want to think about it."

"Of course," she says. "You shouldn't rush it. It's a big decision."

All the same, I feel she is disappointed as she shows me out of the shop. She's afraid I won't come back because of what she said earlier and I can't think what to say to reassure her. I get back into the car and drive back to Barr Dubh House. On the way I think about the colours

33

she showed me, and how beautiful the fabrics were, like jewels.

But what I really wanted was lavender.

Chapter Five

James is due home after midnight. I have a long hot bath in the brand new claw-footed tub, listening to music that echoes tinnily in a room with no soft furnishings – we still have to buy curtains and rugs for it. A dining-room chair stands incongruously next to the tub, so I have somewhere to put the glass of wine and the book I brought upstairs with me. Some more elegant solution will have to be found in future, but for now the main thing is to have the book and the wine at hand. Everything is a bit like that at the moment: temporary solutions cobbled together until we have finished decorating and unpacked everything.

I lie in the tub and stare at the ceiling. The bathroom is huge and beautiful; it even has an opaque stained glass window. The whole house is huge and beautiful. It's perfect. Our life here will be perfect.

The incident in the town this morning is still on my mind. Things feel out of kilter. I want to draw a line under all of it; I want James to come home.

I pick up the book lying on the chair and look at it. It's a really ancient paperback copy of *Jane Eyre*. I've read it loads of times already and I don't think I'll ever be bored with reading it, but right now I can't seem to settle to anything at all – except the wine, and I'm not having any more of that either or I'll have a headache in the morning. I put the book down again and reach for my towel.

When I've finished in the bathroom I go downstairs to wait, wrapped in my robe and with damp tendrils of hair sticking to my face and neck. It's completely dark outside now and I imagine how the house must look from a distance with its illuminated squares of window. But probably nobody sees it; there is a barrier of trees between us and the distant road.

My phone is lying on the kitchen counter so I check for messages but there's nothing. I chew my lip, running my thumb over the screen to check there's nothing I've missed. No news is good news, I suppose; if James were running late I guess he'd let me know. I don't want him to be held up because I don't want to have to go to bed without him; I don't want to lie down alone in the place where I awoke last night, struggling and fighting for air. I'd rather sit up all night than do that. So I wait, prowling the half-finished rooms, and eventually, impatiently, I open the front door and stand there, looking out.

It was a mild autumn day today, warm even, but now the cold air makes me shiver. Beyond the patch of light from the open doorway it is very dark, the moon a thin sliver. Experimentally, I lean back inside and turn the light off, then look out again, into the night, hoping for distant headlights.

The darkness is vast and uncompromising. It does not smell like London nighttime does, a mixture of grime and spices. It smells like a river, cold and damp and subtly organic, a scent that makes me think of dank green moss. The blackness is alive with sporadic sounds: throbbing cries and tiny scufflings and something that sounds like a metal blade scraping against a strop. I do not know what any of these sounds are, what makes them, but they are all around me, filling the dark.

36

I stand there for a while, but even when my eyes have become used to the darkness, there is very little to see. The land is dark and the sky is simply a deeper shade of black above it, dusted with stars. My hair is still slightly damp and my scalp is beginning to tingle with the cold. There is nothing for it but to go back inside.

I'm on the point of turning to do that, when lights *do* at last become visible, some distance away to the north-east, where I know the main road is. So I wait, pulling my robe closer around myself.

The headlights sweep in an arc and begin to follow the lane that leads towards Barr Dubh House. The car makes slow progress; the lane is eroded with enormous potholes in places. Eventually it comes to the turning into the drive that leads up to the house. There are massive stone gate posts on either side of it, gateless now. They are relics of some obsolete topography; Barr Dubh House itself is new.

The drive runs at an angle to the house before following a long curve that leads right up to it. The first section is lined with trees and the bright beams of the headlights illuminate each pale trunk in turn as the car passes them. I find myself counting automatically: *one, two, three, four, five...* Then of course it should be *six* and *seven* but instead I'm staring into the darkness that was lit up only a second before, my eyes wide and my hand over my mouth, thinking *Did I really see that?*

The brief splash of light against the fifth tree showed someone standing there, pressed closed to the trunk; someone so fleetingly visible that I have only the impression of a twig-thin upper body, and below that, some kind of billowing drapery. I have no sense of what the head was like at all, beyond a dark patch that might have been hair or perhaps just the momentary play of shadows on the bark. I saw enough, though, that my breath catches in my throat.

37

There is no chance to look again. The headlights have strobed on along the tree trunks, leaving inky blackness in their wake. I can hear the car now, the rumble of the engine, the crackle of gravel as it turns up towards the house.

Get a grip, Fen, I say to myself. *It was a plastic bag blowing in the wind, or a clump of overgrown weeds.* But the image is indelibly imprinted on my mind's eye: an unnaturally thin arm and torso, the surge of loose fabric. It is an effort to put it aside, but I must, because here is James, James whom I have been waiting for, and I don't want some figment of my imagination, born of bad sleep and loneliness, to spoil the moment. Instead I concentrate on watching the yellow headlights coming closer and closer until they sweep right across me like a searchlight, and the car stops on the gravel.

Then the engine dies and the lights go out at the same time, and the car door opens.

"Fen," he says in a voice that sounds both weary and amused, "You'll freeze."

It is very, very late before we finally get to bed – so late, in fact, that it might almost be called early instead. There can only be a few hours until dawn. We talk first, catching up on all the things we didn't manage to squeeze into texts and brief international calls. It's too late for coffee, even for James, so we have tea, which we drink sitting on the sofa without bothering to remove the dust sheets first; like much of our other stuff, it is newly bought, and like a Christmas present, has to be kept until the decorating is finished before being unwrapped.

I sit with my legs folded under me, watching James over the rim of the tea cup while he tells me about Madrid. He has been on television *and* the radio, with the help of an interpreter. Someone read an excerpt from the Spanish translation of his book and that was strange, he says, because he could see the other people in the room reacting to what was being read, to the words he had written, but he couldn't follow it himself.

He's still wearing the smart clothes he had on for the last interview. The navy blue shirt is somewhat wrinkled now but with his dark eyes and hair and his high cheekbones he still manages to look ridiculously debonair; I think so, anyway.

I tell him about what I've been doing, too. I describe my disastrous attempt to paint one of the bedrooms yellow. The paint was supposed to be daffodil, but once applied it was a nasty shade of mustard.

"I'm going over it with rose pink," I tell him. "But I can only do a bit at a time because the colour clash is so awful. The room looks like it's been papered with slices of breaded ham."

James laughs at that, and I smile too. We talk and we laugh, and we hold each other's gaze in a way that gives me butterflies in the stomach. James puts out a hand and touches my bare foot, running a finger along the instep so that I can't help shivering like a cat. I think that soon there will have been enough of talking.

Throughout the entire conversation and everything that comes after it, I say nothing about the terrible nightmare I had: not a word. The memory still intrudes into my conscious mind. I don't *want* to think about it – I am *determined* not to think about it – but it is always there in the background. It's not even the dream itself that bothers me, because I know that it is meaningless, a freak of the imagination. It's the fact that I have not told James about it, and that I am not going to tell him. It feels wrong to have a secret. I say to myself that it will soon be forgotten and that if I am not thinking about it, I am not hiding it from anyone.

Forget it, I tell myself. *Forget it.*

One thing I do ask him, though. Later, when we are lying side by side in the darkness, I say, "James?"

"Yes?" he says sleepily.

"When you were coming up the drive tonight, did you see anyone – I mean, any*thing* – over by the trees on the right?" I hesitate. "Maybe a deer or something? I thought I saw something over there as you drove up."

He takes such a long time to reply that I think he has already fallen asleep. Then he says, "No, I didn't see anything," in a voice that is slurred with tiredness. I wait for a long time, but he doesn't say anything else, and at last sleep claims me too. I sleep through the night, and if there are any dreams, I don't remember them.

Chapter Six

"You'll go mad, Fen," is the first thing Belle says as she gets out of her car, pushing her magenta hair back from her face so she can look at me properly. She has lipstick to match the hair, and I see that she is wearing boots that are completely impractical for the country.

"Thanks, Belle," I say ironically.

"Seriously," she says, her grey eyes round. "This is the middle of *nowhere*. This isn't even the *arse* of beyond, it's..." She tries to think of a suitable simile. "...the *appendix* of beyond, or something. Do you have any idea how far away from civilisation this place is?"

By *civilisation* I'm not sure whether she means Edinburgh, or London.

"It's only twenty miles from Perth," I protest. "About twenty miles," I add lamely.

Belle isn't listening. "I couldn't believe it," she says. "I turned off the motorway onto this dual carriageaway, and then I turned off again onto this little A road, and I thought, well, I must get to something soon, a services with a Costa or something, but – not a thing. And then," she goes on, "I had to turn onto a little B road, and you know, it was getting like a horror film or something – smaller and smaller roads until you get stuck and you can't turn round. As for that last bit, I think I left my back axle in it."

She reaches into the car. "This is for you. I think you probably need it."

"Wow," I say. "I've never seen a bottle of gin that big before."

"I hope you've got tonic," Belle says severely.

"Loads," I say, truthfully.

"Good." She hands me the gin, then tilts her head back. "So this is Barr Dub House, is it?"

"Barr *Dubh*," I say. "It means 'black hill'."

She raises her eyebrows. "It's certainly impressive, I'll give you that."

"Thank you–"

"–But it's still miles from anywhere."

"It's only a couple of miles to the town," I point out.

"But is it near enough to walk back when you've had a few?"

"Not really," I admit. "No."

Belle sniffs. "I suppose James wants you all to himself. Like *Bluebeard*." Suddenly she smiles broadly. "Oh, *hello* James."

James is at my elbow, looking as improbably gorgeous as I've ever seen him, but as grim as an undertaker. Clearly he has just heard himself being compared to Bluebeard. Then his face breaks into a grin and I realise he was doing it on purpose.

"Hello, Belle," he says easily. "Welcome to Barr Dubh House."

Belle has brought an incredible quantity of luggage, considering that she is only staying for the weekend. James offers to carry it into the house, but when he opens the car boot and looks inside, he announces very gravely that this may take some time.

Belle takes my arm very firmly. "You can show me over the house," she says. So I do.

There is still a faint smell of emulsion, and our footsteps echo crisply as we walk around, weaving our way around removers' cartons. All the same, it's fun to tour the house, and I don't feel too bad about showing off, because I know Belle thinks we live lamentably far away from the bright lights. But then Belle is utterly a city girl; to her, anything with sheep in it is a kind of dystopian badlands. For me, London had begun to feel like a trap.

I show her the charcoal grey kitchen with its stainless steel range and the fridge freezer that is tall enough to be a pharaonic sarcophagus. We wander through the dining room where a huge gilt-edged mirror is standing against the wall, waiting to be hung. It reflects an ivory-coloured wall halfway across which a tide of dark bottle green has swept and then suddenly been arrested – yet another work in progress. Then I take Belle into the living room, where she looks at the enormous window and says, "Wow." While she is gazing out at the view, I stand next to her and look at the spot on the treeline where I saw the person in lavender. Of course, there is nobody there today. You wouldn't expect a local walker to be in exactly the same place every time you looked out. After that, we put our heads around the door of James's study.

A little later I take Belle upstairs and show her the bedrooms, including the one I've prepared for her. It's the pink one, the last of the repulsive mustard colour having been painted over in a hurry. It's at the other end of the corridor from ours, and it has its own ensuite.

"Shame," says Belle, when she sees that. "I quite fancied a dip in that bath with the feet."

"You can anyway," I tell her, but she's already drifted away, towards the window. From this side of the house you can see the drive with its line of trees, and beyond the fields, a wooded hill. There's a fitful sunshine today, brightening the landscape for twenty minutes at a time before lapsing into brooding cloudiness again. In spite of the capricious weather, the view is undeniably beautiful. Sometimes I see birds of prey hovering in the air currents over that hill.

"It is amazing here," says Belle, without turning around. "You're very lucky, Fen."

I wait for her to follow this up with, *but you're still miles from anywhere* or *but you'll still go nuts out here*, but she doesn't. I'm glad about that, because it's true, and it doesn't need any qualification. It *is* amazing here, and I am very, very lucky. I wouldn't want anyone to think otherwise.

We spend what's left of the afternoon sitting at the back of the house, in a corner that's sheltered from the breeze but traps the autumn sunshine. James brings us drinks – coffee for Belle, tea for me, and later a glass of wine each – but otherwise he leaves us to it. He knows we are going to talk for hours about people he doesn't know, and besides, he wants to get back to the book he is working on. I can tell that from the slightly preoccupied air he has; his body may be wandering about Barr Dubh House, but his imagination is somewhere else altogether. Weekends as a concept are meaningless to him. So we wave him away and let him get on with it, although Belle takes care to get the bottle of wine from him first.

Although Belle has never worked at the same office I did, she knows a lot of people who do, mainly because she has been on-off dating one of them.

"Genghis Caan is spitting feathers," she tells me. "You know the bloke who wrote that thriller you were always moaning about? He's written another one, and it's even

44

worse. I don't know why anyone keeps publishing them. Maybe he's sleeping with someone important." She rolls her eyes. "Anyway, she's supposed to be copyediting it, and she's not happy about it. Take care you don't end up with it, Fen."

"I can always turn it down," I point out. "I'm freelance now."

"Well, don't say I didn't warn you." Belle upends her glass, and holds it out for a refill.

"I'm my own boss now," I tell her. "And believe me, I'm not touching that thriller. I'd rather copyedit a telephone directory."

"Good," says Belle firmly. She picks up the wine bottle and shakes it gently. "This one's empty. Is there any more of that? It was rather nice."

I fetch another one and we sit there talking an increasing amount of nonsense until the day begins to slide into twilight and the midges become troublesome. Then we go indoors, to find James making dinner – some kind of stir fry, which he is shaking about with cheerful vigour. He is actually humming to himself. I deduce from this that the writing has been going well.

"Sit," he says, nodding at the breakfast bar which we have mostly been using for meals, until such time as the dining room shall be entirely and not just partially green.

"House-trained too," remarks Belle, as she slides onto one of the stools.

It is very late by the time we decide to call it a night. I drink a huge glass of tap water before I go upstairs, in the hopes of fending off a headache in the morning. I'm faintly annoyed with myself; I never normally drink this much. *Perhaps I really am terrible at saying no*, I say to myself. I fill the glass again and carry it upstairs with me, doing my best not to slop it everywhere.

I creep into the dark room, trying not to wake James. The curtains are open a little way, casting a bar of cool moonlight across the room and the bed. I go over and set the glass of water down on the windowsill. On impulse, I lean close to the window, staring out into the night. The moon is full and very bright tonight. Beyond the fence the pasture is pale and silvery and bisected by a thin dark stripe that runs from the distant trees to the edge of what will eventually be our garden: a rabbit track, I suppose, invisible by the strong light of day but revealed by the shadowy contrasts of night. I stare at it for a while. Nothing moves out there.

At last I undress and slide into bed. I lie there thinking that I should have closed the curtains properly, that the moonlight will keep me awake, and while I am thinking about that, sleep claims me.

Chapter Seven

When Belle comes down very late the next morning, James is making us an enormous fried breakfast, including slices of lorne sausage and potato scones. A lot of melted butter seems to be involved.

Belle looks at it, and says, "Get thee behind me, Satan." She turns her back on us as she pours herself a large black coffee, but then she says, "It's no use, I can still smell it," and holds out her hand for a plate.

I'm already spearing fried mushrooms with a fork. "James," I say between mouthfuls, "I love you."

"So do I," says Belle.

After breakfast we roll up our sleeves and paint the rest of the dining room green. This was Belle's idea; she says she wants to be useful, although I think she's already being useful just by being here. I'd forgotten how nice it is just to see a different face and indulge in a bit of scurrilous gossip.

That thought brings me back to the encounter with Seonaid again. I haven't mentioned it to James, because I didn't want the first report I made of the town to be something negative. So eventually I tell Belle about it instead – about lavender being unlucky here.

She listens to me patiently, and then she says, "Bollocks. I bet you anything she made that up."

"I did wonder," I tell her. "But why would she do that?"

"She probably has a job lot of nasty white satin, and no lavender fabric in the shop," says Belle.

I snort with laughter. "It can't have been that."

"I bet it was," says Belle robustly. "Unlucky, my arse."

"Well," I say, "I've kind of gone off the idea of lavender anyway."

"What are you having instead?"

"I don't know. I was thinking maybe blue."

"Well," says Belle, "Sod what anyone else thinks. Just have whatever you want. Except maybe beige."

"I was thinking of keeping beige for the bridesmaid's dress," I say, straight-faced, and enjoy about two seconds of seeing the horror on Belle's face before I can't help grinning.

We carry on that like for much of the day, painting and bantering with each other, until all four walls are dark green and we also have flecks of dark green on our hands and our clothes. I'm for stopping after that, but Belle has her usual relentless energy; she starts opening boxes with "dining room" scrawled on them in black marker, and unpacking the contents. Of course the flat in London had no dining room; it had a tiny table shoved up against a wall. The boxes are from somewhere else, somewhere that is still packed up in a corner of my mind with *do not open* marked on top. Up until now I've put off looking inside. Belle, however, is fearless. She rips the tape off the boxes with the grim determination of someone ripping a sticking plaster off a wound. She unpacks a silver candelabra, a set of crystal wine glasses, and an entire gilt-edged dinner service.

All of these things require decisions, but I'm not ready to make them, so I put them in the sideboard.

It's a new one, big enough to swallow everything except the candelabra. Out of sight, out of mind.

"What's this?" says Belle as she opens the third carton. "It's kind of weird if it's a table decoration."

Reluctantly, I go over and take a look. I recognise all the other stuff, right down to the tarnished silver teaspoons, but I don't recall ever seeing this before. It's an arrangement of artificial flowers, made of what appears to be white porcelain. It looks vaguely bridal because of the colour, but I can't imagine how it would be used, as it is too big for anything but the most extravagant wedding cake. The thing is a small mystery within the wider mystery of other people's tastes and choices and perspectives, even those who should be closest to us. I touch one of the snowy petals with a finger; it is smooth and very cool and I cannot bring myself to like it. Flowers should be real or not at all. I don't even really like hothouse flowers, grown for sale, because there is something artificial about them. *When I marry*, I decide, *I shall have wild flowers*. I'm tempted to tell Belle to bin these china blooms, but in the end I bottle out.

"In the sideboard," I say, and she slots them in on top of a silver plated tray.

It's my turn to cook this evening, but I can't be bothered after spending the day painting and sorting, so Belle and I drive into the town for fish and chips. The three of us eat at the dining room table in spite of the fresh paint smell, just so that we can admire the green walls. We even have a bottle of Prosecco to go with the food, but none of us overdoes it.

The sun is going down by now, so I light some candles, creating an incongruously gracious effect in contrast with the fish and chips boxes littering the dining table. I don't talk very much this evening.

I lick salty chip grease off my fingers and sip Prosecco and watch the other two. I don't need to listen to the words to follow the flow of the conversation. James talks with energy and enthusiasm, and he argues well, but sometimes he is prone to letting his writer's imagination run away with him, and then Belle demolishes him with savage glee. There is an edge to these skirmishes, but I can tell that James likes Belle because she doesn't let him get away with anything, and Belle likes James because he still believes in things; he hasn't become as cynical as some of our acquaintances. The candlelight gilds their faces and when the discussion becomes more heated they draw shapes in the air with their hands.

I watch them and I think: *I love these people. These are my real family – my oldest friend and the man I'm going to marry.*

It's such a simple thing – to belong to certain people, and have them belong to you – and yet so many people take it for granted. Not me, though; I will *never* take it for granted, and I will never let anything spoil this.

Chapter Eight

On Sunday morning, Belle is late downstairs again. James eventually goes off to his study; he is itching to get on with the new book. I stay in the kitchen, drinking tea and looking out at the fields and the distant trees. The land is so lush and green now, but soon the leaves will be turning the colour of flames; the days will be colder and the nights longer. I wonder how it will be here at Barr Dubh House in the middle of winter.

At last I hear footsteps on the stairs. When Belle comes in, it seems to me that she is missing a little of her usual bounce. She looks tired, and when she smiles I have the feeling that it's an effort. Her grey eyes meet mine for a second, then her gaze slides away.

"Coffee?" I say.

"God, yes," says Belle. She slides onto a bar stool and sits there rubbing her face with her hands.

"Are you okay?"

"Yes," she says. "I just... didn't sleep very well."

I raise my eyebrows. "Dr. Munro prescribes carbs."

Belle doesn't argue, so I cut a couple of doorstop slices of bread and stick them in the toaster. I set out butter and go off hunting for a jar of marmalade that I've put in one of the many new kitchen cupboards, if only I could remember which one. While I'm opening and closing doors, Belle says nothing at all. Then I look up and catch her watching me, with a peculiar expression on her face.

I stand there with the jar of marmalade in my hands and say, "Are you *sure* you're okay, Belle?"

There's just a tiny pause before she says, "Yeah, I'm fine. I just need more coffee."

So I pour her another cup and make myself a mug of tea, and then I slide onto the stool opposite her.

"What do you want to do today? We could go out somewhere."

"I'm not going for a *walk*, if that's what you're thinking," Belle says firmly. "I've already seen three fields, one hill and eleven sheep from my bedroom window. That's quite enough."

In the end we settle on a drive into the town to look for an armchair for the spare bedroom, followed by lunch at the sprawling Victorian hotel. Lunch is enormous and very hearty – big slabs of roast meat and potatoes and heaps of vegetables liberally glazed with butter – and also very lively. There is a buzz of voices around us all the time – clearly the hotel is a very popular place for Sunday lunch. In this cheerful atmosphere, Belle begins to look a bit less wan.

Afterwards, we drive up the winding single track road that leads to the dam. We're both ready for somewhere a bit quieter after the bustle of the hotel, but more than that, I want to show Belle why I want to live here. I know I'm never going to persuade her to walk up any mountains with me – not with *those* shoes on – but I want her to see the magic of the place anyway. The dam is the best spot for that; you can drive up high above the town until the road runs out and the entire view is filled with the glittering waters of the loch, and the surrounding hills.

I only know about this place because in our first few

days here in Perthshire we took a wrong turning on the way back from a grocery shopping trip, and when there were no more houses and the road began to ascend steeply James drove on anyway, to see where it went. I remember sitting in the passenger seat saying, "But we have frozen food in the back." James stopped the car and I said, "No, go on, it doesn't matter," and he nodded at the road ahead and said, "I can't unless you open the gates." There were Highland cows close to the road, those big shaggy ones with enormous curving horns. I had no idea whether they were dangerous or not (I still don't), but I got out anyway and opened the gates. We drove all the way up to the dam that day.

Now I drive up there with Belle in the passenger seat, laughing at her alarm when she sees the same enormous beasts so close by. I haven't the heart to make her get out and open the gates, so I do it. We rumble over the cattle grid, and then of course I have to stop and get out and close the gates behind us.

"It's like a safari park," says Belle when I get back into the car.

"Except those things mostly don't sit on the bonnet and pinch the windscreen wipers," I say.

"Mostly...?" says Belle.

The road – well, it's a track really, and in places the surface has crumbled away completely – leads right up to within sight of the dam. There it comes to an abrupt end next to a small parking area. When we get out of the car, I can feel that the air up here is a degree or two colder than it was down in the town.

There's a breeze, too, that blows our hair back from our faces. There is nobody else parked up here today. We have the place to ourselves.

Even Belle can't complain about the very short walk

to the edge of the dam, where a stone wall topped with green moss separates us from the dark water. The loch stretches away into the distance, with heather-covered hills sweeping up on either side of it into cold blue skies. In all the vastness spread out before us, there is not one human being visible. Far away on the hillside I can see white dots which are sheep, moving very slowly across the slope, and high above us a bird of prey is coasting on the air currents. Otherwise, we are alone.

When I was a child, I used to find it confusing when adults called a landscape "beautiful". To my childish self, "beautiful" meant something gold or silver or pink, something that gleamed or sparkled; I couldn't see how it could be extended to fields and cows and the gnarled trunks of trees. I can't call this view "beautiful" either, because the word is completely inadequate. All my life I've loved words but there aren't any for this. I know that those hills are savage. They are wild and often trackless and to be caught up there in the dark or the cold is to risk death from exposure. But I feel the pull of them; I feel something like new love – a tingling in the skin, a cold feeling of excitement in the pit of my stomach. I want Belle to feel it too.

We stand side by side with our elbows on the wall, gazing up the loch towards the distant bulk of Ben Chonzie, the breeze ruffling our hair.

After a minute or two I say, "Amazing, isn't it?" I wait for Belle to say yes, or at least to laugh at me and my enthusiasm.

But Belle says nothing at all. I glance at her, and she has her head down, only her profile visible to me, and her lips pressed together as though she is considering something difficult. She is silent for such a long time that I begin to wonder what is wrong. Have I been so wrapped up in my own concerns that I haven't noticed that Belle has something on her mind?

"Belle–" I begin, and as I speak she suddenly turns to me, as though she has made up her mind to say something. Her expression is so grim that my own words die in my throat.

"Fen," she says, "I wasn't going to say anything about this."

Her words strike me cold. "That sounds serious," I manage to say.

Belle doesn't smile. "You'll probably think I'm off my head. But I've been thinking about it on and off all morning and I can't just go back down to London without saying anything."

"About what? I'm starting to feel worried."

"About Barr Dubh," she says. "I don't like it."

Whatever I expected, it wasn't that. I look at her blankly. "You don't like the house?"

"Yes. No. It's not the house, it's the place."

"The place?" I repeat, blankly. "Look, Belle, I know you love living in London, and I really don't expect you to understand–"

She's shaking her head. "It's not that. It's beautiful here – in Perthshire, I mean. It wouldn't be my thing but I can see why you would love it. It's the place where the house is."

"What's wrong with it?" I say, staring at her.

"I don't know. But something *is* wrong. Look, you know I said I slept badly? It wasn't just a crap night's sleep. Something happened during the night." She hesitates, and then takes the plunge.

"I know it's hard to believe, but I woke up, and the house was different. It had changed – I mean, completely changed."

"What do you mean, changed?"

"The room I was in didn't have pink walls any more – they had patterned wallpaper with birds and flowers on it. And there was a lot more furniture. All of it was heavy, old-fashioned-looking stuff. It made the room look crowded. There was a little wooden table with a bowl on it, with a jug standing in it, like people used to wash in before there was running water. And the bed I was in was different too. I wasn't lying under a duvet any more, there were sheets and blankets."

"You must have been dreaming," I say.

"I know it sounds that way," says Belle, "But it didn't feel like a dream at all. It felt absolutely real. I could feel the texture of the cotton sheets and the roughness of the wool blanket. And when I got out of bed I could feel the floorboards under my feet. They were cold."

I look at Belle carefully, studying her expression for any sign that she might not be serious, or that she might not be sure of her ground. But so far as I can tell, she is absolutely in earnest.

She says, "I couldn't work it out. I knew I ought to be in your place but it wasn't anything like it was when I went to bed. But it really was just so *real*." She shakes her head. "So I decided to go and find you. I opened the bedroom door and the hallway had changed too. You've mostly got plain painted walls, but now there were wooden panels, and more patterned wallpaper. I thought, okay, Belle, maybe you went out through the wrong door and this is an old part of the house that they haven't done up yet. But the house isn't that old, is it? I mean, it looks new."

"No, it's not old," I say. I'm surprised how calm my own voice sounds. "It was built two years ago. We're only the second people to live in it. What did you do then?"

"I went down the hallway but I couldn't find your room.

56

All the doors were open but I didn't recognise any of the rooms, and I didn't see anyone at all. I could see where I was going alright – there were these weird-looking lamps on the walls – but there was nobody in any of the rooms. I thought about shouting to you and James but it was so quiet I felt funny about doing that. I felt... I don't know, like it wouldn't be such a great idea to draw attention to myself. So I just carried on looking.

"I got to the top of the stairs and I thought, well this definitely isn't the same house at all, because there was this wooden staircase that took several turns on the way down, and it had these big bannisters with posts at the top and bottom."

"Did you go downstairs?" I ask her. I have a cold feeling in my stomach.

Belle nods. "Yeah. There didn't seem to be anybody downstairs either, but it was still lit up everywhere with those same funny-looking lamps. And there was this big picture on the wall." Belle puts up a hand and rubs her face. "Not a photo," she says. "It was one of those old types of picture – an engraving or whatever you call it. Black and white. It was a picture of a house – not a modern house like yours, but an old one with sort of little towers on it. Only I think it was here, or very near here, because I sort of recognised the land – the hill at the back, and the trees."

I can't stop staring at Belle.

"Go on," I say.

"You know I said it was quiet? Well, it was at first. When I was upstairs, I couldn't hear a thing except my own footsteps. But while I was downstairs looking at this picture, I started to hear something. A knocking sound, like someone banging on a door. Bang, bang, bang. It started so quietly that I could hardly hear it, and then it got louder.

I looked down the hallway and there was a door there at the end, so I thought whoever it was must be on the other side."

"Did you go and open it?"

Belle shakes her head. "No way. I just stood there, looking at the door and listening to the knocking. I thought: *someone really wants to get in*. But I had this very strong feeling that it would be a really, really bad idea to let them inside. The whole thing – I can't describe – it felt *wrong*." She heaves a sigh. "So I turned my back and went upstairs again, as quietly as I could. I still felt it would be best not to be heard. I managed to find my way back to the room where I'd started, so I got back into the bed and pulled the covers over my head. I thought I could still hear the knocking, even there, but it was much fainter. I lay there listening to it with my eyes closed for ages and ages, and then eventually I realised I was listening to footsteps going down the landing, and it wasn't the knocking any more, it was you or James getting up. I put my head out and everything was back to normal."

"So it was a dream then – a horrible, frightening dream."

"I don't know," says Belle. "It didn't feel like one."

There is a long silence after this, broken only by the soft sighing of the wind over the loch. Then I push away from the wall, and start walking back towards the car. The atmosphere is broken, the beauty of the scene tainted as though clouds have come over.

Belle trots beside me. Neither of us says anything. I take the car keys out and there is a *click* as the doors unlock. We climb in and for a moment we both sit in silence, staring out through the windscreen.

Then Belle says: "Fen..."

Her voice trails off.

"Yes?" I say softly.

"I'm just... worried about you."

"Belle, it was only a dream. I mean, you can't just wake up and find yourself in a completely different place."

The words are hardly out of my mouth when I think about the night when I thought that exact thing had happened to me.

"Just a dream," I tell her firmly. "What else could it possibly be?"

"You know I've always been... sensitive," she says, in a low voice.

"No," I say, shaking my head. I start the engine, as though I can just drive off and leave this conversation behind. "I'm sorry, Belle, I don't want to hear any more."

The tyres crunch over gravel as we turn onto the track leading back down the hill. Both of us sit in silence as I drive back down, carefully circumnavigating the potholes. When we get to the gate with the cattle grid I get out and open it, and the fresh air is a welcome change from the uncomfortable atmosphere in the car. I get back in and drive through, get out again and shut it. I glance around me, at the rolling land and the dense strip of forest, as though looking for escape. Then I trudge back to the car. Belle says nothing as I get back in.

It's true that she has always claimed to be 'sensitive', as she calls it. It's never really bothered me before, probably because I've never really taken any of it seriously: feelings about places and people, omens and premonitions. I felt about it the same way as I feel about horoscopes – I don't really believe in them, but I find it fun reading them anyway, picking out the best bits and saying, "Yes, that's totally me." Belle and I have never fallen out over this stuff, because it's always felt like a harmless quirk. But this feels personal. She's telling me there's something wrong with the place I live. My *home*.

When we get to the bottom of the hill, there's a small, muddy layby, and I pull in. We have to finish this conversation before we get home, because I don't want to have it in front of James.

I sit for a moment, thinking.

"Belle," I say in the end, "You have a right to believe whatever you want to believe. But Barr Dubh is our home, mine and James's. When you tell me you don't like it, and it feels wrong... It's kind of hurtful."

"I'm sorry," she says, in a small voice. "I just..."

I wait. "Just what?"

"I just felt I had to... warn you. Something felt off."

"It was a dream. It *had* to be a dream, however realistic it felt."

"It wasn't..." she begins, and then her voice trails off. For a minute or two we both just sit there, not saying anything at all. Then she says, "Just be careful, Fen."

I think about that for a moment. "Alright," I tell her. "If we can agree that whatever you thought happened, it was a dream, then I promise if any monsters or serial killers come knocking, I won't open the door. Okay?"

"Okay," she agrees, and then she hesitates, as if there's something else to come, but nothing does.

I start the car again and we drive back to Barr Dubh. With the heater on and music playing, the atmosphere soon becomes more mellow.

I point a few things out to her as we pass them, until the topic of last night is far behind us. By the time we get back to the house, and find James in the kitchen making coffee, it's not too difficult to act as though nothing has happened.

Okay, I said to Belle, and she agreed: *Okay.* But somehow, in spite of our smiles and chat, it isn't okay – not quite.

Chapter Nine

"Did you and Belle fall out?" says James the next morning, as we watch Belle's car disappearing down the drive.

"Well, not exactly," I say, uncomfortably.

James looks at me quizzically, eyebrows raised, but he doesn't push it, and I'm glad.

Have I fallen out with Belle? I'm not even sure myself. From the moment I drove out of the layby until Belle's departure a minute or two ago, we didn't mention her dream, or whatever it was, again. All the same, I'm not surprised James detected something amiss in the atmosphere between us. We were friendly enough with each other – but not quite natural. There was something a little strained about Belle's manner, as though she was afraid the mood would plummet if she let up with her relentless cheerfulness. She looked tired this morning too, as though she hadn't slept well last night; under her magenta hair she was drawn and pasty. As for me, I felt as though James and I were on probation: if we seemed to be anything less than perfectly happy at Barr Dubh, Belle might think that her dream meant something, that there really was something wrong. And there *isn't*.

When we said goodbye, some of the real warmth

returned. Belle is my best and oldest friend, after all. We hugged each other for a beat longer than usual.

"Come back soon," I said.

She said, "I'll call you."

And then she was gone.

James says he'll make coffee – and tea for me. He asks where I want it, which is a tactful way of saying that we both need to get to work.

"In the kitchen," I tell him. I am going to have a study of my own but I haven't quite settled where it will be. For now, I'm happy with my laptop on the breakfast bar, where I can look out of the kitchen window at the green land beyond, so deliciously empty of people. I boot the laptop up and open my emails.

The one that catches my eye immediately is from my former employer, and it's ominously titled *Availability?* It sits there amongst all the promotional offers and requests to sign online petitions, like a hand grenade in a bed of roses.

Belle was right, I think. I click to open it, and sure enough, it's a crafty attempt to sell me the idea of copyediting the terrible new thriller. *I know you're taking a short sabbatical, Fen,* it says, *but this is such a great opportunity.* There's a lot of stuff about the unique skills I'd be bringing to this high profile project and how they'd really, really like it to be me. Nowhere does it mention the fact that Genghis Caan said she'd eat her own iPhone before she ever touched another manuscript by that author.

I sit there for a bit, just looking at that email and thinking. I'm certainly not going to write back with *Hell yeah,* but on the other hand, an emphatic *No* might have its disadvantages.

I'm freelance now, so I have to consider carefully

before turning work down. We could certainly manage without the income from this particular job, but if the work dried up, what would I do with my time? That is too big a question to be answered in an instant. In the end I take the coward's way out and defer the decision until later. Perhaps someone else will have volunteered to do the work by then. Or whoever the thriller writer is sleeping with will have thrown him out on the grounds of disservices to literature, and then cancelled the book. Or the apocalypse will have happened. Anything, really, so long as I don't have to untangle any more of that horrible prose.

There are a hundred and one things I could be getting on with now – like looking for suitable wedding venues, for example. The good ones always get booked up ages in advance, so it's not something I can put off for long. Instead, I raise my head and listen carefully for a few moments, to make sure James is safely in his study and not prowling around. Then I click over to a search engine and type in *Barr Dubh House*.

I get a clutch of estate agents' listings for the house. I click through some of those and read *property no longer on the market*, although one of them still has photographs of the house, including some of the interior. We've painted some of the rooms since they were taken, and cluttered the place with furniture covered in dust sheets, but it's still instantly recognisable. This makes me feel a little uneasy. Anyone could look over our home, as easily as leafing through the pages of a book.

Why would they want to, Fen? I ask myself sternly. I guess I'm just jumpy, because of the things that have happened over the last few days – my dream, Belle's dream, the conversation in the dress shop, and the night I thought I saw someone or something on the drive. But what do those things add up to? Nothing really – nothing concrete. Bad dreams, a silly local superstition, a trick of the light.

I think about that trick of the light, or whatever it was. I think about the drive, lined with trees; those didn't grow to that height within the last two years. Beyond the trees are the massive stone gate posts that mark the end of the drive, weathered and lichenous as gravestones. Those aren't new either. I've never really thought about them before. When you drive around Perthshire you're constantly passing stretches of mossy wall, overgrown gateways and tumbledown lodges – relics of the past that no longer have any meaning for any living person. The walls trace boundaries that no longer exist, the gates lead onto nothing discernable at all.

Perhaps, I think, *there was something here before this house.* I think about what Belle said about the house in her dream. *Not a modern house like yours, but an old one with sort of little towers on it.* I know the style she means; it's called Scottish baronial.

Idly, I draw circles on the mouse pad with my fingertip. *What are you thinking, Fen? Are you thinking Belle dreamed about a real place, a building that stood here in the past? You know that's nuts.*

But is it? I wonder if there is any rational way she could have, and then I try to think of one. Could the buried foundations of an earlier house create hotspots or coldspots or an electrical field? I'm a copyeditor, not a physicist, but that idea feels far-fetched. Anyway, even if the footprint of an older building could be felt in some way, that wouldn't account for Belle imagining *turrets.*

A more logical explanation is that Belle has read something about the area in the past and simply forgotten that she did.

You're assuming that there really was an older house, I remind myself. *Maybe there wasn't.*

I sit forward. After a moment's thought I type in *Barr Dubh House + history* and run a new search. This time I get more hits, but none of them useful. As far as I can tell, they are all about the history of properties with vaguely similar names. I click through several pages of them, but it's clear there's nothing about our little patch of Perthshire. I try *old Barr Dubh House*, but that's the same story. If there ever was another house on this piece of land, there doesn't seem to be a scrap of evidence for it anywhere.

"Fen?"

I jump as James comes into the kitchen, carrying his empty coffee cup.

"You look like you've seen a ghost," he says.

"Really?" I say, but it comes out as a squeak. I try again. "Really? It's so quiet here. You made me jump."

"I'm glad it's that," he says, "And not that I'm inherently terrifying."

"No, not terrifying," I tell him. "More like slightly alarming."

I can see he's going to come over, so before he can do so, I slide off my bar stool, taking care to close my laptop first.

James puts his coffee cup down. "Let's go out," he says.

"Where?"

"Anywhere," he says with a sly grin. "Just out."

I deduce from this that he's struggling with whatever he's writing and wants a break; these urges come over him whenever he reaches a sticking point with his work. I don't have to think about it too long anyway, because I've reached a dead end myself. That's not the real reason I say "Yes," though. James can say he's going *anywhere* and I'll go along too, just for the joy of being with him.

I was wrong; sometimes it *is* terrifying, loving someone this much.

Chapter Ten

There is a ceiling rose directly above me. I have been studying it for long enough to memorise every detail: the design of fruit and roses, executed in bone white plaster that stands out against the grey-green of the ceiling; the border of stylised foliage. I stare up at it, unblinking. Fruit. Roses. White. Green.

I think: *There is no ceiling rose like that in Barr Dubh House.*

I know I'm not mistaken. Barr Dubh House is a modern building; there is nothing in its construction that is as antique-looking as that ceiling rose. It's a mystery that I can be lying here looking up at such a thing. I puzzle over it without feeling any impulse to move, to look around me at the rest of the room. There are other questions to consider, as well as *Where am I?* – for example, *What time is it?* It should be nighttime; I have a dim recollection of getting into bed beside James. But it is the clear light of full day that is showing me the ornate plasterwork above me.

It is very quiet here, and cool. Tiny sounds carry well. Somewhere in the distance I hear the harsh caw of a crow. An insect bumps gently on a window. Then there is a stretch of silence broken at last by a faint metallic rattle. Keys in a lock – not in this room – somewhere else in the house.

Still I don't move. I listen to the distant sound of hinges creaking, and then the crisp sound of a door closing. Whoever has entered the house does not bother to announce their arrival by calling out. Instead I hear one – no, I think two – pairs of boots or shoes, low-heeled ones, crossing a hard floor, and then a rug, judging from the way the sound is suddenly muffled. The footsteps come closer and still no words are spoken.

Now they are in the room. I hear one of them breathing heavily: an older man, I judge, or someone very unfit. There is a whisper of coarse cloth. A soft grunt as someone exerts themselves a little, lifting something perhaps. A scraping sound.

I can smell something. A blend of odours, I think. There is a faint human smell of perspiration but the strongest scent is tobacco – familiar, but not often smelt these days.

A shadow falls across me. One of them is standing between me and the daylight streaming through the window, a long dark shape at the very edge of my vision. If I turned my head, I would be able to see him clearly, but I don't do it. I keep lying there, eyes wide open, staring at that ceiling rose. I don't even blink. The entry of the men into the room has stirred up dust, and now I see motes of it descending gently through the air towards me. Some of them land on the surface of my eye and still I don't blink.

Deep inside me, there is a silent shriek of terror. It is unaccompanied by any burst of adrenaline, urging my muscles into life. My fear is frozen inside me, like a stinging insect trapped in amber. I have guessed who these men are now, and what they are here to do.

They lift it into view: an ominous geometric shape that is instantly recognisable. The lid that will exactly fit the casket that encloses me. I hear it scraping against the side as they heave it up and begin to slide it into place. They do this with care. Respectfully. Slowly, slowly, the lid slides across, narrowing the light.

I want to scream so badly – so very badly. But the desire is somehow theoretical. I cannot translate it into sound or movement. I lie there in the coffin and let them cover me.

When the lid is halfway across, and half my face is in shadow, half in light, the men pause for a moment. The older man is wheezing. It is the younger one who speaks, his voice brittle with distaste.

"Why'd they no' shut her eyes?"

The other man mutters something under his breath. Then the lid resumes its grim passage across my face, the gap narrowing until the light is cut out altogether. I am in darkness.

Sounds from the room around me are muffled now, but pretty soon I hear something very clearly. The descent of the hammer on the very first nail, sealing me in forever.

This time I awake screaming. James is holding my shoulders, shaking me gently, saying my name. At first I feel his grip and I think in my panic that it is the coffin restraining me, pinning me down. I fight him, flailing, struggling. Then I roll away to my side of the bed. I am convulsed with a fit of coughing. I hang over the side of the bed and cough until I am almost retching. I have screamed myself hoarse; my throat is burning.

"Fen," says James. "Fen, calm down."

There is a *click* as he turns on the bedside lamp and the room is flooded with soft yellow light. I roll onto my back again and stare at him wide-eyed, my chest heaving. I try to tell him why I was screaming, but at first I can't say anything coherent at all. "I," I say, "I was..." Then I'm choking and shivering, unable to get the words out.

James sits right up in bed.

"God, Fen. What's the matter? Shall I call 999?"

"No," I manage to say, grasping his arm before he can turn away and reach for his phone. "Don't. I'm okay."

This is patently untrue, since I'm still panting and shaking, but he doesn't pick the phone up. He waits, but his eyes are wide with alarm. His dark hair is sticking up all over the place. At this moment he does not look like a suave literary author; he looks like an onlooker at the scene of a terrible accident.

Eventually I get my breath back and calm down enough to be able to speak properly.

"I had the most horrible, horrible dream."

"Jesus, Fen. A *dream*? I thought you were having some sort of fit."

"It was awful." I plunge my hands into my hair, pulling at the roots. "It was so real. I thought I was..." I hesitate. It's the resolve I made last time, not to tell James I had dreamed I was buried alive, that stops me saying it now. I'm still too shocked to think it through logically. "It was like being dead," I say. "I wanted to move but I couldn't, and I kept trying to scream but I couldn't do that either."

"You definitely managed to scream," says James. "I can vouch for that. My ears are still ringing." He tries a grin, somewhat unconvincingly.

"It's not funny," I snap. Then I stop, dismayed. I don't want to be snapping at James. Not now.

"Hey," he says, unperturbed. "I know it's not funny. Look, since we're both wide awake now, why don't we go downstairs for a bit, make some tea or something? Don't try to go to sleep again until you feel better."

"Okay," I say. In truth, I don't think I could go to sleep again right now, even if I wanted to.

James comes round to my side of the bed, a dishevelled vision in hastily-donned boxers and t-shirt, his feet bare. He puts his arms around me.

"Come on, Fen," he says into my hair. "What's up? You've been funny all day, since Belle left. Did something happen?"

Put on the spot, I have to say something. "I don't know," I tell him. "We unpacked a lot of stuff... you know. Their stuff. Belle wanted to do something useful."

James is silent for a moment. "Yeah," he says at last. "I can see that that would feel weird. You know, Fen, maybe that's why–"

I reach up and put a finger to his lips. I don't want to hear him say that that's why I dreamed about being dead.

"Don't let's talk about it," I say.

So we don't.

Chapter Eleven

The second time I ever met James it was winter, the end of winter too, when the parties were all behind us and the grim weather felt unending. Towards the end of the working day the offices, which were in an Edwardian building, became so dark that we all existed under strip lighting, like items in a supermarket freezer. I spent a lot of time in the kitchen, making myself comforting cups of tea.

Things weren't going well outside work. As well as the parties on the ground floor, there were various shady characters hanging around at all hours. It was uncomfortable to come home after dark and have to go up to my flat past sullen-looking men who leaned against the scuffed walls and stared at me as I passed. Mrs. Khan confided in me that she and her family were planning to move, which meant I would be deprived of my one ally. I had begun to look for another place myself, but everything was so expensive. Sometimes on Sundays I would walk through the park, muffled up in a winter coat and scarf, past bare brown flower beds and disreputable pigeons pecking at cigarette ends. I thought of moving right out of the city, somewhere wild and green, but the idea felt like a mirage. It would mean a new job as well as a new place to live, and I had so few free hours to spend investigating those things, so little energy left over after work. More than that, though, I had no idea where to go. I was like a compass at magnetic north, the needle swinging wildly and never coming to rest anywhere.

I suppose I should have guessed that James might be at the offices that day. I'd seen emails circulating about a lunchtime event involving several authors, but it hadn't really registered with me; it was something that editors and publicists would attend, not staff like me. The hubbub when they all went out to it was simply an annoyance. I wanted to work flat out that day, and leave on time, and the fewer interruptions the better.

It was shortly before five o'clock when they all trooped back in again. I kept my head down. Some people would be picking up their things and leaving, but others would be staying late to catch up and I sincerely hoped I wouldn't get dragged into anything just as I was about to get away myself. There was a buzz of voices in the corridor, which I mostly ignored, until I heard my name.

"We should invite Fen," said a male voice.

I recognised James's voice at once, even though we'd only ever had one conversation before. I stopped what I was doing and waited, my hand still on the computer mouse.

"Fen Munro?" said someone else. I was pretty sure that was James's publicist, Delia. She made it sound as though there were half a dozen Fens it might have been. "I don't think she'd want to come."

"Why don't we ask her?" said James. A moment later he was in my office, with Delia at his shoulder.

"We're all going out to dinner," announced James, before Delia could cut in. "And I think you should come too."

"The booking's for eight people," said Delia.

"I'm sure the place has an extra chair," said James. He looked at me. "Coming?"

I glanced at Delia, who was giving me the sort of look that would make house plants wither and birds drop dead from the sky. That was what made up my mind, really.

"Alright," I said. "Yes."

I grabbed my coat and bag. On the way out of the office, Delia came up beside me.

"You realise we don't have the budget for this?" she hissed in my ear.

"That's okay," I told her. "I won't eat much."

When we got to the restaurant, I noticed that Delia managed to get the seat next to James's. I ended up diagonally opposite him, where I could see him perfectly well but couldn't exchange a word with him without leaning across the table and raising my voice, effectively copying in everyone else on every exchange. Someone ordered wine while we were looking at the menus. I took a glass, and over the rim of it I watched Delia snuggling as close to James as she decently could. I decided that Delia was a cow, and also that I liked James, but that I wasn't going to get anywhere near him while Delia was all over him like wisteria. When the waiter came back, I ordered the most expensive thing I could find, venison with chestnuts, just to see whether Delia would notice. Of course, she didn't. By the way she was looking at James, I suspected she would have eaten *him* all up, if she could have.

Eventually, I became tired of the whole thing, and increasingly nervous about getting home. The later it got, the greater the likelihood of having to run the gauntlet of dodgy characters on the communal stairs. I shot another look at James. He looked as though he was settled for the rest of the evening; his jacket was hanging over the back of his chair and he had a full glass of wine in front of him. I doubted he would notice when I left and I wondered why he had bothered to ask me to come along. At last I pushed back my chair, said my goodbyes in a tone of faux regret, and left the restaurant, slipping my arms into the sleeves of my coat as I pushed my way out through the door.

Outside, the sky was dark, though tinged with the yellow of the city lights. The air was cold. I stopped to button my coat, and then I set off towards the tube station. The street was well illuminated and there were plenty of people out and about, so when I heard footsteps behind me, I wasn't particularly alarmed. All the same, I glanced around. To my amazement, it was James.

"Slow down, Fen," he said.

I stopped and stared at him. He was jacketless, his sleeves rolled up – far too lightly dressed for the chill air – and he was very slightly short of breath.

"Did I forget something?" I said.

"I don't know," he said, smiling at me. "Did you?"

"Where's your jacket?"

"In the restaurant, hanging over the back of my chair, I should think," he said.

"But why is it – I mean, why did–?" I couldn't work out exactly what I was trying to ask, so in the end I just shut up.

"I wanted to talk to you," he said. "Do you want to go for a drink?"

I was looking at him when he said this, and for a moment he looked different – more serious, less confident.

"Okay," I said slowly. "Do you mean... now?"

"Why not?"

"What about your jacket?" I asked.

James shrugged. "Someone will bring it into the office tomorrow. I've got everything important in my pockets anyway. And besides," he added conspiratorially, "As long as it's on my chair, they'll think I'm coming back for it.

That should give us a good head start."

I couldn't help laughing at that. "You'll freeze, though," I said.

"We'd better find somewhere quickly, then."

We went to a pub; there was less chance there of running into the others, who would probably go to a wine bar if they went on anywhere. James ordered a beer; I went for a soft drink, having had wine already. I wanted to keep my wits about me – the evening had already taken an entirely unpredicted turn. In spite of James's apparent interest, I couldn't help suspecting that once we started talking properly it would turn out that he wanted to pick my brains about some professional question. Perhaps he wanted the inside dirt on his publisher. In that case, it would be very embarrassing if I had taken his invitation to have a drink with him as some kind of personal declaration. With these thoughts going through my mind, I was a little subdued at first. Gradually, however, I realised that it wasn't publishing he was interested in. It was me.

I'm used to James and his impulsive nature now. He makes up his mind very quickly; if he likes something, if it interests him, he pursues it. He doesn't worry about where the pursuit is going, but more often than not it leads him somewhere useful. The idea for *The Unrepentant Dead*, for example, came from a chance remark from a folklorist he met in a bar in the Highlands; once he'd heard about the *sluagh* he wasn't content until he'd learnt everything he could about them, and once he'd done that he had to put it into a book.

Back then, I didn't know any of this. I was mainly bemused; I kept wondering if I'd got the wrong end of the stick. The feeling wore off, though. The sharpness and sense of mischief that had made him pick up on the Genghis nickname the first time we met made him very entertaining company. By the end of the evening, I felt as though we'd swapped life stories. I'd even told him about my secret desire to pack it all in and go and live in the country, which was something I never, ever mentioned at work, in case it marked me out as lamentably unambitious.

It was late by then, so James offered to get a taxi and drop me off at home before he went back to his hotel. I was grateful, but I wondered what he thought of the block when we stopped outside it. By the look – and sound – of it, there was another party going on in the ground floor flat.

I kissed James – on the cheek – before I got out of the cab, and I guess we must have said something about meeting again very soon. But mostly I remember looking up at the apartment block with its dark upper floors and then glancing back into the cab at James, and wishing I could have left it all behind and gone with him instead.

Chapter Twelve

The next morning, I wake up late, to find pale Scottish sunlight streaming through the window. I'm alone. James's side of the bed is empty and when I put my hand on the sheet it's cold.

For a little while, I just lie there. The memory of last night is like a hangover: it makes me feel weak and drained. I feel as though I've lied to James, although I didn't really lie – I just didn't tell him everything. All the details. I could rectify that, of course. I could get out of bed right now and go downstairs and tell him everything. But I know I'm not going to do that. I can't even get things straight in my own head.

What is happening to me?

I'm not a superstitious person. I've always thought dreams were just random things my brain threw up like driftwood, tattered scraps of stress and hope and anxiety with no particular logic to them. I didn't think of them as omens or messages. But I've never had dreams like these before, reoccurring and gruesomely specific. They're so realistic that while I'm dreaming them they are indistinguishable from real life. I don't just see and hear things in exquisite and painful detail, I smell and feel them, too. And then there's this repeating theme of being in my coffin, being buried alive.

I rub my face with my hands, like someone trying to rub away sleepiness. It's no use; the memories *will* press in on me: the curious old-fashioned ceiling rose, the scent of old tobacco, the sound of nails being hammered down. The whole experience was so intensely and agonisingly vivid that it is hard to avoid the conclusion that it means something – that my subconscious is waving a red flag at me for all it's worth.

What about Belle's dream? I say to myself defiantly. *That didn't come from my subconscious.*

For a moment I feel the relief of self-reassurance, but then the misgivings come creeping in again, gnawing like evil insects at the edges of my fragile complacency. Perhaps Belle dreamed what she did because she is my oldest and closest friend and she sensed the same *wrongness* that spawned my own dreams.

No, I tell myself. *There is no wrongness. I chose to leave London and come here, to Barr Dubh House. I've chosen to spend the rest of my life with James. I'm happy with my choices.* I think about these things, examining them carefully, and I know that this is true. There is no lurking doubt, quietly obtrusive as grit in my shoe. I love living in Scotland, I love Barr Dubh House, and most of all I love James, with all my heart.

James. I glance at his side of the bed, empty, the hollow in the pillow where he laid his head still visible.

I throw back the covers with an energy that is almost angry. Sliding out of bed, I grab my robe and shrug it on. I'm halfway down the stairs before I've finished tying the belt.

James is not in the kitchen; the lights are off and the hob is cold. I pad through into the living room and he's not there either. I pause by the big plate glass window and stare out at the land beyond, remembering the day I saw someone walking along by the distant treeline. I often find myself looking towards that same spot, but I have never seen them again, and I don't now.

The door of James's study is open just a crack, and so I go softly up to it and peep through the gap, not wanting to disturb him if he's engrossed in his work. Yes, he's in there, sitting at his desk with his laptop open in front of him, but he isn't working. He's gazing out of the window, at something I cannot see from here. I know he's not working because the laptop's screen has gone dark. So I knock lightly, and then I push open the door.

It takes James a beat longer to react to my knock than I expect. For a moment, his gaze remains on the view through the window, and at this apparent preoccupation my heart sinks a little – has what happened last night disturbed him too? But then he turns and smiles at me, and I can see at once that it's alright.

"Sleeping Beauty awakes," he says drily.

"Ha," I say. "I've almost certainly got bed hair."

"Hard to tell from here. Perhaps you'd better come a bit closer."

"'Come into my parlour, said the Spider to the Fly'?"

"Something like that."

I cross the room and stand by his chair, looking down at the laptop. "How's the writing going?"

"Oh," says James, "You know. Fits and starts." He puts his head back and looks at me. "And how are you this morning? That was one hell of a fright you gave me last night."

"I'm fine," I tell him, not quite truthfully.

"It sounded like you were being murdered."

I smile uneasily at that. It's on the tip of my tongue to say that the problem wasn't that I was being murdered, it was that I was not dead *enough* when they started nailing the lid down. But in the end I say, "It was just a really horrible dream."

There is nothing I want to add to that, so for a moment there is silence. Then I say, "Where did *that* come from?"

James follows my gaze. "I thought you put it there."

"No," I say, shaking my head. I lean over the desk for a closer look. The thing is a kind of small casket, about eight inches across, with two squat little glass bottles slotted into the top of it. Apart from the bottles, it is entirely made of some smooth black material that I'm pretty sure is ebony. So the thing is old; that wood is protected nowadays. It stands on four tiny clawed feet and on the front face of it there is a relief carving, of a limp hand holding a wreath. The entire effect is deeply funereal. I think it is horribly ugly. "I didn't put it there."

"That's a relief," says James. "I thought I was going to have to pretend I liked it."

"James! Why would I give you something as ugly as that?!"

"Because it's for a writer. It's an inkstand. Look." James lifts up one of the little bottles and shows me the dark stain of ink in the bottom of it.

"Well, it may be apt but it's still ugly," I say. "And I've never seen it before."

We both look at the inkstand.

"Belle must have put it there," James says. "She probably unpacked it from one of the boxes." He glances at me. "You don't have to love it just because it was theirs, you know."

"I know," I say.

The silence that follows makes me uncomfortable. "Shall I put it away?" I say eventually, in the lightest tone I can manage.

"Sure," says James. "I can always put it out again if I

decide to start writing with a quill pen." He grins, and I smile uneasily.

I reach over and lift the inkstand. It's heavier than I expected, and the glossy wood has a waxy feel to it that I find unaccountably repulsive. If it weren't so obviously an antique, the proper place for it would be the dump. Instead I carry it into the dining room. The sideboard is already crammed with stuff, so I set it down on top. Then I look at the inkstand again and decide I don't want it where I can see it. I open the sideboard, take out an innocuous box of tarnished silver napkin rings, and put the inkstand in its place, next to a stack of gilt-edged plates. I shut the door on it and straighten up, instinctively rubbing my fingertips together as though I've been handling something sticky. It's no use; once the idea has got into my head, the idea of *contamination*, I can't let it go until I've washed my hands. I go through into the kitchen and run the tap until the water is hot. The feeling of the water running over my hands is comforting, and I stand there for longer than I need to, listening to it pattering down into the sink.

You're making too much out of this. The inkstand is only a thing. The other stuff in those boxes, the ones you haven't opened, are only things. They have no meaning other than the meaning you give them.

I turn off the tap.

The dreams, too: they can't hurt you unless you let them.

I tell myself: *Change is hard. Even good change is hard. The dreams are just a by-product of normal stress. Industrial waste from your brain.*

I know that this is the most plausible explanation, but it still leaves me with the question of what to do about it. I consider that while I make myself a very strong, very sweet cup of tea and two slices of toast. The obvious answer is: *keep yourself busy.* It's a strategy that's worked well for me in the past. Consume yourself with work and there's no capacity left for thinking about other things.

There is loads to do, of course: decorating, unpacking boxes, eventually gardening, and of course, a wedding to organise. As regards most of those things, I am my own foreman. I could do any of those tasks today or tomorrow or in a month's time. The wedding is more urgent; we haven't even set an exact date for it, because we don't have a venue yet. But I can't spend every moment on that; James has to come with me to view places. That leaves my freelance work. If I had a deadline, that would be something to focus on. Something to give shape to my time.

I think about this some more when breakfast is finished, when I'm upstairs pulling on my clothes and fastening my hair into a knot at the back of my head. I stand in front of the mirror applying eyeliner and sheer lipstick and doing my best to avoid catching my own eye. I know what Belle would say about the decision I'm close to making – I even pick up my phone, debating on calling her, before putting it down again.

In the end, though, I do it. I go downstairs and boot up my laptop. Then I email my former employer back and tell them I'd love to copyedit that thriller.

Chapter
Thirteen

I don't remember that ebony inkstand, the same as I don't remember the white porcelain flower arrangement that Belle put into that sideboard. But I do remember the gilt-edged dinner service that is also stored in there. There is one plate missing from that service, and I know why.

I remember sitting at the highly polished table in the dining room with one of those plates set out in front of me, flanked by silver-plated cutlery that was cumbersome for a child's hands. I remember this very clearly. It is strange how selective memory is: there are so many days that have vanished completely, yet specific incidents remain, as though varnished into a state of perfect and unchanging preservation.

To my right, at the end of the table, sat my father, the judge, broad-shouldered, grey-haired and florid, with his hands placed palm down on the table top, as though he might propel himself to his feet at any moment and deliver a blistering tirade. At the other end of the table sat my mother, straight-backed and as grim-faced as a gorgon. Opposite me sat my older brother, Stephen. I was afraid to look at either of my parents, but once I raised my eyes

83

from my plate and glanced at Stephen. He was terribly pale and kept biting his lip to try to keep his composure. I didn't want to catch his eye in case he broke down.

I looked down at my plate again. Arranged on it were slices of lamb, which I hated, three small potatoes and a large heap of boiled vegetables. There was also a comma of pale brown gravy, already congealing. It was a meal that a child was *supposed* to eat, but almost certainly wouldn't like. I had still fared better than Stephen though. The plate set in front of him was empty, as clean and white as a bone. That was part of his punishment: to be sent to bed that evening without any dinner. The other part was to watch the rest of us eating ours – not just the loathsome cut of lamb but the pudding, too. He was not to be allowed to go until the last drop of coffee had been drunk at the end of the meal and my father had set his cup down on the saucer.

None of us was eating at that moment. My father was watching Stephen, to ascertain that there would be no protest, and no attempt to leave the table. My mother was watching my father, her hands smoothing the napkin over her lap. I did not dare to begin without them.

I think the three of us thought that Stephen would submit to his punishment and say nothing at all. I hoped he would, because it would mean less trouble in the end, and I think my parents expected it. And for a moment it seemed that he would. But just as my father sat back and reached for his knife and fork, Stephen said, "They were only mocks."

He spoke in a very low voice, hardly more than a mutter, but my father heard him all the same. He leaned forward again with deliberate slowness, fixing Stephen with his cold gaze.

"They were only mocks," my father repeated. He paused. "Only mocks. *Only.*"

I clenched my fists in my lap. *Don't say anything, Stephen. Just shut up. It will just make it worse.* But it was already too late.

Unbelievably, Stephen didn't shut up, although he winced under my father's glare. He spoke up, this time quite clearly, although he didn't look at either of our parents. He looked straight ahead, at me, but not seeing me.

"I'll do better in the proper exams."

"Really? You'll do better in the proper exams?" There was a silkiness in my father's tone that I recognised as dangerous even then. I suppose it was a trick he had acquired in his days as a barrister: to make his voice soft and encouraging, to lure a defendant into saying something very unwise. Stephen should have known better than to fall for it, but he did.

"Yes. I'll work really hard, honestly I will."

"Well, Stephen," said our father, "This is a very laudable intention, on the face of it at any rate. But I think we have to examine the balance of probabilities here. You have made the statement that you intend to work really hard, but what evidence do we have to support it? Is it probable that someone who lacks the motivation to make an effort on one occasion will miraculously discover it on the next? Is it probable–"

"I *promise* I'll work harder," said Stephen, his voice rising.

"Don't interrupt your father," said my mother.

"But I will. I–"

"Stephen," said my father, and my brother instantly fell silent. "Nobody knows better than I do how important it is to offer a second chance, nor indeed how often such chances are wasted–"

He went on in this way, as though he were summing up

the case for the prosecution, and of course Stephen didn't have a hope of defending himself. Perhaps it was the fact that he tried to, uselessly, at the beginning, that made our father go on for so long. Both of us knew very well that the best way to deal with one of our father's scathing lectures was to endure it without interrupting, as though it was a bout of savage weather passing over our heads. Arguing back was fatal.

At first, I gazed down at the unappetising slices of lamb and gelatinous gravy and prayed silently for Stephen to stop talking. But as my father went on and on, I began to feel indignant. There was nothing I could say. I could not think of any argument strong enough to counter what my father was saying. It was probably true that Stephen hadn't worked hard enough for his mock exams; I knew he liked picking out a tune on the piano or lying full length in the long grass at the very end of the garden, watching insects going about their business, more than he liked poring over his school books. It was logical to think that no miraculous change was going to come over him before he sat the actual exams. Quite possibly he would fail some of those, too. I could not refute any of this. But at the same time, I felt that my father was wrong. He was brilliantly good at arguing – there was no way that a fifteen-year-old and a twelve-year-old were ever going to win – but that didn't mean that he was *right*.

Then I looked up again and saw that Stephen was going to cry. I could see it in his face. He started to say, "I'm sorry," and he choked on the words.

It was a long time since I had seen my brother cry. I cried often, partly because it usually defused whatever trouble I was in, but I had not seen Stephen cry since before he turned fifteen the previous year. I was horrified, and that made me reckless.

"He's said sorry," I burst out. It came out more loudly than I expected. My father stopped speaking. Everyone looked at me.

"Be quiet, Fenella," said my mother.

I looked at her and then at my father. "No. He's said sorry. Stop telling him off."

"Silence." My mother was turning pink in the face.

"*No.*"

"What?" said my father incredulously.

"No." I was hot with terror at my own boldness, but I was committed now. "You're being mean."

"Fenella—" began my mother, but there was no stopping me.

"He said he was sorry, so you should leave him alone. Stop telling him off." I was breathing very quickly now and I was near to tears myself. "And let him have his dinner. It's cruel to starve somebody."

"It's alright, Fen," said Stephen quickly. "I'm okay."

"It's not alright," I insisted.

"How dare you?" said my mother.

"You're not being fair," I said. Now I really was crying. "If you want him to pass his exams he has to do his homework, and how can he do it if he hasn't had any dinner?"

"Very well." There was a scraping sound as my mother pushed back her chair and stood up. When she leaned over me, I flinched back, but she didn't lay a hand on me. She picked up my dinner plate with both hands, and then she walked right around the table to where my brother sat, picked up his knife and scraped the whole lot onto his plate. "There." She came back round to my side, and slid the empty plate in front of me. Then she went back to her own place and sat down.

For a moment there was silence except for my own

muffled sobs. Then my mother picked up her cutlery and began to cut up one of her own slices of lamb with quick, abrupt movements, as though it were a live thing she was trying to finish off. She glanced at Stephen. "Eat."

Stephen looked down at the tumbled mess of food on his plate. A globule of gravy was suspended on the rim of it; as I watched, it oozed languorously onto the table top.

"You heard your mother," said my father. "Eat."

"But..." Stephen began, but his voice trailed off. We looked at each other, and I could see the indecision in his eyes. I think neither of us could imagine what would happen if he refused to eat. Would my mother get up again and scrape the food back onto *my* plate? I could not face such a terrifying farce. Hungry though I was, I didn't think I could eat that scrambled pile of food any more.

Inevitably, Stephen caved in. "I'm sorry, Fen," he said in a low voice as he picked up his fork.

My father's fist came down on the table top with a thump that made the cutlery jump on the polished surface. He didn't need to say anything. He simply glared until Stephen put the first forkful into his mouth.

I heard the muffled choking sounds my brother was making and knew that he was crying. My fifteen-year-old brother, three years older than me, was *crying.* I curled my own hands into tight fists under the table. I didn't look at Stephen. Instead I looked at my plate. It was empty except for a few unappetising streaks of gravy where the food had slid off it.

I made up my mind there and then that I wouldn't sit there until the coffee had been drunk at the end of the meal. I was in trouble already, right up to my neck, and now I became actually reckless.

My mother saw what I was about. "Sit *down,* Fenella," she snapped, before I was even properly out of my chair.

I didn't obey. The legs of the chair screamed on the floorboards as I pushed it back. "I'm going to my room," I said.

"Sit down."

"No," I said. "I've got nothing to eat now anyway." I snatched up the plate to show her. It was slick with gravy; some of it had somehow got underneath the plate too. It slipped from my fingers, dropped to the floor and broke into three large pieces.

For several moments I simply stared at the fragments. I was afraid of what I had done. I knew it was no use saying I hadn't meant to do it; I *had* done it, and it would be taken as deliberate misbehaviour. It passed through my head that I could bolt for the door and run upstairs to my room before anyone could stop me, but it was already too late. My mother was on her feet again. She grasped me by the upper arm, her fingers digging into the flesh. Then she dragged me to the door. Her strength seemed superhuman; there was no fighting against it. When we got to the doorway she hurled me out of the room with such force that I fell against the wall on the opposite side of the hallway. My head came into contact with the oak console table that stood there, and for several seconds I was dizzy with pain. Then I heard the dining room door slam shut, and the sound of my mother's footsteps on the boards on the other side as she stalked back to her seat.

My head ringing, I did not trust myself to stand up immediately. Instead I crawled as slowly and quietly as I could to the dining room door and pressed my ear to the panel. What was happening to Stephen?

I could not hear a sound from him. I supposed he was forcing down the slices of lamb and the mushed-up remains of the potatoes and vegetables. I heard a brief exchange between my parents; the actual words were muted by the door but the terseness smacked of self-righteousness. Justice had been served, at least for the time being, but I was sure there would be more of it later.

My head ached. I knew I should get up and hide myself upstairs before the meal was over. If I got up now, I would have time to go into the kitchen and take some biscuits or a slice of bread up with me to stave off the hunger pangs. Still I huddled there against the door a little longer, and soon I heard my father begin to speak again. His voice rose and fell with studied skill. I knew that he was pointing out my brother's deficiencies to him in exquisite and pitiless detail. It went on and on, until I crept away to my room.

I was angry with my parents, but I was indignant with Stephen then too. Why didn't he stick up for himself – or for me? It was no use saying *Sorry, Fen.* I didn't see then how crushed he was. I didn't know that some things, once broken, can never be mended.

Chapter
Fourteen

It is evening, and we are walking up through the town towards a pub that promises traditional live music; that's something else we have to organise for the wedding, so I suppose it counts as research. It has finally stopped raining after a downpour that lasted two days and we are both grateful for a reason to go out. Even in the town, things have a wet, bedraggled look: water runs down the gutters and into the drains with a gentle gurgling sound, carrying leaves and litter with it, and the streetlights are reflected in the glossy wet pavements. I glance back, and beyond the limits of the town I see the dark bulk of the hills, a few lights faintly visible on their lower slopes.

The pub door is closed, keeping the heat in, but as soon as we push it open we can hear the buzz of voices. It's warm and well lit and already I can feel my spirits rise. I look up at James and smile.

He smiles back, pleased to see my low mood evaporating. "Let's get a taxi back," he says. "Then we can both have something."

"I don't think there are any taxis," I say. I haven't seen a taxi rank anywhere in the darkened town.

"So let's walk."

"It's miles, James!"

"Good thing you've got boots on, then. What are you having?"

I give up. "Gin. We'll probably regret this."

"Probably," he agrees, cheerfully.

The bar is crowded and as we edge our way sideways through the packed bodies I cannot see anywhere to sit. James squeezes in between two other people to order the drinks while I wait, surrounded by strangers engrossed in their own conversations. I've barely spoken to anyone in the town before, so I'm taken by surprise when my own name rises above the hubbub. I turn, and there is Seonaid McBryde, vivid in jeans and an emerald green top that sets off her mass of auburn hair.

"It *is* you," she says. Then she looks past me and says, "And is that–?"

"Yes," I say. "That's James."

"Oh my God!" she says, all agog. "You have to introduce us! I mean, as long as you weren't planning on a quiet evening together or anything."

"In here?" I say, raising my eyebrows.

She laughs. "I suppose not. But honestly, you don't have to if you don't want to."

I'd have to be quite hard-hearted not to, considering the star-struck expression on her face. So when James pushes his way back through the press of people with a gin for me and a whisky for himself, I say, "James, this is Seonaid McBryde. She runs the wedding shop in the town."

"Can I just say..." begins Seonaid.

...*how much I loved The Unrepentant Dead,* I think, amused.

"...how much I loved *The Unrepentant Dead,*" says Seonaid, who has gone a little pink in the face. "It's one of my favourite books." She has actually clasped her hands together, like a Victorian lady about to swoon.

"There are so many things I want to ask you about it. Please, please come and sit with us."

This is an offer we can't refuse, mainly because there won't *be* anywhere to sit unless someone makes space for us. So we follow Seonaid to the far corner of the room, where an improbably large number of people are crowded round a single table covered in glasses. Two stools materialise as if by magic.

"This is James Sinclair," Seonaid announces. "He's a famous author." Then she remembers me. "And this is Fen. She's going to marry him."

This piece of news provokes a small and slightly inebriated cheer. We sit, and I smile into my gin while James good-naturedly fends off all the usual questions, both the regular ones – where do you get your ideas? how long does it take you to write a book? – and the completely unanswerable ones like: have I heard of you? and, would I like your work? Someone goes up to the bar for more drinks – I get another gin, without asking – and after what seems like a very short time, someone else goes for another round. It is very warm in here and already James is in his shirt-sleeves. I am nursing my coat on my lap because if I put it down anywhere I can't imagine ever being able to find it again. The gin is burning a warm trail down my throat.

There's not much chance of my talking to James because he has been appropriated by half a dozen other people. But there's a friend of Seonaid's – Holly – who's dying to ask me about the wedding.

"Where are you having it?" she says, and I have to admit that we haven't decided – either where we'll have the ceremony, or the reception venue. I can almost see her and Seonaid rolling up their sleeves.

They have an argument about the big Victorian hotel in the town – Holly says it's the best place for a reception if you're inviting loads of people; Seonaid says it's "too obvious".

"Fen's looking for something a bit different," she announces, and I wonder if she's going to bring up the subject of the lavender dress, but she doesn't. Instead, the pair of them start brainstorming the most unusual places they can think of for a wedding ceremony: a ruined castle, or a handfasting by a Pictish stone. When Holly suggests a boat in the middle of the river Tay, I feel I have to cut in.

"I was thinking of something more traditional than that."

Their faces fall, but then Holly says, "I know *exactly* the place." She tells me about a mediaeval chapel out in the middle of the countryside, with views of the distant mountains. It does sound interesting, so I get her to give me directions, wondering whether I will remember them in the morning after all this gin.

Meanwhile, James is just in the middle of explaining that he got the idea for *The Unrepentant Dead* from a conversation in a bar some distance north of here when a long wavering note, the sound of a violin being tuned up, drowns conversation out. The musicians have arrived, though I can't think where the bar staff have put them. The next moment they launch into what sounds like a very energetic reel, though there isn't anywhere to dance. After that there's no point in trying to say anything, not even *honestly, I really can't* when yet another drink appears in front of me. Seonaid digs me in the ribs and I look at her – we laugh at each other and I pick the glass up, knowing this is going to mean a headache for sure in the morning but not really minding.

After the reel we have a couple of modern folk songs I

don't recognise, and then *Loch Lomond* followed by *The Skye Boat Song*. By this time, we are all in a pleasant haze of warmth and bonhomie. People are clapping and singing along, James included. So it's a surprise when the next song strikes up and there's a noticeable drop in the sound levels. At first I think they're all just trying to listen, because this one is a ballad – it's slower and softer, almost melancholy. I pick out fragments of the words: *dark, dark the night... she will come back to you...*and something that sounds like *she'll put ye on like a suit of clothes*, though perhaps I have misheard that because it doesn't make any sense. I look from face to face and see that the grins have been wiped right off them. Some look neutral, some downright stony. Nobody likes this song, for some reason. A few heads shake. And Seonaid gives me a sidelong glance.

It's a wary glance, the sort of glance you give someone if you know someone else has said something potentially offensive in front of them. In spite of all the empty glasses crowded onto the table top, she's not so drunk that she doesn't notice me react. She looks down, quickly, and then away.

At that moment, the band launch into the chorus and I know why.

Lavender lady, lavender lady...

There's a buzz of conversation and the rest of the words are drowned out. It feels as though people are purposely talking over the song.

I guess the musicians have got the message, too: they hurry through the rest of the chorus and then stop abruptly. There is very little applause this time. It's a relief when they launch into a raucous-sounding reel. After that, we get *A Red, Red Rose*. By the time they have started on a cover of *Caledonia*, any awkwardness has been forgotten – well, everyone else seems to have forgotten it, anyway.

I shoot a look at James. He isn't looking my way. He's doing his best to listen to the band while the man on the other side of him explains something at great and rather drunken length. I turn to Seonaid.

"Seonaid, that song–"

"What song?" she says, but I can see from her expression that she knows exactly which one I mean.

"The lavender lady song. Is that why lavender is unlucky?"

"I suppose," she says reluctantly.

"What does it mean, she'll put ye on like a suit of clothes?"

She shrugs uneasily. "I don't know." Her pale skin is flushed. We've all had far too much to drink and I don't think she's capable of lying about anything.

"But the song is about a lady who dresses in lavender?"

She nods. "The song is from here," she says. "The band aren't, though. That's why they didn't know not to play it."

"But why don't people like it?"

"They just don't. It's bad luck. I guess..."

"Yes?" I say, expectantly.

"It's old. Stuff that happened a long time ago. People have forgotten."

And that's all I can get out of her. I try asking Holly, but she knows even less than Seonaid does. The band are finishing their last song. Shortly after that, Seonaid is on her feet, shrugging on her jacket, and people are looking for their coats and bags, and a few minutes later we are out on the street.

I was right about the taxis; there aren't any. I have a ridesharing app on my phone and that says the nearest one is Edinburgh.

"Looks like a walk," says James, peering over my shoulder. "It's only three miles."

"Three and a half," I say, faintly.

"At least it's not raining any more."

That's true, but there's still a damp chill in the air. It's remarkable how quickly everyone has dispersed, now that the pub is closed. As we walk down the hill, I see someone far ahead, turning off into another street, but otherwise the place has rapidly become deserted. There is no-one to cadge a lift from. The pavements are still shiny but without the sound of falling rain we can hear our footsteps echoing. We stop at the car so that James can get the torch out of the glove box, and when he shuts the door the sound is incredibly loud in the silence.

"This is nice," I say, shivering.

James laughs briefly, but the cold night air and the quiet have a dampening effect, even on his good humour. He takes my hand, and we set off. The dark shops and cafes are soon left behind. We pass houses, most dark, a few with lights on, and then the park. The gates are closed. Beyond the railings I can dimly make out trees and bushes and the faint metallic gleam of the children's play apparatus. The road snakes on. This feels a lot further than I thought. We come to the smaller gate that marks the other end of the park, and here the street lamps run out. For a moment we pause there, under the last light, and contemplate the blackness ahead.

James takes the torch out of his pocket and switches it on. The effect is not what we would have hoped. Shone directly on the ground, it would help you to avoid stepping on anything, but that's about it. If you direct it ahead, the beam dissolves into the impenetrable dark. I wonder whether it is actually possible to walk several miles in this without falling into a ditch or something. The warm haze of gin has evaporated completely. I hold onto James's arm.

"Right," he says, more resolutely than either of us feels, and we step into the dark.

After another couple of hundred metres, the pavement

runs out and there is tarmac under our feet. There are potholes too, full of rainwater that gleams like ink in the torch beam. Wet vegetation overhangs the edge of the road, so we walk a little further out. If a car came, we'd see the headlights long before it reached us, but nothing does come.

Neither of us says much. We are too busy concentrating on where we put our feet. I am alive to every tiny sound – every rustle and scurry. We hear something far off, a brittle cry that I think might be a fox. Once, something passes overhead and in the light of the torch that James directs upwards we see the white wing of an owl. The cold damp air seems to press very close.

After what feels like an interminable time, we come to the turning that leads towards Barr Dubh. The surface underfoot is worse here, but at least the house is visible in the distance; we left the outdoor light on for when we came home. We toil our way slowly towards it. Mostly, I look at the ground, afraid of stumbling, but then I look up, at the house.

"James," I say.

"Mmm?"

"Is that someone outside the house?"

He stops for a moment and looks towards Barr Dubh. Once again, I am struck by how quiet it is.

"I can't see anyone," he says at last. "It's a bit late for anyone to come calling, anyway."

I look too. "Just to the left of the light," I say.

He shakes his head. "I can't see anything."

"Maybe it's just a shadow," I say, to convince myself as much as him. We watch for a few moments and then we start walking again.

I am tired and my head is starting to throb, so when I glance towards the house and see it again, I don't quite trust my eyes. It looks as though someone is standing there, outside the door, someone thin and crooked; they stand quite still, but a wind I can't feel makes their clothing billow out for an instant, raggedly.

I blink hard, and now all that I can see is the patch of light at the front of the house, and the shadows that shift and blur from a shrub planted near the door.

We turn in at the gateway and trudge up the drive, crunching over the gravel, James fishing in his pocket for the keys. Of course, there is no-one here. I wait while James finds the right key and fits it into the lock, looking around me into the dark. I see nothing, hear nothing. The darkness is like a holding of breath, a waiting. A watching.

James opens the door, and we go into the house.

Chapter Fifteen

No grey Perthshire rain today; cool bright sunshine filters down through the coppery autumn leaves as James and I travel through the countryside. I am driving; James is map reading. We are going to see the little mediaeval chapel Holly told me about. The directions are distinctly hazy in my head, and the chapel is on a country lane so insignificant that it isn't on the mapping software on my phone, so James has a map spread out on his lap. I can tell that if we decide to hold the wedding ceremony there, we are going to have to give the guests some very specific instructions on how to find it.

"There's a stone circle up here," says James, scrutinising the crumpled paper as we take a left turn onto a narrow road. I can hear the relish in his voice.

"James," I say, "What about the chapel?" I am alert to the risk of being sidetracked into investigating a fascinating potential story location.

"Second left," he says, sounding dangerously preoccupied.

Luckily for me, the chapel is signposted with one of those brown signs they use for historic places. We make a very sharp turn onto a track that is even worse than the one that leads up to Barr Dubh House.

The car bounces and rattles so much over the ruts and holes that my teeth chatter.

I can see the chapel ahead of me, just before the road takes another sharp corner, leading off towards some farm buildings. It is a very plain grey stone building with a stubby tower. It is nothing like the picturesque English church in the town where I grew up, with its pale golden stone and elaborate stained glass windows. All the same, I like it. It looks at home in its setting, with the mountains in the distance beyond it. A low stone wall encloses the kirkyard but outside the wall, the ground is rough and overgrown. I cannot see anywhere to park.

Eventually, after driving up and down, I decide to leave the car at the side of the road, with two wheels on the grass, and hope that nobody decides to drive a combine harvester down the track or anything. I look at James, who is folding the map.

"Forget getting a Rolls for the wedding," he says. "We should get a four by four."

"Who said anything about a Rolls? I thought we were having a small, intimate wedding."

"A tractor, then."

"A white one."

"With a muck spreader on the back."

"Romantic," I say, and James grins.

We get out of the car and walk towards the chapel, circling puddles on the way. When we get to the gate, I'm surprised to see that there is a battered-looking bicycle leaning against the wall. So we are not alone, although there is nobody in sight as we go into the kirkyard. It is completely grassed over; there is no path leading to the main door. Our feet whisper through the grass, making barely a sound. James's hand in mine is warm, his grip firm.

The door is truly ancient-looking, made of thick wood studded with black iron nails and set into an arch-shaped stone frame with carvings so weathered that you can't tell what they are supposed to be any more. It stands ajar, and inside I can only see darkness.

James pauses to study the outside of the building, so I let go of his hand and go first, pushing the door open with a great squeal from the hinges. I step inside and immediately discover that it is colder indoors than out. It is less dark than I expected. Although the windows are small, they are made of clear glass, and the light streams through them, illuminating a bare stone floor. The chapel is entirely empty: there are no pews, and no pulpit. I can't even tell where the altar should be. If we marry in here, we will have to have chairs brought in.

And lights, I think, glancing around me. There is no sign that the chapel is lit by anything other than natural light from the windows.

I slip my phone out of my pocket and take a few snaps; I know Belle will want to see this.

I am not sure how I feel about it as a place to get married. It is cold, stark and dimly lit, a shell with few traces of its past usage. There is a faint minerally smell of damp stone. On the other hand, it is a kind of blank slate that could be adapted to whatever style of wedding we wanted. We could arrange the chairs in lines in the traditional way, or have them in a circle, facing inwards; we could have untidy bunches of the wild flowers I fancied, or trees in pots. I think that I would like it to be as different as possible from a conventional wedding. There would be too many elements missing from that: nobody to give me away, for example. I shall give myself away.

The church takes the form of a cross, which means that not every corner is visible from where I am standing. It is

102

several minutes before I realise that I am not alone. Even then, I hear his halting footsteps on the flagstones before I see him: a tall, thin, rather stooped old man in a shabby tweed suit with a startling crimson tie. He is carrying a ring with several large keys on it; when he sees me, he holds them up.

"You've timed it well. I only opened up five minutes ago."

"Oh," I say. "I thought–"

He shakes his head. "Yes, it's supposed to be open from ten. But most days nobody bothers to come at all, so I thought I'd finish my coffee first."

"Is that your bicycle outside?" I ask him. It's hard to imagine him riding it around the lanes; he doesn't look fit enough.

He nods. "One day it will pitch me off into the ditch," he says, as though the bicycle were a live thing. "Anyway, miss, is there anything I can tell you about the chapel before I take myself off home?"

"We just came for a look around, really," I say. I glance behind me and yes, James is there in the doorway. "We're looking for somewhere to hold our wedding."

"And you've come up specially?"

He's noticed my English accent, of course.

"No," I say. "We live here."

"Well," says the old man, "This is a fine place for a wedding... in the summer."

"It's a beautiful old place," says James. "When was it built?"

It takes the old man quite a long time to answer this question. James listens to an extensive history of the building, which may or may not have replaced an earlier one, and has had various additions and repairs over the centuries. The history is peppered with references to local places and families I have never heard of, and James rashly asks some further questions. Judging by the avid way in which the old man replies, he is thrilled to be asked. I suspect he will not be off home for another coffee any time soon. I only half listen to what he is saying, occupying myself instead with imagining what it would be like to get married in here. It certainly wouldn't be the place for an off-the-shoulder dress. I pull my jacket closer around me, shivering a little.

The old man seems to know an unimaginable – some might say indigestible – amount of local history. So I wait until he has come to the end of his account of Perthshire history, and say, "I wonder if you know anything about the area where we live? We'd love to know something about its past."

"You can try me."

"It's called Barr Dubh House. It's not old – just a couple of years – but I think it's named after the place, or maybe after an older house that was there before it."

I catch James's eye as I say this, and I see him raise his eyebrows questioningly. Of course, he doesn't know about Belle's dream, or mine. I'll have to think what to say about that later.

The old man is silent for a few moments, considering. At last he says, "Where would this be, Barr Dubh House?"

I do my best to describe the location, which is neither in the town itself nor properly in the next village, and not directly on the main road either. All the landmarks I can think of are natural ones, and that's not very helpful because everything around here is a short distance from either a hill, a forest or a river.

The old man listens, and then he says, "Hmmm. I thought so. You're talking about Barr Buidhe."

I shake my head. "It's definitely Barr Dubh."

He looks at me for a long moment, sharp grey eyes peering from under bushy eyebrows. "Barr Dubh is what local people call that spot. Have done for a long while. But Barr Buidhe is its real name."

I must look unconvinced because he continues.

"Look," the old man says, "The place is named for the hill near it. Barr Buidhe, the yellow hill – because of the gorse that grows there."

"Oh." That makes sense. I remember seeing the yellow gorse when we first came to look at the house, earlier in the year. "But why would they call it Barr Dubh, the black hill, then?"

"I can't say. But you are right that there was an older house there, a long time ago. Perhaps the owners thought Barr Dubh sounded grander."

So there *was* an older house. Just like in Belle's dream.

It means nothing, I say to myself. *You shouldn't even be surprised. You've seen the old gate posts – they had to belong to something.*

"Do you remember the house, the older one?" I try to keep the edge out of my voice.

Up go the bushy brows. "I'm seventy-seven, young lady, not one hundred and seventy-seven. There's been nothing there in *my* lifetime, not until they built the new one, which is your home."

"I'm sorry," I start to say, but he waves away my apology. "Never mind. I dare say I look one hundred and seventy-seven to *you*. And I'm too old to stand about in this damp building blethering all morning. I'll be off, and leave you two to think about your wedding plans." He pauses. "If you'd lived at Barr Buidhe in times gone by, when the old house was there, you could have got married in your own chapel, you know."

"Really?" says James, sounding interested; he has

evidently recovered from the torrent of local history poured out on him a few minutes ago.

"Oh yes. As I say, the house was gone long before I came along, but the chapel was still standing when I was a lad – well, the remains of it, anyway. I expect it's gone now."

"Whereabouts was it?" asks James.

"Let me see. Are the gates to the old estate still there? They are? Well, it would be south-west of there, I suppose. But it's no use thinking of holding your ceremony there. I doubt there's one stone left on top of another after all this time."

During this conversation, we have been drifting towards the doorway. James opens his mouth to ask something else, and then all three of us hear something from outside: a loud irritable blast on a horn.

"Parked on the road, are you?" asks the old man. "You'd better go and move it, quick."

I've already got the keys. I hand them to James and he takes off at speed. Whatever the horn belongs to is making an ominous rumbling sound. As the old man and I follow James out into the kirkyard, I see the most enormous tractor in the lane, looming over our car.

"Don't worry," says the old man, unperturbed. "He'll let your young man move the car. Angus has only had that tractor a couple of months. He won't want to scratch it."

I have no idea whether he is joking or not. We stand side by side and watch James reversing the car down the track, until he reaches a spot where it is wide enough for the tractor to pass without crushing it.

"Can I ask you one more thing?" I say, without taking my eyes off the car.

"If you must," says the old man drily, and then, more warmly: "Of course you can."

"Do you know why the colour lavender is unlucky around here?"

There is a slight pause before the old man says, "Where did you hear about that?"

"In the town," I tell him. "Well, in the wedding shop. I went in to chat about wedding colours. And we heard a song in the pub, *Lavender Lady*, and I thought it might be connected."

"Hmmm," he says. "Well, if I say it's true, you're not to put us down as a lot of superstitious teuchters."

Teuchters? I don't know what that means but it doesn't sound flattering and I'm not inclined to ask.

"But why is it unlucky?"

The old man glances at me. "Well, that's a question. A hundred and fifty years ago, lavender was a mourning colour. Half-mourning, they called it. I should say it was something to do with that. Not the colour for a wedding, hey?"

"I suppose not," I say slowly.

"Well, I must be getting on," says the old man abruptly. "It was nice meeting you, miss."

"My name's Fen–" I start to say, but he's already stumping away across the grass, heading for the gate. I watch him go, hugging myself against the chill breeze. I feel as though I have been snubbed.

He probably didn't hear you, I say to myself. But I am pretty sure he did. And I don't believe he told me everything he knew about the lavender superstition. I noticed the way he hesitated when I asked about it.

It's just bad luck, Seonaid told me. But I feel sure there's something more. As I pick my way across the kirkyard, I see the old man walk past the car, wheeling his bicycle. James has just got out and is standing next to it, waiting for me. He says something to the old man as he passes, but the old man doesn't stop. He raises a hand in acknowledgement and carries on past James, his head down. It is not until he is perhaps fifty metres further up the track, well out of conversational distance, that he stops and climbs very carefully onto the bicycle. Then he pedals away.

"Do you want to drive, or shall I?" says James when I get to the car.

"You drive." I climb into the passenger seat and reach for the discarded map. As James starts the engine, I unfold the map. It's not new enough to have Barr Dubh House on it, but I find the place pretty easily anyway. I study it carefully but can see no trace of a chapel marked anywhere on it. There are other things marked: a memorial, several cairns. But there is nothing to show that there is – or was – a chapel at Barr Dubh.

Perhaps the old man was mistaken, I think. *He could have mixed it up with somewhere else.*

The more I think about it, the more likely that seems. The estate agent never mentioned any other buildings on the land and there is nothing on the map. And if there is no chapel, perhaps there was no house either.

The map crackles as I fold it again.

"Did you find anything?" asks James.

"Not a thing." I slide the map into the side pocket.

"How on earth did you know there was an older house there?"

"I didn't," I say. "Not really. I just thought there must have been something, because of the old gate posts." I glance at him. "There still might not be anything. Maybe the old man was thinking of somewhere else. The two different names, that's fishy."

"He was right about the yellow gorse, though."

108

"There are probably hundreds of hills with gorse on. *Thousands.*"

"Well, there's one way to settle it," says James. "Look for the remains of the chapel."

I sit back and watch the fields and trees slide past the windows and think about that. We will look for the chapel. Of course we will. But do I want to find it?

Chapter Sixteen

Rain is falling when we arrive back at Barr Dubh House. Within seconds, a few light drops on the windshield of the car have turned into a heavy downpour and neither of us can see through the glass. There's no point in trying to sit it out. I know from experience that rain like this can go on for ages. Instead, I open the car door and dash for the porch. The rain is coming down so hard that it stings the skin of my face and neck.

James joins me a moment later, raindrops sparkling in his dark hair. He has the keys in his hand, his knuckles white and shiny wet. I am leaning on the door, trying to shrink back from the water that streams off the top of the porch and splatters onto the gravel.

"Hurry up."

When he opens the door, the pair of us nearly fall into the hallway, scattering a handful of letters that are lying on the floor.

"Ugh," I say, shaking my hands so that droplets fly. "I'm soaked." I push back my hair; even in the short distance from the car to the porch it has got very wet and is clinging unpleasantly to the side of my face. My skirt is sticking to my legs.

James comes up close and puts his arms around me. "Isn't this the bit where you have to take off those wet clothes?"

I push him off, laughing. "That's the all-time cliché, James. You really should know better. Call yourself a literary writer?"

"I was thinking about a change of genre," he says. "Erotic memoir, maybe."

"Can't you pick something useful?" I say. "Like cookery books? I could murder a bacon sandwich and a cup of tea right now."

"I have to go where inspiration takes me," he says, straight-faced.

This time, when he puts his arms around me, I don't protest. His lips are grazing mine when the phone rings, echoing shrilly in the long hallway.

"Ignore it," says James, kissing the side of my neck.

And I would, except something occurs to me.

"Isn't Laura calling you today?" Laura is James's agent.

"Yes, but later." All the same, James lets go of me with one hand so he can look at his watch. The other is still around my waist. "Shit," he says. "It's now."

"Go," I say, but he's gone already. A door closes and the phone abruptly stops ringing. I'm left standing alone in the hallway, with water dripping off me onto the floor.

I pick up the letters, which are damp now too, and dump them on the little table that stands there. I'll look at them later. First I want to get into some dry things and make myself a huge cup of tea.

My steps make a sound like a series of gavel blows on the wooden treads as I run upstairs. The bedroom is very cool; I must remember to turn the heating up. I unzip my damp skirt, let it drop to the floor, and then drape it over the side of the laundry basket to dry. Something warm and dry is needed instead; I pick a pair of fleecy-lined tracksuit bottoms that I only ever wear for lounging about. Then I wander into the bathroom and rub my hair ineffectually with a towel. The result is unsatisfactory, more scarecrow than sleek. I make a face at myself in the mirror.

Then I go downstairs again, put the kettle on and open my laptop. I suspect James will be on the phone for ages, so I think I'll do a little more research. While the kettle boils, I wander over to the window and look out at the distant treeline, tinged now with the coppery shades of autumn. If the old man is right, and this is the place they used to call Barr Buidhe, and the chapel is to the south west, I guess it's somewhere over there. More or less, in fact, where I saw that person – for I'm pretty sure it *was* a person, although all I can remember is the billowing of pale fabric – walking that time. Their presence suggests that at the very least there is a path along there, perhaps an interesting walking route. Certainly it must have fine views towards the house and the land behind it. Ruined chapel or not, it is worth investigating.

Once I've made the tea, I slide onto a stool and get to work, the mug steaming gently beside me. Last time I researched the house, I was looking for *Barr Dubh*. This time I type in *Barr Buidhe*, and sure enough, a whole lot of completely different stuff comes up.

I scroll down. Local history sites, database entries, book references. Where to start? I click on *images* and there it is: a black and white engraving of a country house in the Scottish baronial style, stone built with corbie steps and those little corner turrets. I click on the thumbnail to go to an enlarged image. There is a legend underneath the picture reading: *Barr Buidhe House, Perthshire.*

I sit and look at the engraving for a long time. I begin to see little details that I didn't notice at first glance: a sundial, a heraldic stone shield over the doorway. There are tiny figures, too – a man in a long fitted coat and breeches, and a woman in a dress with a tight bodice and a huge skirt, a curl of hair visible below her bonnet. Long shadows suggest that the view is intended to be an evening one. The windows of the house are dark, with tiny flashes of white to represent reflections.

Behind the house a hill is visible, and trees. The setting could certainly be Barr Dubh, but it could probably be a dozen other places, too. There's no handy blasted oak tree or jagged rock face or anything else to distinguish it.

I go to the website where the image is, but it's simply an online store selling antique prints. There is no information about the pictured house, other than the name. So I backtrack from *images* and scroll through some of the other results. Immediately something snags my attention. It's an entry in a database of historical sites, headed *Barr Buidhe House*.

A couple of clicks later and I'm looking at a small gallery of pictures, the first of which is the same engraving I looked at a few minutes ago. There is also an interactive map, with a dot representing the location of the house. I zoom in as much as possible, but there is only ever that dot. There is no plan of the house, because it no longer exists. I zoom out again, and now I know that the location really is our Barr Dubh. I can see the road from the town to the north of it, and I can trace the tracks that connect with it. Zoom out a little further and the town itself is on the map. I zoom in and out a few times, trying to orient myself, but it's soon clear that the old house was in pretty much the same spot as the new one – our home. In the world of that map, I'm sitting right under that dark dot, at this very minute.

I click back to the engraving of the old house, with its dark windows and tiny human figures. I stare at it for a few moments. Then I get up, abandoning the laptop, and pace the kitchen, rubbing my hands together. Cold unease drifts through me, sliding queasily through my stomach and raising the tiny hairs on my arms. I have to keep that feeling tamped down, because otherwise it might ignite into real dread, and that's no good, because I have to *think*.

What difference does this make? That's the question I ask myself. Before, I wondered whether there really was an older house on the site of our home. Now I know for certain that there was one.

As for how Belle could have dreamed about it – shouldn't that be *more* explicable, now that I know it was real? There are images of the house, a database entry, a map – all kinds of evidence that could have been seen at some past time and simply forgotten. There's nothing mysterious about that.

I go over all of it, rationalising everything. That feeling Belle said she had, of *wrongness,* that doesn't have to mean anything, except perhaps that Belle is worried about me, and Belle is only worried about me because she doesn't understand my life here. It wouldn't be good for her, so she doesn't see how good it is for me.

So far, so very sensible. But what about my own dreams? That is a box I don't want to open.

I go back to my laptop and look at the engraving again. I could call Belle. I could tell her she was right. I could talk this over with her. I could do that.

Seen and forgotten, I say to myself, firmly. I click out of the site, and close the laptop. My tea is now warm rather than hot; I drink it in several long swallows. Then I go off to collect the post from the table in the hall, before it disintegrates altogether from the wet.

Chapter
Seventeen

There's no sign of James emerging from his study. As I pass the door, I can hear the rise and fall of his voice, although I can't make out the words. I linger for a moment, the memory of his kiss on my lips, but the discussion is clearly in mid-flow; no chance of him coming out any time soon. I sigh a little, then go down to the end of the hall, where the letters are lying on the table. When I get close to the front door, I can hear the rain outside, still running off the porch and cascading onto the gravel.

The letters are a sodden heap; I can see that even before I pick them up and feel their wet pulpy texture. One of them – addressed to James – even has a muddy footprint on it. I hold that one by the corner, and as I walk back to the kitchen, it drips rainwater onto the floor. I put the whole lot down on the draining board and look at them.

I never normally open James's post, any more than I would read someone else's diary. But I can't see any harm in opening everything that's arrived today and leaving it somewhere to dry, before the whole lot turns into papier maché. The one with the footprint on it looks positively disgusting and I can't imagine James would want it dropped on his desk in its present state. It's also so waterlogged that I don't really need to tear it open at all – the envelope more or less disintegrates in my hands.

I uncurl the folded sheets inside and spread them out on the work surface, and as I do so I notice two things. Firstly, it's a card statement. There's no missing the well-known logo at the top of the page. Now it does feel uncomfortably intrusive to have opened it, so I consciously turn my gaze away, but it's too late, because the second thing has snagged my attention. The account balance.

Suddenly I'm hot all over, shocked and guilty at the same time, as though I have been caught looking at something obscene. Seconds slide past as I force myself to keep looking away, my gaze turned towards the window although I can't take in anything that's out there. Then I can't help myself. I have to take another look. I have to know whether I saw what I thought I saw.

A little over twenty-two thousand pounds.

James owes twenty-two thousand pounds.

Now that I've looked down at the statement, I can't look away again. I stare at that horrific total, willing it to be a mistake, but it isn't a mistake – it's there in stark black and white.

It's not the amount – though that's bad enough. It's the fact that until a few seconds ago, I had absolutely no idea that he was in debt at all. Isn't that the sort of thing people tell each other when they're getting married?

Maybe some of it is work expenses, I think, clutching at straws. There was the trip to Spain, amongst other things. There have been other trips too – to book festivals here and abroad. Perhaps he had to pay all that and claim it back from his publisher? It couldn't come anywhere near to that grisly total, but it might account for a bit of it.

I'm terribly tempted to turn the statement over and read the list of transactions. It would set my mind at rest if I knew.

Maybe it won't, says a sharp little voice at the back of my mind. *What if he's spent it all on—*

—On what? I snap back at myself, angry and dismayed at the same time that I'm even speculating like this. It shouldn't make any difference, anyway, what James spent the money on. That's definitely James's business. We're both grown-ups, after all, and if I go any further, if I turn over the statement, I'm into snooping territory. No. The issue is whether we are being open with each other, not where the debt came from.

Still, I find myself thinking of Bluebeard's wife, who looked into the one room she was forbidden to enter, and saw something she would rather not have seen. Is it better to live in blissful ignorance, or to know the truth, however ugly?

I turn the paper over. *Previous balance from last statement: £21,973.88,* it says. The rest is interest.

I let out a long breath. I could still find out, of course. I could wait until James is out, and go hunting for the previous statements. But that would very definitely be stepping over a line. I am one hundred per cent *not* going to do that. Where would I stop, once I started with that? I'm pretty sure James has more than one credit card. Would I look at those statements too? *No.* Opening one letter because it was falling to pieces with wet is fair enough; poking about in someone else's things absolutely isn't. *Walk away from the locked room; throw the key in the moat if it's the only way to stop yourself looking.*

Then it occurs to me that I've already got a problem. However innocently, I've opened James's private mail and seen something he hasn't told me about – something he didn't want me to see. I can hardly claim to have opened the envelope and *not* noticed the contents. What am I going to say to him?

I sag against the kitchen cabinets. I try to summon up Imaginary Belle. I'm pretty sure I know what she'd say. "Have it out with him. This is the perfect opportunity to do it." But I'm not Belle. The happy place I've made with James feels like an island I've crawled up onto after a shipwreck. I don't want anything to spoil it. I *can't* let anything spoil it.

I pick up the soggy statement and tear it into pieces. It isn't difficult, it's so soft and wet. I open the lid of the kitchen bin. It's nearly full. I push the torn fragments into the bag, stuffing them down the side of the other refuse so they won't be obvious to anyone – *anyone* being James – who opens the bin. It's not enough, though; I can still imagine pieces being visible through the plastic when the bag is lifted out. In the end I haul the whole sack out, tie the top together, and haul it to the wheelie bin outside the back door. It is still raining heavily and I am pelted by drops as I open the bin. I don't care. I lift out the topmost bag, stuff the one with the pieces of the statement in it as far down the bin as I can, and then replace the other bag on top of it. The lid drops shut with a hard report. I go back into the house, close the back door and turn the key. It's hard to shake the feeling that I've done something wrong, but the strongest feeling is one of relief.

James will notice that his card statement seemingly hasn't arrived – I'm pretty sure of that. He'll probably think it's gone astray, or perhaps been sent to his old address. If he doesn't notice, the company will remind him soon enough if he misses the payment date. Either of these things might prompt him to say something to me, and then it will be out in the open.

Twenty-two thousand pounds, I think, dismally. A year ago, that would have been a disaster. I could barely cover my rent and living expenses, let alone find the cash for anything else, and James's income is always unpredictable. Now – well, now we *could* find the money to pay it off. It would pretty much clean us out, but we could do it. I might be glad that I said yes to copyediting the terrible thriller. But to do anything about it, James has to tell me. He has to trust me.

I sit thinking about this while the rain beats down, streaming down the kitchen windows until the world outside is a blur, shades of autumn gold and green and grey running into each other. The bright sunshine of this morning has gone; now the clouds are so heavy that it is almost dark indoors.

Some time later, James comes into the kitchen and switches on the lights. He is smiling; the conversation with Laura has gone well. I feel a twinge of something I can't quite define. I wonder fleetingly whether she knows about the debt or not – she's his agent, after all. It's her job to make him money.

"Why are you sitting here in the dark?" he says.

"I... don't know. I was on my laptop for ages and I didn't really notice it getting so gloomy." I make an effort to keep my tone light. "What did Laura say?"

"She wants to know when she can see the new manuscript. I said: not yet. And–" He pauses for dramatic effect. "She's had an offer for film and TV rights for *The Unrepentant Dead*."

"Wow." In spite of my melancholy mood, I'm genuinely impressed. "That's amazing."

"Yes." James is trying not to show too much excitement, but I can tell that he's thrilled. He starts telling me what Laura told him, about the company who've made the offer, and all the wonderful things they've said about the book. He knows – and I know – that the offer isn't a guarantee of anything; there's a long way to go before he sees his work on film. But it's impossible not to pursue the thought of it; it's like chasing butterflies.

I sit on the stool at the breakfast bar, with my chin on my hand, listening to James talk. His enthusiasm is infectious; soon I'm smiling too, quite naturally. He probably can't see anything amiss in my manner – can't see that I'm waiting. I'm waiting for him to say, *If this comes off, there will be money, and I'm glad about that, because there's something I have to tell you. Something I probably should have told you before.*

I smile at him, and I wait, but he never says it.

Chapter Eighteen

After James has gone back to work in his study, I can't settle to anything.

The die is cast, I remind myself. *It was cast the moment I tore up James's credit card statement and stuffed it down into the bin. I've already made the decision not to say anything – not now.*

What about later? That is the question, and I don't have an answer ready. I'm sick at heart, and the only thing I can think of right now is to push the whole problem away from me. If I can't keep my feelings out of my face James will see them, and then we'll end up having the discussion whether I want to or not.

Calm down, I say to myself. *What has really changed? James is still himself: kind, good-looking, talented. You have your dream home in the place you've always wanted to live. None of that has changed because you looked at a piece of paper.*

But it has. That's the trouble. James has kept something from me. There's another thought too, circling me like a shark, one that I have to keep pushing away. I know James loves me. I *know* he does. But supposing the money was the deciding factor? Would he have proposed if I hadn't had any?

I move about restlessly, until it occurs to me that my endless clattering about may attract James's attention and bring him out of his study. So I go upstairs, into the room we share, and open the window.

The rain is still sheeting down. I rest my arms on the windowsill and gaze out. The hiss and rattle of the rain is strangely comforting. The air is cool and fresh and also damp, even though I am protected from the downpour by the eaves. My nostrils flare as I draw in the scent of wet vegetation. The land is very green, even though it is autumn. This is why I wanted to be here. *Peace*, I think. Nobody wanting anything, nobody expecting anything, no bustle and scurrying to keep up. The lights and the traffic sounds and the grimy stink of the city feel like some kind of aberration here, where it is often so quiet that I can hear the breeze shivering through the leaves on the trees. It makes me feel as though I have been ill, and now I'm well.

I remember a day long ago, the day when I walked into the loch.

I'd reached the end of something, driven into the borderlands of what I could stand. I didn't argue or cry or say *shut up, stop it, leave him alone, leave us alone.* I don't think my parents even noticed me go, not at first. I put my hands over my ears and walked out of the room, out of the atmosphere that was as oppressive as the stink of blood. The holiday cottage had French windows which were standing open, and I walked straight out through them.

Outside, the sky was a flat opaque grey, a Scottish summer sky, but the air was warm enough. I went down the stone steps onto the lawn. The grass was springy under my bare feet. I pushed my way between overgrown shrubs until I came to the loch's edge. The water stretched out in front of me, smooth and glossy, and in the distance I could see the little island that was in the middle of the loch. It was thickly clustered with trees, so that it looked like a little forest, growing up out of the water. Something from a fairytale.

I stood there gazing out at it for a long time. I wished I could be there, or anywhere at all but where I was. There was no way of winning; I knew that. My parents were not religious, so back then I had never come across the concept of Original Sin, but if I had, I would have recognised it at once. Stephen and I, but especially Stephen, would always be wrong. It hardly mattered what we actually did. The question was how much punishment either of us could stand. I thought of my big brother crying, while they picked at him like vultures tearing at a carcass with their hooked beaks. I wished we were orphans in a storybook. Yes, I wished that. I didn't think it could be worse.

After a while, of course, I was missed. First they sent Stephen out to find me. I didn't turn round when I heard someone coming over the grass. I already knew it was him because he was sniffing from having wept.

"Fen, you have to go back in," he said.

"I'm not going."

"You have to," said Stephen.

"I hate them." My hands curled into fists.

"Fen..."

I turned to look at him. "Don't you hate them too?" I said savagely, my voice rising.

Stephen dropped his gaze. "It doesn't do any good."

"I don't care. And I'm *not* going back in."

For a moment there was silence, and then I heard my mother calling, first Stephen's name and then mine, her tone ominously insistent. I looked at Stephen for a moment and saw him tentatively reacting to her calling. He made small helpless movements, as though he were struggling to resist but was drawn anyway, like iron filings to a magnet. He would give in, I saw that plainly. I turned and walked into the loch, deliberately.

The water was cold, even though it was August. I could feel the line of definition between the part of myself that was submerged in it, and the part of myself that was in the warmer air, as clearly as if I had been cut in two. Under my feet the bed of the loch was soft and silty, with a sprinkling of small stones. My toes sank into it, releasing lazy clouds of brown silt into the clear water.

"Fen–!" Stephen's voice was urgent, afraid of the further trouble I was bringing on myself.

I took no notice. I kept wading further out. The slope into deeper water was gradual at first, but as the water rose over my knees I could feel the drag on my legs with every step. Stephen was still calling my name but I didn't look back at him. Instead I looked at the clear smooth water ahead of me, and the little island in the distance.

"Fenella!" That was my father bellowing my name. From the sound, I judged that he was now on the bank with Stephen. No matter. I was more than an arm's length away from the edge now and I didn't think he'd follow me in, not with slacks and socks and shoes on. I kept going.

When the water reached my breast the bottom of the loch began to fall away more sharply. I paused for a moment, looking at the vitreous surface of the water, the way the spreading ripples died away when I stopped moving. The cold wasn't so bad now, and anyway, there was a cleanness to it. The loch would drown me if I swam into the middle and became too tired to swim, but there was no malice in it. It was simply there, whether I swam across it and climbed out the other side, or slipped under the water and never came up again.

My mother was shouting now too. "Stupid, stupid girl!"

I took a deep breath and launched myself forward, my toes leaving the bottom. I kicked out, actually swimming now. The cold of the water seemed to coagulate around me, encasing my body in its frigid embrace. My breath came in hard little gasps. I kept my head up, looking at the island, the trees crowded on it.

Behind me, the voices of my family rose and fell but I was not tempted to turn around. My parents sounded very angry, and Stephen was drowned out altogether. I could not think of a single reason to go back. Besides, I needed to concentrate on staying afloat. The clothes I was wearing – a t-shirt and cropped summer trousers – were light and fairly close fitting, but there was still a noticeable drag on my limbs as I moved. I was not used to swimming fully clothed, and it was more of an effort to keep my head out of the water.

The island still looked a long way away. I had not consciously meant to aim for it when I went into the loch, but now I struck out for it. Water slapped at my face; I shook damp tendrils of hair out of my eyes. The first cold shock was over and the feeling of my arms and legs sliding through the cool water was almost pleasant, but still I didn't want to put my face in.

For a moment I paused, treading water, and tried to touch the bottom, but there was nothing there; my bare feet cycled without meeting any resistance other than the water. I was well out of my depth now. I wasn't afraid. I thought that I could swim the distance, if I took my time and paced myself. It was better anyway than going back. If I swam far enough out, the angry voices behind me would fade away altogether.

I concentrated on the movements of my arms and legs, on keeping my fingers pressed together, my breathing regular. The water made tiny lapping noises as I cut through it. The ends of my hair floated like delicate water weed. The taste of the loch was on my lips, subtle as a kiss.

After some time I began to flag a little. I didn't seem to be getting as close to the island as I'd have expected after swimming for this long. Perhaps it was simply that my progress was so gradual that I wasn't really aware of it. I tried closing my eyes and swimming vigorously for a minute or two. I thought that when I opened my eyes again I would see a difference, but instead I was dismayed: the island seemed no closer, and I had changed direction without realising, my face towards open water. If I kept swimming this way, I would swim right past the island without ever putting my feet on it.

I trod water again for a moment, and risked a glance behind me. The shore looked a long way away now. There was one figure on the bank – Stephen – and from here he looked tiny, a doll. I felt cold, a sensation that had nothing to do with the cool water: the loch was suddenly huge, and I a tiny speck in the very middle of it.

There really was nothing for it but to keep swimming. I put my face to the island again. Either Stephen had stopped calling or he was too far away for me to hear him; all I could hear now was my own breathing and the water itself – the increasingly uneven splash of my strokes, and the slap of little waves against my neck and shoulders.

Slowly, slowly, I struggled towards the island. After a few minutes in the water, I had acclimatised to the temperature, but now I was beginning to feel cold again. Swimming in waterlogged clothes required all my energy; it made the water feel clinging and gelatinous. I was sinking into its embrace; water slopped into my mouth and made me splutter. The first jagged spikes of panic pierced me.

I trod water again, shaking back damp hair. The island *was* closer now, but it would take determination to reach it. I swam, grimacing against the cold water. My fingers were acquiring a pale waxen look and I could feel my toes slowly turning numb. If I got a cramp now—

Don't think about it.

I kicked harder, trying to force life back into my limbs. My lower jaw was juddering, my breath hissing in and out as I shivered. The effort had become agonising; for a while I didn't really think at all, but floundered through the water like a drowning animal, fighting to keep my head up.

I was still some ten metres from the island when my feet struck something underwater with painful force. A rough surface scraped against my skin. I looked down and saw that I had swum into the branches of a fallen tree, almost completely submerged in the loch. I grasped at it with my hands and clung on, breathing heavily. It was a while before I had recovered sufficiently to make my way through it to the edge of the island itself, and even then it was a struggle. Some of the branches bounced or sank when I put my weight on them, and others were slick with weed and algae.

At long last, I crawled up the bank on my hands and knees, grabbing handfuls of grass and weeds to stop myself sliding back into the loch. I wanted to cry, but I didn't have the energy. I lay on my side on a patch of bare brown earth, my mouth opening and closing uselessly, my whitened hands curled into fists.

Cold. So cold.

I knew I couldn't lie there forever in my wet clothes. When I had stopped gasping, I forced myself to sit up, hugging my knees to conserve what little warmth I had. Looking out over the water, I could see the shore far away, and the white rectangle of the holiday cottage. Was

Stephen still standing there, looking out over the loch? At this distance it was hard to say. I saw a thin dark shape that might have been my brother, or a post or tree trunk. I waved feebly, but saw no movement in return.

After a while, I stood up, with some idea of running – or at least walking – around to warm up. My teeth were chattering. I knew that there was absolutely no possibility of swimming back again. I didn't have it in me to swim that far. And then I looked at the black limbs of the tree poking up out of the shallow water and shuddered. I doubted I could even make my way back through that tangle of submerged branches. To be here on the bank, freezing cold and wet, was bad enough, but becoming stuck in there would be worse. I imagined someone coming out here later in a boat and peering over the side, to see my dead white face looking up at them from the dark water, like some ghastly reflection seen in a tainted mirror.

I walked away from the water's edge, stepping carefully to avoid stones and nettles. Almost immediately I saw what was not visible from the shore of the loch: the remains of a building. It was hidden by the trees that clustered around it, and I saw that they were growing up through the floors and out through the empty windows too. It was old – very old. That was clear. I picked my way all around it and saw nothing but desolation. The ceilings had fallen in, and most of the rooms were full of rubble. Even if I had dared go inside such an unstable-looking building, it would hardly have provided any shelter, with the rooms open to the sky. I wasn't afraid of it, though, in spite of its grim appearance. When I stood on the shore, I had thought that the island looked like something out of a fairytale. Now it seemed as though it really was, but the fairies had gone long ago. I was delirious with cold and exhaustion and it seemed to me that perhaps they would come back, if only

I waited long enough. Perhaps when night fell.

I kept walking around and around the ruined building, until I could barely focus on what was in front of me and I was falling over my own feet. I still didn't feel any warmer. At some point I suppose I sat down in a corner of the tumbledown walls and closed my eyes.

It was a light that woke me. It was bright – too bright. Dazzling. My eyes felt as though they were sealed with a crust of frost; it was an effort to open them. I thought about putting up a hand to shield them from the light, but somehow the thought did not translate into action. Everything seemed to be seeping into my consciousness very slowly. I saw that there was not only one light, but many of them, beams dancing over the ancient stonework and the trunks of the trees. The effect was strange and beautiful.

Fairies, I thought.

But it was not. Someone was close by. I heard the rustle of his clothing as he squatted down next to me. When he spoke, his voice was kind, and very definitely human.

"So we've found you, lassie," he said. "You've given everyone a fright, that's for sure."

I didn't even have the energy to turn my head to look at him properly, but in my line of vision I could see white teeth and a beard with a lot of grey in it, and under that, some dark material with a stripe of reflective stuff on it.

"I thought it was the fairies," I said, but I think I didn't say it out loud, only in my head, because he didn't react to the words. Other people were coming now; I could hear the crackle of the undergrowth as they trod it down. I knew why they were coming. I had hoped for fairies, but they were coming to take me back to the ogres.

Chapter Nineteen

I have another dream – if dreams are what they are. Belle was right. They don't feel like dreams. They feel like real time spent in some other place, some other life – and death. But they can't be real. They *mustn't* be.

This time when I come to myself, I am gazing not at a ceiling rose, nor into darkness, but across a room. I don't recognise this room. It is peculiarly old-fashioned, fussily decorated and yet neglected-looking. There is a faint musty odour, and motes of dust drift lazily in the sunlight that slants through the windows. The room is papered in a bold ugly design of intertwined vegetation, in shades of green and brown. Directly opposite me is a white marble fireplace, with a tiled grate. It is elegant but cold; there is no fire burning. Above the fireplace is a large mirror in an ornate gilded frame, the glass tarnished with dark spots. The backs of the clock and the china ornaments clustered on the mantel shelf are reflected in it. I can see armchairs, their overstuffed upholstery studded with buttons, and a little spindle-legged side table. I can also see half of a large oil painting in a heavy gilded frame, but that is all I can see of it, because I cannot turn my head. I cannot even shift my gaze; the things at the periphery of my vision are impressions, indistinctly seen.

Judging by my line of vision, I am sitting, and not standing. But as I cannot look down it is impossible to be sure. I cannot say what I am wearing. I can't feel it, and since I am unable to make even the tiniest movement, there is no rustle or crackle of fabric to tell me anything.

I sit for a long time. The light from the windows takes on a golden hue and the shadows in the room grow longer, the contrast between dark and light more marked. As the sun sinks, the shadows grow and merge, until I am sitting entirely in the dark, my face still angled towards the fireplace, my gaze still fixed, long after there is anything to see. It is quiet too. The soft bump of a moth on the window pane can be heard from outside, but inside the room there is nothing, not even breathing. My thoughts become as thick and slow as sludge. I stare stupidly into the dark until the first grey light begins to pick out the shapes in the room again, ever so faintly.

When it is full light, a series of creaks announce that someone is moving about the house. A door opens behind me. I do not turn my head; I do not move a muscle, even when she bustles past me: a young woman in what looks like an old-fashioned servant's uniform, a dark dress of some rough fabric with a white apron over the top of it, and with a white cap perched on her auburn hair. She has a dustpan and brush in her hands. She hitches up her long skirt a little so that she can kneel comfortably on the hearth and sweep up the ashes of the long-dead fire. While she is doing this, she hums to herself very quietly. When the task is finished, she stands up, the dustpan full of ashes in one hand, brush in the other. She turns and sees me.

The dustpan falls from her hand and hits the floor. I hear the soft *whump* as the ashes land on the carpet. There is one moment of silence and then she screams, so loudly that the room seems to vibrate with it. She runs past me, heading for the door, and now she makes no effort to be quiet; her feet thunder on the floorboards. I hear her progress all down the hallway outside the room – the frantic footsteps and the screams for help that fade as she puts as much distance as possible between herself and me. A door bangs violently.

I don't scream. I continue to stare ahead of me as I have done all night. After a while I hear scuffling and whispering in the passageway outside the room, and then they come in: two of them this time. One is the maid with the auburn hair, who comes in reluctantly. I hear her sobbing. The other is an older woman by her voice, which is harsh and determined as she urges the girl to enter the room. The pair of them come and stand in front of me, but I cannot see their faces, only the fronts of their aprons.

Then the older one stoops to peer closely at me. Her face looms large in my vision. It is very wrinkled, like a withered fruit, and the whites of her eyes have a yellowish tinge, like ivory.

"She's gone, right enough," she says, grimly. "Though I suppose we should check. Go and get the mirror from her dressing table." She waits until the girl has hurried off, glancing over her shoulder to be sure she has gone. Then she plucks something from my lap. As she straightens up, I see that it is a small green glass bottle. *Laud* I read. The rest of the text is under her calloused thumb but I know what it says. *Laudanum.* She stuffs it deep into the pocket of her apron.

"Nae need for anyone else to be seeing that," she mutters in a disapproving tone.

The footsteps of the younger woman come pattering back. She has brought the mirror. The two of them huddle close together and put the glass close to my face. It is a hand mirror, a silver-backed one. I can see the rim of chased silver around the oval glass. The old woman is breathing heavily – I can hear her wheezing – but I do not think *I* am breathing. They put the glass very close to my lips, but no breath mists the surface of it. They tilt the mirror, trying different angles, and suddenly I see a reflection in it. *My* reflection. Only it isn't me, Fen, with my dark hair and dark eyes and still smooth skin. It's someone older, her faded skin creased with fine wrinkles, the hair that frames her face streaked with grey. The eyes that stare back at me, unblinking, are pale and filmy. The mouth sags open, dark and cavernous. For a brief moment we gaze at each other, and then the mirror is angled away.

Inside, I am screaming. But it is as though the part of me that is screaming is at the bottom of a dark well, hundreds of feet deep, so far below the surface that nothing can be heard. My lips don't make a sound; I cannot so much as flutter my eyelids. My face is absolutely immobile. No matter how hard I try, however much I strain to move, I cannot achieve so much as a tremor in those dead features.

If I can't let out the scream that is building up inside me, I feel as though I will shatter into little jagged pieces. I *will* myself to scream aloud; I strain with every part of my spirit to do it, until something seems to burst inside me and the world turns dark.

It is still pitch dark. It takes me a few moments to realise that I can hear myself breathing, taking in great gulps of air and hacking them out again in ragged sobs. I can feel a textured surface under my hands. Fabric. The arms of a chair. My fingers curl over the ends of them. I am not lying in my bed; I am sitting up.

Am I still in that place? I strain my eyes, gazing into

the blackness. Gradually the room takes form around me, dimly at first, and then more clearly as my sight adjusts to the dark. I know this room. It's across the downstairs hallway from James's study – it's one of the rooms I'm considering for my own study. Currently, though, it's full of boxes and furniture that we're storing while we finish decorating Barr Dubh House. The chair I'm sitting in is a spare armchair that doesn't match the other things in the living room. It's an old-fashioned high back wing armchair, upholstered in shabby tapestry. We just dragged it in here and left it, so it isn't facing the window or the fireplace, just a blank wall. I could touch that wall with my bare foot if I stretched my leg out. But I don't. I shrink back into the chair, and for a long while I huddle there, shuddering, and listening to my own breath going in and out in little hisses. I put my hands up to my face and explore my own features in the darkness, running my fingertips along the familiar curve of my cheekbones, touching my lips and my eyelids. I put my hands in my hair and pull strands of it over my face, seeking the scent as well as the texture of it, reassuring myself. I am me, Fen Munro, my own self, and not that hideous reflection I glimpsed in the glass. I convince myself of this at last, but it's not enough.

Why am I down here, huddled in a chair we never use, in a room we hardly ever enter? The last thing I remember was going to bed upstairs, in our own room. I *know* that's what I did. I can remember it perfectly clearly. James was still in the bathroom when I climbed into bed; the door was ajar and light was spilling out of it. I could hear the tap running. I meant to stay awake until he came to bed, but I was very drowsy. I must have fallen asleep with that bar of light across the bed and the sound of running water in my ears. So how did I get here? Did I sleepwalk? I can't think of any other explanation, but I can't believe I really made it all the way out of our room and downstairs and in here without waking James or breaking my neck on the stairs.

I want to think that I'm imagining this too, that if I close my eyes again I'll wake up safe in my own bed, pressed up against James's warm sleeping body. But I'm cold. The room is freezing – the radiator is turned off because we never come in here. I was shivering with shock before, but now I'm shivering with cold. All I'm wearing is a thin nightdress, and my arms are bare. It doesn't matter how much I hug myself, I'm bleeding out warmth with every passing moment.

I force myself to get up, uncoiling myself with difficulty from the chair, my body stiff with sitting for so long. I stagger a little as I feel my way to the door. Under my bare feet the floor is as cold as a butcher's block. The door is closed – did I really do that in my sleep? It takes me a few moments to find the handle and open it.

The hallway is dark. It seems my sleepwalking self could open and close doors, but not turn on lights. I don't step out of the doorway immediately. Instead I stand there, looking into the darkness, and listening. There is a cold feeling in the pit of my stomach and the skin of my arms prickles in the chill air. I should hurry back to the warmth of the bedroom, but I am unnerved; I cannot hurl myself precipitately into the hallway. It is so quiet that the tiniest sounds are audible if I listen carefully. There is a faint hum from the kitchen, where the dishwasher is still running. The ticking of a clock. An occasional soft scratching of twigs on glass: a bush planted too close to the window, moving gently in the night breeze. I can hear nothing untoward and yet suddenly my heart is thumping.

I step into the hallway, feeling for the light switch on the wall outside the door. Before I turn the light on, I close my eyes, not wanting to be dazzled. There is a click, and I open them slowly. There are still no lamp shades here, and the bright artificial light is both brutal and comfortless. I pad along the hall towards the kitchen. I could cut through the living room, where at least there is a rug underfoot instead of cold boards, but I don't do that. I'm still too shocked from that dream, and from finding myself somewhere I didn't expect to be; my nerves can't stand up to the thought of passing those huge plate glass windows with their view out into the night. Supposing I looked towards them and saw – what? I imagine a white face looking in, dark holes for eyes, pale hands pressed to the glass. I chide myself silently for my childish fears, but at this moment I think the merest thing – a tree moving in the wind, or a night bird fluttering close by – would be too much to bear. So I go along the passage instead and whenever I pass an open door I keep my gaze fixed straight ahead; I don't look in through any of them, towards the windows. There is a big window near the bottom of the stairs and I turn my face right away from that. I don't turn off the downstairs lights either. I go up leaving them all blazing.

There is just enough faint light to see my way into the room James and I share. James is breathing softly, deep in slumber. Clearly, when I got out of bed and went downstairs it didn't wake him. Would he have slept on until morning, not noticing I'd gone?

It's warmer in here than it was on the ground floor, but by now my teeth are chattering. I lift the edge of the duvet carefully and do my best to slide into bed without rousing James. It's no use. I'm so cold that I can't resist moving close to him for warmth, and the moment I touch him he wakes with a yelp.

"Jesus, Fen," he says, pulling me into his arms. "You're like a corpse."

Chapter Twenty

I remember the first time I woke up next to James. It was a very bright morning in June and the room was very light, even though it was early. The cheap curtains were too thin to keep out the sunshine; the sun's rays poured around and right through them, illuminating the room with brutal clarity.

When I opened my eyes, the first thing I did was shield them with my hand, and when they adjusted to the strong light, I found that I was looking straight up at a stain on the ceiling. It was the remnant of an old leak, a spreading splotch that reminded me of a map of some rambling island. My gaze slid from that to the yellow light shade suspended from the middle of the ceiling. It was the landlord's, not mine, so I wasn't responsible for its insolent ugliness, but the continuing presence of the drooping cobweb attached to it was down to me. I felt a twinge of guilt, but not a very strong one. The flat was so depressing that it cried out *not* to be dusted; its natural state was grim and apathetic.

I was further over than I normally was, because James was lying next to me. I could feel the wall against my shoulder. On the other side, the back of my hand was lightly touching James's warm skin. I heard him give a long sigh in his sleep.

For a while I just lay beside James without turning my

head to look at him. I was almost afraid to do it, as though the prince might have turned back into a frog during the night. I had wanted him for such a long time that it seemed impossible that it had actually happened.

Instead I lay there, thinking about the night before. Every year, the company threw a summer party at which staff and authors were supposed to mingle. It was always at a venue cunningly chosen for its "originality": once they held it on a houseboat, and this time it was in a converted church, lit up with red and blue lights which rather jarred with the Gothic arches. As usual, there was a lot of alcohol, inadequately soaked up by small but elegant canapés, and as usual, everyone crowded around the bestselling authors.

It was like being at a high school dance, watching the cool kids partying in the middle of the dance floor. I doubt I would have been able to get close enough to James to speak to him at all, except he was somewhat eclipsed by the writer of the spy thrillers. The first of the terrible thrillers had sold spectacularly well, and now someone was going to make a film of it. I really hoped the thriller writer wasn't going to do the screenplay. At any rate, he was enjoying his moment of glory. I could see his bouffant head of hair above the cluster of publicists and envious fellow authors; I had never seen anyone so blow-dried in my life before.

While I was observing this, James was deep in conversation with his editor in another part of the room. Then I looked away from the mesmerising sight of publicists swarming around the thriller writer, back towards the spot where James was, and he had gone.

A moment later he appeared at my elbow, so suddenly that I almost jumped.

"Fen," he said, and I said, "James," trying not to look too embarrassingly lovelorn. It was a struggle. I had seen James exactly three times since the evening in January when he had followed me out of the restaurant. Each time he had been in London for a daytime meeting of some sort, and we had met briefly before he caught the train home. Twice we had had coffee together, and on one occasion we had managed lunch in a restaurant deemed safe from interruptions because it was not cool enough for the publicity department. None of these meetings was long enough; it was like trying to sate a ravenous hunger with the tiny canapés currently being carried round. After the lunch, I had gone to the station to see James off and he had kissed me goodbye, so lingeringly that it was agonising when we had to peel ourselves apart.

Now, however, it was seven thirty in the evening and James, like quite a few of the other authors, was staying in London overnight. This knowledge was so fraught with interesting possibilities that it made me feel quite lightheaded. I had to force myself to concentrate on what James was saying.

"I had to talk to Jennifer. She's trying to tell me in the nicest possible way that I need to get my arse in gear and finish another book."

"Oh," I said.

"I've promised her all sorts of improbable things," James said. "Anyway, now you've got me all to yourself."

"Good," I managed to say. After that, I can't really remember *what* I said; probably the most inconsequential things. The canapés were, as usual, a hopeless replacement for an actual meal, so we waited until the point in the evening when the Managing Director began a long speech about the magic of literature, and while everyone else was listening, cradling their glasses of Prosecco in their hands, we sneaked out and went to a restaurant. I didn't eat much there, either; I was too much on edge, like a gambler on a winning streak who knows the odds may go against them at the last. I toyed with my main course and barely touched the pudding; I kept thinking about what was going to happen at the end of the meal.

Eventually the waitress came over and said, "Would you like coffee?" and I spent so long thinking about it that she said, "I'll give you a moment, okay?" and went off again.

James and I looked at each other.

"You could come and have coffee at my hotel," he suggested.

"Everyone's staying there," I said, imagining the pair of us running into a gaggle of his fellow authors. For a moment there was silence. Then I said, "You could come back to mine for coffee. If you like," I added.

Once we were in the taxi on the way back to the flat, I said, rather guiltily, "I don't actually have any coffee, you know. I mostly drink tea."

James looked at me and then he looked out of the cab window. A moment later, he tapped on the glass separating us from the driver.

"Can you pull over here for a moment?"

The taxi veered sharply toward the kerb, and James got out. He was briefly silhouetted against the lighted shopfront behind him, and then he was gone. I stared after him in dismay.

The cabbie looked over his shoulder at me. "Do you want to wait?"

"I..." I stared at him. "I don't know."

He shrugged. "Give it a minute, then. As long as you know the meter's running."

I sat alone in the back of the cab and fidgeted. Was it possible that James had thought I was genuinely offering coffee and after dinner mints? That seemed wildly unlikely, but as the seconds ticked by I began to feel more and more uncertain. Perhaps it wasn't that. But what if it was something else?

Then the door opened and James climbed back inside, clutching a jar of coffee. I couldn't help it. I laughed, more from relief than anything.

"You really can't do without coffee?"

He grinned. "I could probably manage without it at this time of night. But I'm like a bear with a sore head without my cup of coffee in the morning." Then he said, "I mean–" and stopped short, with the grace to look slightly embarrassed.

I bit my lip, turning my head to hide my smile.

After that we didn't speak until we got to my flat. Small talk was absolutely impossible and anything else risked being overheard by the cabbie. But my hand was on the seat and I felt James's fingers covering mine. My heart was so full that I hardly dared look at him; I thought the naked desire would be visible on my face. The streets slid past in a blur of lights and all I could feel was his touch; all I could think about was the journey's end.

For once, astoundingly, the ground floor flat was dark and silent and there was nobody hanging about in the stairwell. Our footsteps rang out loudly as we climbed the stairs to the top floor. I opened the front door with James at my shoulder. We stepped inside and James set down the jar of coffee on the tiny table that stood in the hallway. I had a lightweight summer coat on and I had begun to take it off when James put his arms around me and I simply let it fall to the floor. We kissed each other for a long time, there in the hallway, until my heart was racing and I was dizzy with the desire to go further. I knew James was, too. When we came up for air I could hear how rapidly he was breathing. Still I wondered why he made no attempt to move until I realised that he had never been here before; he didn't know the layout of the flat at all. So I pushed back the hair that was falling over my face, took his hand and led him to the bedroom.

I kicked off my shoes and then we fell onto the bed. I tried – I think we both tried – to take things slowly, to savour every moment, but I was struggling against myself. I think I had known almost from the first time I met James that I wanted him, and we had spent far too much time waiting. We undressed each other in such violent haste that I actually pulled one of the buttons right off James's shirt. When my dress was off, I heard James draw in a breath with a sharp little hiss. "Oh, Fen," he said, and I gasped as his lips touched my skin.

We made love twice that night, the first time in a frenzy: I think I astonished him with my energy. The second time, in the small hours of the morning, we moved slowly and thoughtfully. I lay there in the darkened room with the light from the street lamps below seeping around the edges of the curtains and the rattle of the window frame when the night bus passed by, and the hands that had written the books I loved so well traced out their own tale of love and longing on my bare skin.

I remembered all this the following morning, as I lay there beside James, gazing at the ceiling of my shabby room. After a while I did turn my head to look at him. James was confident in sleep: he lay on his back, his face exposed. His dark hair was rumpled. That made me wonder what *I* looked like: a panda, very probably, with eyeshadow smeared all over the place.

It was difficult getting up without waking James, but I managed it, by pushing back the duvet on my side and climbing out of the bottom of the bed. I put on my robe and went through into the bathroom to inspect the damage. *Gruesome*, I decided. I didn't feel properly human until I'd cleaned my teeth and wiped off the remains of my makeup and dragged a brush through my hair. After I'd finished in the bathroom, I padded down the hallway to get the jar of coffee, which was still standing forlornly on the little table.

I was waiting for the kettle to boil when James came into the kitchen in his boxer shorts and his crumpled shirt; he was still doing the shirt up and I saw him look down when he came to the missing button. I turned back to the tea and coffee, biting my lip to hide my smile.

"Morning," he said as he came up behind me and kissed me on the side of the neck.

"I thought you were in a horrible mood until you got your morning cup of coffee," I observed mildly.

"Generally I am, yes," he said, his arms around me.

"So what's different this morning?" I enquired.

"Hmmm," he said. "I don't know. Fine summer morning, I suppose." But he kissed me again before he took the cup of coffee.

It was strange, that morning. Perhaps there is always a faint sense of unreality when we get something we have wanted for such a long time. I felt as though I could have leaned against the scuffed formica cabinets with my tea cup in my hands and watched James moving around the flat for hours. He was interested in everything: the view from the windows, the little stack of vinyl records and of course the books, which were everywhere – double stacked on the bookcase and piled up everywhere else. No booklover can ever visit another's home without examining the bookshelves. He touched the battered spine of my copy of *The Unrepentant Dead* with his forefinger, but he didn't comment.

Of course he looked at the photographs on the window sill too. There was one of me and Belle, our heads together, both holding up glasses of wine. There was one without any people in it at all, a photograph of the Quiraing on the Isle of Skye. And there was an old photo of Stephen. When

143

he saw that one, James glanced at me, perhaps wondering whether it was an old boyfriend or something.

"That's Stephen," I said, with quiet reluctance. "My brother."

"I didn't know you had a brother," said James.

And I stared at him as the moments slid by, wondering whether to say: *I don't.*

Chapter Twenty-One

The call came very early on a Sunday morning in the springtime. I was in my university room, face down in my pillow, sleeping off three quarters of a bottle of wine that Belle had made me drink the night before, on the basis that I needed to let my hair down *some time*. It took a few moments for the irritating riff of my mobile phone ringing to penetrate the heavy fog of sleep. Then I decided to ignore it; there was no good reason for anyone to be calling at that hour. The phone fell silent and I had just turned over in bed when it started up again. Wearily, I raised my head, my hair hanging over my face in tangled clumps, and fumbled for the phone on the desk adjacent to the bed. I flopped back onto the pillow, the phone to my ear, and said, "Yes?"

"Fenella?" It was my father, his tone terse.

"Dad?" I was conscious of a dull ache in my temples. I pressed the heel of my free hand to my forehead. "Is that you?"

"Yes." There was the merest pause before he said, "Fenella, your brother's gone."

"Gone?" I repeated, stupidly. "Gone where?"

My father was silent for a few seconds. Then he said, "You should come home immediately."

I sat up in bed and the ache in my head briefly intensified into a throb. I couldn't make sense of what my father was saying.

"It's the middle of term, Dad. I can't come home yet." I began to grope around for my dressing gown, with some idea of getting up and making myself some tea. "And where has Stephen gone?"

"Your brother is dead." There was a tightness in my father's voice. He sounded angry, although whether with me or Stephen I could not tell. "Is that clear enough?"

Still I didn't take it in – not really. I felt curiously numb. "Yes," I said, and then, "No. How can he be – what's happened?"

"We are trying to ascertain that," said my father. *Ascertain*, he said, as though he were a spokesperson for an official enquiry. The formality of his words added to the sense of unreality; what he was saying had still not really sunk in. "You should come home," he repeated. "If you need money for the train fare, we will reimburse you."

"Dad?" I was fully awake now. "Can I speak to Mum?"

"Your mother isn't able to speak to you at the moment," said my father. There was a slight edge to his tone, as though the request had been unreasonable. "Will you come home today?"

"I suppose so," I said into the phone. The logistical details of how I would do this crowded into my head, trying to push out the unwelcome information my father had delivered. I thought of buses, and train times, and packing. I did not want to accept the news about Stephen at its face value; it seemed impossible. Instead I said to myself that I would go home and get to the bottom of the matter. I would surely find out that there had been some

146

mistake. I tried to recall the train timetable. Perhaps I might even be able to travel back again tonight, after I had seen my parents. "Yes," I said.

After the call had ended, I got out of bed, dressed and set about packing a bag. I struggled to think what to take; my mind seemed to have lost focus. I picked up a rather heavy book I had been reading for my current assignment and for perhaps half a minute I just looked at it, unable to make a decision about whether to take it with me or not. In the end I put it into the bag, but after I had finished packing I changed my mind and took it out again.

I might be back tonight, I reminded myself. My hands trembled as I fastened the zip on the bag.

It was not until I was outside my room, locking the door, that I began to think of things I had forgotten to do. I had not eaten or drunk a thing since I got up – not so much as a glass of water. My mouth was dry and my head was still aching dully. Unless I had something it would undoubtedly get worse. I considered going back inside, but decided against it; I could buy something at the station or on the train, I supposed. More urgently, I needed to tell someone I was leaving. If I had to stay overnight, I would miss a seminar on Monday morning...

Dragging the bag behind me, I went up the corridor to Belle's room and banged on the door.

"Go away," said Belle in a muffled voice.

"Belle? It's me, Fen."

"Go away, Fen. I mean that nicely."

I leaned against the door with my shoulder. Trying to think of the right words to persuade Belle to open it felt like an exhausting prospect. "Please," I said into the wooden panels.

I thought perhaps she had gone back to sleep, but then I heard her undoing the lock from the inside and I stepped back from the door. Belle looked out, her unmade-up face pale and her hair sticking up.

"What the fuck, Fen? It must be, like, seven o'clock in the morning."

"I have to go home, Belle. Can you tell Dr. Edwards?"

Belle stared at me. "Why? What's happened?"

"I don't know," I said. "My dad phoned and said Stephen's gone, and he said I have to go home right away. Can you tell Dr. Edwards, in case I'm not back tomorrow morning?"

I waited for Belle to say yes, so I could set off for the station. But she kept looking at me, and then she said, "Your brother Stephen? What do you mean, gone?"

"Dad says he's dead." It made me feel strange to say that: weirdly lightheaded and disconnected. "I don't think he can be, though," I said. "I'm going home to sort it out. Will you tell her that's where I've gone?"

"Of course," said Belle. "But Fen–"

I had already turned to go, but she caught hold of my arm. "Wait a minute. Your *dad* phoned you and said your brother was – that he was *dead*? And he told you to come home? How are you going to do that? Are your parents driving up to get you?"

I shook my head. "Dad said to get the train." I looked away, up the corridor. "I should get going."

"Fen, how far away do your parents live? An hour's drive? An hour and a half? Why the fuck aren't they coming to get you?"

I could hear the anger in Belle's voice, but I couldn't deal with it. It was too much, on top of everything else. At last I felt the pricking of tears in my eyes.

I tried to pull my arm away, but Belle wasn't letting go. She stepped right out into the corridor.

"Fen, come in for a minute."

"The train," I said miserably.

"You can get the next one. I'm going to get dressed and then I'm coming with you, okay? At least as far as the station. I'll come on the train too, if I can afford it. You shouldn't be going off on your own."

I didn't have the energy to argue. I let her lead me into her room, where I stood with my bag, waiting for her to be ready, until she told me tartly that I was making the place look untidy. Then I sat on the battered armchair, bolt upright, until she was dressed. I kept fidgeting while I was waiting, as though it made a difference how quickly I got to the railway station; as though if I managed to get home fast enough some evil spell would be broken and my father would say, *Why did you come home, Fen? Your brother is perfectly fine.*

There was no bus due, so Belle walked to the station with me. When she got there, she made me sit on a bench while she went off to buy tickets. She came back scowling – "it's exorbitant" – and it wasn't until I was on the train on my own, rattling through the countryside, that I realised she hadn't asked me for the money back. She'd paid for my ticket, which was why she hadn't been able to come any further with me. I was glad, though, even in my numb state of misery, because I couldn't face showing Belle my parents.

So I went home, and when I walked up to the house it was like sinking to the bottom of a dark ocean. The pressure on my chest was so great that I felt as though I was going to suffocate. In books, haunted houses are grand and sinister affairs with Gothic turrets and grinning gargoyles. This was just an ordinary suburban house.

Still there was something draggingly awful about walking up the garden path towards the dowdy green front door. Once inside, my family would swallow me again, and what had happened to Stephen would become real.

I rang the bell and the door opened instantly. My father must have been standing right behind it, although he hadn't opened it until I rang. He stood there for a moment, looking at me, and there was something faintly challenging in his expression, as though he was wondering why I was there. Then he stood back to let me inside. I only glanced at his face once. It told me all I needed to know. He hadn't changed. Stephen, my brother, was dead, but my father had not changed.

Of course, I didn't go back to the university that evening, nor the next day. I stayed until the funeral, which was a functional affair at a local crematorium. There were too few of us, in a large room decorated in pale cream and pine wood, as though having light colours and a bland atmosphere would deny the grim reality and somehow make the dear departed less dead. The eulogy was given by the headmaster of Stephen's old school, who was also a friend of my father's. It was delivered carefully but was strangely dispassionate, as though he had plundered Stephen's CV for the content. None of the family wept. My parents were as grim and silent as statues, and I had cried so much in the previous days, in the solitude of my old bedroom, that I felt hollowed out. The only person who sobbed aloud was Stephen's godmother, and when she did so, I sensed my mother's head turning like a pitiless searchlight of disapproval. I don't remember much of the wake. I stayed that night at my parents', and the next morning I went back to university.

Travelling back on the train did not make me feel any better. I did not feel as though I was escaping from the oppressive environment of my parents' house to a welcome sanctuary; I felt like a dumb beast transported from one pen to another, the shadow of the killing bolt always hanging over it. I wondered if that was how Stephen had felt: corralled. Trapped.

His death was not intentional. That was the conclusion that was meant to make the family feel better, as though we were still living in the days when suicides were buried at a crossroads or on the north side of the churchyard and a death *not* being suicide was somehow supposed to be a good thing. It didn't help me at all. My brother was gone – out of my life, out of his own life.

I'd heard all the details now. Stephen had been working for his Finals – working flat out nearly every hour he was awake. His marks at university had always been good – excellent, even – but still he kept pushing himself, harder and harder, as though a moment with his attention elsewhere would lead to certain disaster in the exam hall. His friends barely saw him outside the classroom or the library. At some point, applying himself for long hours was not enough. Perhaps he became too exhausted to concentrate. He began to self-medicate, using a prescription drug with a stimulating effect. Where he got it from was a question yet to be answered. Eventually he took too much of it, or had an adverse reaction to it. He died there in his student room, with his books piled up around him, probably on the Friday afternoon or early evening. The cleaner had knocked and emptied his bin for him that morning, and Stephen had seemed tired and groggy but most certainly alive. Nobody saw him after that. On Saturday night, a couple of his friends had decided to make him come out for a break. After knocking for a long time with no reply, one of them had helped the other to climb up and look through the little semi-circular window over the door. Stephen was slumped on the floor between the desk and the bed, dead.

All through that train journey back, I kept thinking about it – about Stephen in his student room. I'd visited him several times so I knew it well. There was a big sash window behind the desk, and outside there was a cherry tree. As the train sped through the countryside, I saw trees in blossom everywhere, and I knew the tree outside Stephen's window would have been like that too, a mass of pink petals. Had he noticed it? When we were both little, he had loved playing in the garden. Sometimes he didn't really even play; he just lay there, looking at the plants growing up all around him and the clouds scudding across the sky. I wondered if he had ever looked up from his interminable studies and looked at the cherry tree in all its spring glory. I hoped he had. I thought some mention had been made of the curtains in his room, whether they had been open or closed when his body was found, but I couldn't remember which it was. I wanted them to have been open. I wanted the tree to have been the last thing he saw – not another dry page of a law book.

When I got off the train it was early afternoon. The station was quiet. There was no bus waiting, and I had no Belle to walk with me this time; I hadn't even texted to let her know I'd be back. I set off slowly. At the other end of my walk there was a stack of law books waiting for me too. Of course there was; my parents wouldn't have countenanced supporting me through any other kind of degree, and it had seemed worth it just to get away from home. Now, I saw it differently. I saw that there would never be affection and approval; there would simply be more and more pressure, until one day I was flattened by it, squashed out of shape like one of those artefacts you see in a museum, once graceful but now crushed by the tons of earth lying above it, the dead weight of centuries bearing down on it.

The corridor was deserted when I got back to my room. I unlocked the door and when I opened it there was a sour smell in the air. Something had been rotting while I was away – a plate unseen behind a curtain, or scraps of food in the unemptied bin. I left the bag just inside the door, which I closed behind me, sealing myself in with the odour of hopelessness. For a while I just stood there, in the middle of the room, looking at the stacks of books and papers on my desk. In a couple of years they might have been replaced by the very same titles Stephen had been reading – the ones he had died amongst. Something broke inside me. I saw the trap, I felt its jaws closing on me, and like an animal I would have gnawed off my own limb to escape.

The building was old and there was a fireplace in the room, although the chimney was long blocked up. I took a stack of books from the desk and piled them into the grate. One slid off the pile; I put it back on. I fetched the rest and piled them up too. They wouldn't all fit; I had to stack some of them on the tiles in front of the fireplace. I fetched the pages of the essay I had been working on, now a week overdue for submission, screwed them into balls and stuffed them in between the books. When everything was there, I found the box of matches I used to light joss sticks. This was strictly forbidden and I could only ever put them by the open window, in case they set the fire alarm off. Now I didn't care about that. I didn't even think about it. I struck a match and set it to one of the essay pages. It flared satisfactorily and a faint singed smell arose from the volume above it. I struck another match, and another: it is harder to get a stack of books burning properly than you would think. When they simply smouldered, I rummaged amongst my toiletries until I found a bottle of nail polish remover, poured it onto the books and threw a new match onto it. This time the fire ignited with a *whoomph*, so that I stepped back hastily, and a moment later the fire alarm went off.

I could feel the warmth on my face now, and smoke started to fill the room. The stink of incinerated legal knowledge filled my nostrils. I began to cough, and then I couldn't stop coughing. There were footsteps in the corridor outside, and then someone banged on the door. Even over the sound of the fire alarm I heard someone yelling.

"Fen? Fen!"

I opened my mouth to reply but all I managed was a croak before I was seized with another fit of coughing.

The door opened; I had forgotten to lock it when I came in.

"Shit," said someone. It was Alice, the girl who had the room next to mine. She only hesitated for an instant, then she stepped into the room and grabbed my arm. By the time she had dragged me out into the corridor, she was coughing too. The door swung closed, shutting out the flames. "What the fuck?" she said.

One of the accommodation staff members, clad in a high-vis vest, came striding towards us.

"Out," he said, tersely.

Alice pointed at the door of my room. "It's in there," she said. "It's like a bonfire."

"Okay," he said. "Don't open it again. You two, get downstairs to the assembly point."

There was no fight left in me. I did as he said. As we went down the stairs, Alice grabbed my arm again. "What happened?" she asked. "How did the fire start?"

"I started it," I said.

"Holy crap," said Alice. "Really?"

"Yes," I said.

"Why?" she asked.

I couldn't answer that. I couldn't say: *because I would*

have died otherwise. She wouldn't have understood.

When she realised that I wasn't going to say anything, Alice said, "You're going to be in deep shit, Fen." She didn't sound unsympathetic though. "You're a law student, right? And I guess you've just broken the law. Are they even going to let you go on with it after that?"

I looked her in the face for the first time. "I hope not," I said.

Chapter Twenty-Two

The fire was ten years ago now, but still it's on my mind as I set off for the town. I drive slowly, stretching the journey out, trying to relax. It's no good, though. It's not just ugly memories that are oppressing me.

I can't let James see that something's wrong. If he pressed me to say what it is, what could I possibly tell him? *I snooped into your mail and found your credit card bill, and then I tore it up?* No. If that were all it was, I might get over it. The guilt would fade eventually. It's not as though tearing up a single bill has really made a difference, after all. If James doesn't pay it, the company will send a reminder. The thing that's weighing on my mind is that awful sum, and the fact that he hasn't told me about it. How can I act naturally, knowing that? How can I stop my thoughts from creeping into my expression every time James suggests some new expense? I know he develops sudden urgent desires to have something – a particular book, a piece of music. He likes to make spontaneous plans to go out, to see a film or try a new restaurant. I've always loved his impulsive nature, but now I'm asking myself if it's recklessness. I don't want to think like this. It makes me start wondering all over again about the meaning behind the dreams.

Beside me on the passenger seat, my phone buzzes quietly.

Belle, I think. I could pull over. Now I'm out of the house, out of earshot, I could take the call, and discuss the whole thing with her.

My hands tighten on the wheel. *No*, I say to myself. *I'm going to fix those dreams. That's what I'm going to do.* I try to focus on that. If I were sleeping better, if I didn't lie down every night worrying about what was going to happen after I'd closed my eyes, well, I'd probably cope better with everything else. I'd be able to think about that credit card bill in a more objective way.

I drive through the town to the medical centre, which is a low modern building, decked out inside with light-coloured paint and pine wood, a style with uncomfortable associations for me. I've only ever been here once before, to sign on with the practice. I park outside and sit in the car for a couple of minutes. Part of me wants to start the car up again, turn it around and drive away. What am I going to say to the doctor? I rub my face with my hands. I'm not going to tell her *everything*. There was that night when James came home from Spain and I thought I saw something – or someone – by one of the trees on the drive; I won't be mentioning that. Bad dreams are one thing, outright hallucinations and delusions are another. After the fire, I had enough of talking therapy to last me a lifetime. I don't want anyone else picking over the contents of my brain. No. I'm going to concentrate on fixing the dreams. Maybe sleeping tablets would do the trick. Or maybe it will be enough just to hear that it's a perfectly normal problem – something loads of people suffer from.

Night terrors, I think, pushing away the thought that they don't feel like terrors, they feel *real*.

I get out of the car and go into the surgery. After seventeen minutes sitting between a small boy with a runny nose and an old lady turning over the pages of *The People's Friend* with avid interest, I hear my name called.

Dr. McEwan is a bespectacled older woman, brisk and friendly. As she listens to what I have to say, her smile of welcome is slowly smoothed away and replaced with a frown of concentration.

"That sounds unpleasant," she says, after I've described the dream of lying in my coffin as the lid is nailed down.

"Yes," I say gratefully, squeezing my hands together in my lap. It's a relief to tell someone all this. Just using the word "dreams" seems to make them a little less real. "I really want them to stop. I'm getting a bit nervous about going to sleep."

"Hmmm," she says, and she glances at the computer screen. "I see from your records that you've been prescribed anti-depressants in the past. Those can cause vivid dreaming in some people... but I see that was some time ago. You've not taken them recently?"

I shake my head. "Not for years."

"Any other medication? Non-prescription medicines? Or–" She hesitates.

"No," I say firmly. "I don't even take aspirin very often. And I've never taken... you know, drugs."

"Good," she says encouragingly. "Alcohol consumption – moderate?"

"Yes," I say. "Less than 14 units a week. I mean, mostly. Maybe not at Christmas..."

Dr. McEwan smiles. "We'll let you off on that one. What about stress? Are you under a lot of stress at the moment?"

"Well," I say, "I've got a few things on my mind, I suppose." When the doctor doesn't reply, I realise she is waiting for me to go on. "It's not all that long since we moved up here and they say moving house is stressful, don't they? Even if you're quite happy about making the move. And we're getting married, so there's all the wedding planning to do. I mean, obviously I'm thrilled to be getting married, but it's still a lot of work – organising everything–"

Stop wittering, Fen, I say to myself. I smile tentatively, trying to show that everything is alright; there's no stress in my life that isn't perfectly normal stress.

The doctor looks at me for a few moments and I have the disconcerting feeling that she can see exactly what's going through my head. Then she says, "Well, nightmares can definitely result from stress, so that's a possibility. When things have settled down, they might stop on their own. In the meantime, I'd like you to keep a sleep diary." She grabs a pen and paper and starts writing. "I'd like you to keep a note of when you go to bed, how long you slept, whether you woke up in the night, things like that... There's a website you can look at with all the things you should note, so I'm going to give you the address for that."

"Can't you just give me something temporarily to help with it?" I ask her, dismayed.

She looks at me over the top of her glasses. "It probably wouldn't help," she says. "I sometimes prescribe melatonin for patients who can't get to sleep, but that's not really your problem, is it? The problem is what happens when you *are* asleep. And some medication for poor sleep can actually *cause* vivid dreaming, and occasionally even sleepwalking." I suppose the disappointment is visible on my face, because she adds, "If stress is the cause, it's possible that keeping the sleep diary might help a bit, because it's giving you back a feeling of control. And if the problem persists, there is a sleep clinic I can refer you to, although it's private. But you should keep the diary first."

"Alright," I say numbly. I take the piece of paper with the web address on it. "Thank you."

I walk out of the surgery with my head down, my fingers crumpling the piece of paper in my pocket. The sleep diary is probably a sensible idea, but it isn't going to make the dreams any easier to bear. I think about the first one, about the horror of waking up sealed inside a coffin, dressed in all my bridal glory but boxed up tightly like a doll, feeling the last of the air running out, utterly helpless... I shiver. No. I can't imagine keeping a diary giving me any sense of control.

I get back into my car, and as I start the engine the first spots of rain hit the windscreen. I drive home with the windscreen wipers going and the distant view dissolving into grey mizzle.

Stress, I think. Can I really put my nighttime torments down to that? And what can I do about it, anyway? I can't change anything about Stephen, or my parents. I suppose I could decide how to tackle the question of James's credit card bill. I remind myself that there's the practicality too: once the debt is out in the open, we need to pay it off, and that means saving elsewhere. A smaller wedding. A shorter honeymoon. No honeymoon at all.

The thought of discussing those things freely and making the necessary decisions together is persuasive and comforting, like a postcard from a beautiful and distant island. To cross the distance between here and there, that is the difficult thing – how to bring up the fact that I not only opened James's post but destroyed it afterwards. I rehearse different openings to this conversation in my head and none of them sounds right to me. I grimace, peering at the wet road ahead. Some people would probably say that what James has done is far worse than opening someone else's letter. He has hidden something from me – something that affects us both. *Twenty-two thousand pounds.* The thought makes me want to put my head in my hands. But I don't want to get into an argument about who has been more wrong. I *love* James. I don't want to get into an argument at all. I want to be in the happy place on other side of that conversation, the place where we sort it all out together.

Chapter Twenty-Three

It rains all that day, but the next morning dawns bright and sunny, with a clarity that makes me think of blinking back tears. I am up before James, standing by the kitchen window with a mug of hot tea in my hands, looking out at the landscape gilded by the early sunlight. The light has an unusual quality that I have seen before on clear days, as though the contrast between light and shade has been sharpened, and the autumn colours have been subtly enriched. It makes me think of a striking effect I once saw during a solar eclipse: as darkness moved across the face of the sun, the shadows became more deeply graven and every aspect of the view was thrown into sharper relief. But today there is no dark canker eating into the face of the sun.

My laptop is open on the work surface behind me, its screen dark. If I tapped one of the keys, it would spring back into life and reveal the title page of the thriller writer's latest oeuvre. It landed in my inbox at five o'clock last night, no doubt sent by his editor moments before she left the office for the evening. It is hard not to imagine her shrugging on her coat, clicking on *send* and then scurrying for the door, like a ship going full steam from the site of a depth charge.

I had a look at the new manuscript last night when it came in, and it's just as bad as I expected. It begins with a sex scene liberally peppered with words like *genitals*, which is the least sexy word in the entire world if you ask me – even less charged with erotic force than words like *toenail*. Reading this scene has most definitely not left me gasping for more. It's going to take a considerable amount of effort and concentration to turn it into anything I could read without wincing. I should probably get to work on it as soon as I've finished drinking my tea. Instead, I gaze out at the late autumn sunshine and decide that this morning is the morning when I absolutely have to go and look for Barr Dubh's ruined chapel. This is not entirely a work evasion tactic. If there's one thing I've learned from living in Perthshire, it's that you have to take advantage of fine weather whenever you get it. By this afternoon it may be pouring with rain again.

The aroma of hot coffee drifts through the kitchen; I put the coffee maker on when I came down. There's still no sign of James coming downstairs, so I take a mug up to him. He is in the bathroom, running hot water for a shave, and for a few moments I watch him silently through the doorway. Then he catches sight of me in the mirror and turns.

"You're up early, Fen," he says.

"Not that early," I say, lightly. "Anyway, I have things to do."

"Sounds intriguing," he says.

"I'm going to go and look for that ruined chapel. Do you want to come?"

"Yes," he says, and then, "No. Damn it. I said I'd talk to Laura at nine thirty."

"I could wait," I offer.

"No," he says. "I can see you're dying to go and look. Just make sure you show me where it is, if you find it."

"Sure." I linger for a moment, but I suppose he's right; I should go. I'm already dressed in jeans, a shirt and a sweater; now I put on gloves, boots and a padded jacket to keep out the cold autumn air. Five minutes later the front door bangs shut behind me and I'm crunching over the gravel. It's a very fresh morning; I can see my breath on the air. In the trees, a flock of starlings chitters.

To get to the area where the chapel ought to be – if the old man we spoke to was right – I will have to cross the rough pasture and head for the treeline at the other side. There is a gate in the fence that separates the garden from the pasture, so I head for that. It takes me a little while to work out how to open it: there's a kind of lever, and it's so stiff that at first I think I'm doing something wrong. I pause for a moment, frustrated, and glance towards the spot I'm trying to reach, as though wanting to get there badly enough will somehow do the trick. Then I stop thinking about the gate and stand there staring.

There's someone there again – and if I'm not mistaken, it's the same person I saw once before. I see that same sudden billow of light-coloured fabric, as though the wind has caught at a dress or long coat.

Lavender, I think. Once again I wonder whether this whole thing about lavender being unlucky isn't some spiteful in-joke the locals like to play on newcomers. Whoever it is over there doesn't have any objection to wearing that colour, that's certain. I shade my eyes with my hand. It must be a woman, surely? The volume of fabric and the delicate colour suggest a dress, though one entirely impractical for walking outdoors at this time of year. The fact that it's in the very same spot as before gives

164

me pause. Perhaps I am just seeing a piece of something caught on a branch or wire, animated by the wind.

I glance back at the house. Should I go back inside and call James? That seems like overreacting. I hesitate for a moment, and then I grasp the lever on the gate again and yank it as hard as I can. At last it moves with a metallic screech. I open the gate and slip through, and it closes behind me with a clang that is clear and resonant in the cold air. Then I look towards the treeline again and that patch of lavender has gone.

Scared off? The trespassing laws are more relaxed here than in England, but I suppose most people don't want to get into a debate with a landowner. I watch for a moment, but there is no sign of movement over there. I set off, treading cautiously over thistles and coarse grass. It takes a while for me to cross the field. Soon the exposed skin of my face is tingling in the cold air. My breath drifts after me in a delicate mist.

As I get closer to the treeline, I can see that there is a wire fence separating it from the pasture. The fence has been there a long time: there are tangles of thick brambles growing through it in places. Under the trees there is damp darkness. I cannot see anyone moving about in there. I pause for a moment, my gloved hand on the fence, and listen. I can hear the breeze rustling through the dry autumn leaves and the distant cawing of crows and the sound of my own breathing, but nothing else. No footsteps crunching through the mulch on the other side of the fence. No whisper of fabric flowing with the movement of the body under it.

I test the fence with my hand. I don't think I can climb over it, but by pulling apart the top two wires I can make a gap that is just about wide enough to duck through. The top wire scrapes across the back of my padded jacket; if it were barbed wire it would be impossible to do this without sticking fast. On the other side, I straighten up, dusting my gloved hands together, and look around me.

This patch of woodland looks neglected. Here and there, trees have fallen, and have lain there so long that the trunks are thick with green moss. One of them has fallen against the fence, bending the wires with its weight and loosening one of the wooden posts, but nobody has come to remove it. The ground is so covered with branches and brambles and the remains of summer weeds that it will be difficult to explore. There is no sign of a path. I step further into the shadowy place under the canopy of trees and twigs crackle under my feet, but I can't see so much as a rabbit's track.

This is a surprise. I've seen the person in lavender – assuming it *was* a person – several times here, so I just assumed there was a path. Nobody wearing a long dress or cloak could get over these fallen tree trunks and sprawling brambles without a lot of difficulty. I turn and scan the fence area but there is no sign of anything that could have been mistaken for clothing billowing in the wind – no piece of tarpaulin caught on the wire or on a jagged branch. I frown, biting my lip. *A mystery.*

I venture further in, stepping high over fallen branches, steadying myself on tree trunks that are damp and black. It *smells* damp in here too – a subtle but pervasive odour of wet organic decay. It is hard to imagine there ever having been a building in here, and if there was, the chances of my stumbling over it in this snarled mess of vegetation must be minimal. All the same, I keep going, though more than once I have to stop to disentangle myself. Unhooking the fabric of my jacket carefully from a jagged twig, I glance back towards the field, and Barr Dubh House, and the sunshine. It makes me think of looking out from a tunnel.

Not long after that, I come across the first stone. It is damp and green, and furred with moss like the fallen trees, but the rectangular shape of it stands out. It looks *made*, not grown like everything else. I touch it gingerly with the toe of my boot, feeling the uncompromising solidity of stone. Then I look around for others, and pretty soon I have picked them out; they are scattered across the forest floor, almost meaningfully, like a series of stepping stones leading away from the spot where I am standing. I follow them, picking my way carefully, and soon I see a section of rough stone wall, pockmarked with age.

I clamber my way towards it. There is a strange feeling in the pit of my stomach, the first murky stirrings of unease. I want to get this over with. I can't imagine wanting to hold a wedding ceremony in a gloomy dank spot like this. Life and love and happiness don't belong here. Scanning the ground, I see the shattered remains of a stone cross: a grave marker. This place has belonged to the dead for a very long time.

When I am standing at the end of the section of wall, I can see the layout of the chapel very well, in spite of its ruinous state. It was a plain rectangular building, of which both gable ends are still standing. The walls between them have kept their original height in places, but elsewhere they are tumbledown, perhaps where door and window frames have collapsed. Young trees thrust up through the floor, which is covered in pieces of broken stone and slate tiles from the vanished roof. I kick idly at a flat chunk of slate. Even for someone utterly oblivious to the lowering atmosphere, the chapel wouldn't be the place to hold an event; in the first place, you'd need chainsaws to get rid of the trees. *And a bulldozer to make a path through the woods*, I think.

Even if I had those things, I wouldn't do it. It doesn't

feel right here. I find myself fidgeting, shuffling my feet, fighting the temptation to glance over my shoulder. Something is snagging my sense of spatial awareness. I can hear nothing, and I'm fairly sure that if I turned around I wouldn't see anything either, but there it is, pulsing away at me like an emergency beacon: the absolute conviction that someone is standing behind me, a stone's throw away, and a little to the left. The feeling is as clear as a blip on a radar.

Don't be stupid. You're just creeping yourself out, like a little kid.

But I lived in London too long to ignore my own instincts. Walking around after dark, you listen for footsteps that are too close, or a little too fast. In interactions with strangers you watch for warning signs: unpredictability, overfamiliarity. You keep your hand in your pocket, clutching your keys. Now it occurs to me that if there *is* anyone there – a real person, and not a phantasm – they are between me and the fence. If this is the case, it is better to know. I turn around, sharply enough to catch someone unawares. There is nobody there. I scan the spaces between the damp black tree trunks. Nothing.

I want to go back to Barr Dubh House now. I don't want to spend another moment here. But James is bound to ask me what I've found. Reluctantly, I fumble for the phone in my pocket. Perhaps photographs will be enough, and I won't have to bring him back here with me to look. I take off my gloves and stuff them in my pockets, and start taking pictures, snapping away recklessly at everything. I steel myself and step through a gap in the crumbling wall, so that I can take some more pictures inside. I am determined to be as thorough as possible. After that, I don't care if I never come back.

Slates crunch and clink under my boots. I capture a

crumbling window frame, an empty niche in the stone, the desiccated remains of ivy clinging to a wall. All the time, I still have that sensation, that strong awareness of someone behind and to the left of me. My movements become exaggerated, a pantomime to convince anyone who might be watching that I am simply taking photographs, working as quickly as possible in order to be gone. There is a cold slithering feeling in the pit of my stomach. Once, under the pretence of seeking the right angle for a photograph, I turn around again, but there is still nothing to see. There is no movement anywhere except for the swaying of naked branches in the breeze.

Clustered around the ruined chapel, there are memorials to the dead. A stone cross lies on the ground in several pieces. On a mossy headstone, the words *Requiescat in pace* are still just about legible, although the rest of the inscription is obscure. And when I glance down, I see that I am actually standing on a stone slab, although it is almost covered with broken slates and tiny fragments of masonry and the curling tendrils of dead plants. I step back quickly. Then I squat by the slab and brush the debris away as best I can with a gloved hand. There are letters carved into it, worn and weathered but still clear enough. It reads:

Euphemia Alexander
Died 14th February, 1872
Aged 60 years
RESURGAM

Euphemia, I think. *What a crazy name.* I brush dust off the lettering. That's really what it says. As for *RESURGAM,* I have no idea what that means.

There is something else at the head of the slab: a sad mess of crushed wire and broken glass, the remains of a grave ornament. Under the milky shards something white is visible. I pick up a stick and poke at the glass, trying to move the pieces aside so I can see what the white thing is.

It's flowers. White porcelain flowers. The crevices between the petals are stained black and green with mould or dust, but it's still perfectly obvious what the thing is: a decorative arrangement of white flowers, like the one currently sitting in the sideboard in our dining room. And not merely *like* it, but *exactly like* it, except the one in Barr Dubh House is pristine and this one is old and dirty.

I keep squatting there, looking at those flowers. What does this mean? It must mean *something*. When I found the china flowers in the house, I didn't recognise them, but it seemed logical that they came from my parents' house. There was nowhere else they could have come from: everything else is stuff James and I owned before, or which we have bought. It's possible, I suppose, that my parents might have owned something like this, perhaps not realising what it was – a grave ornament. But an *identical* one? How is that possible?

There is something here that I am not grasping. A feeling of something being very *wrong*.

What am I not seeing?

That conviction that someone is there behind me is even stronger than before; it makes the back of my neck tingle. I hold my breath, waiting for a telltale sound – the snap of a twig, or the rustle of dead leaves. Nothing. The breeze dies.

Then I hear it: a rush of air, almost a sigh, like the sound of a long indrawn breath before a scream that never comes. It seethes and shivers amongst the trees, as though the whole wood is breathing.

I rise to my feet, my heart pounding, and turn my head this way and that, scanning the woods for the source of the sound. Nothing. Naked branches sway gently with the moving air, but there is no sign of any living creature. Not so much as a squirrel running up a tree trunk.

I *know* there is somebody or something there, though. Every instinct is screaming this at me. A prickling at the back of my neck tells me the hairs are standing up.

There is a rustling in the dead remains of the summer undergrowth, as though something is sweeping swiftly and invisibly through them. I can't even identify a direction; the sound seems to be everywhere at once. But I am sure of one thing – it is closing in on me. I don't know what will happen if I am still standing here, by the grave of Euphemia Alexander, died 14th February, 1872, when it reaches me, but I think it will be something very bad indeed.

Panic. I launch myself into flight, stumbling, running for the fence as hard as I can. The ground is treacherous, an obstacle course of slippery slates, mossy stones and fallen branches. My boots skid in mud, on wet leaves. I fall, landing on one knee, and feel the cold damp seep through the fabric of my jeans. Then I'm up again, breathing hard, running for the sunlight visible on the other side of the trees. Surely the chapel wasn't this far in? I dare not look behind me. All I can think about is getting out, away.

The sun is still low enough in the sky to be dazzling when I come to the edge of the trees, and I run straight into the fence. I struggle for a moment before I realise what has happened, and then I duck and try to force my way through the gap between the wires. For several seconds I stick fast, like a fly in a cobweb. Then I hear a ripping sound as the back of my jacket pulls away from the wire, and I'm through. I stagger away from the fence, panting. I think – though there's no logical reason for it – that I'm safe on this side. I listen, trying to control my breathing, but I can't hear anything in there – no rustling of dead leaves, no whisper of moving air.

Safe on my side of the fence, I stand there and gaze into the gloom under the trees. It is bright out here, the cold clear brightness of autumn, and it is hard to pick out anything amongst the shadows. At first I see nothing but the black bars of the tree trunks and the dark mass of undergrowth. Then, far, far back, between the trees, I see something very briefly – a mere flicker of light colour, as swift as the snapping of a pennant on the breeze. Lavender.

Chapter Twenty-Four

When I stumble back into the house, it is ten to ten; I can see that from the clock at the end of the hallway. James will still be on the phone to Laura; those conversations are never brief. I close the door quietly and then I lean against the wall and close my eyes for a few moments.

What just happened?

I ask myself that, and I think James would ask me some version of that if he walked out of his study right now and saw me standing here with mud on my jeans and a big rip in the back of my jacket. There is no sensible answer to the question, no answer that won't make it look as though I've completely lost touch with reality.

I open my eyes and force myself to get moving. I unzip my boots and leave them on the doormat. Then I take off my jacket, and examine the damage. It's a pretty bad rip. There are little downy feathers leaking out of it. There is a row of pegs in the hall with outdoor coats hanging on them, so I take one of them off the hook, put the ripped jacket in its place, and then put the other coat back on top of it. It's the best solution I can think of for now. Then I make my way down the hall and upstairs to the bedroom to peel off my muddy jeans. I let these small practical tasks fill my mind.

When the jeans are safely stuffed down to the bottom of the dirty clothes hamper and I'm dressed in warm dry things, I go back downstairs to the kitchen and make myself another cup of tea. With a warm mug cradled in my fingers and the sunshine streaming in through the kitchen windows I feel more like myself. I feel practical and sensible. I am able to go back to that question.

What just happened?

I try to go over it methodically. The conviction that someone was standing behind me, and to the left. A sound like a sigh. A rustling amongst the undergrowth. There's nothing there that wouldn't be explained away quite confidently by a sceptic. The ruined chapel was lonely, decayed and creepy – anyone would start imagining weird presences, or feel like they were being watched if they spent too long somewhere like that. The sighing and rustling? Random gusts of wind. There's nothing peculiar about those in Scotland in the autumn.

I shiver. I don't think I was imagining the person standing behind me. I *know* there was someone there. It doesn't matter that I didn't see anyone when I turned. The feeling was so strong that I think there was something more than I can remember – something subliminal, like a sound almost out of the range of my hearing, or the merest hint of a scent.

I did see something, I remind myself. *That patch of lavender.*

But that's all I saw: a flash of colour, a billow that was probably fabric of some kind. I rub my eye with the heel of my hand. It doesn't make sense. If someone was lurking around in the woods, they chose a strange colour to wear. Lavender doesn't exactly blend into all that green and brown.

174

Perhaps, I think, *they wanted to be seen.* It's not the first time, after all. I've seen that flash of lavender before.

Then my mind jumps back to that night when James came home so late from Spain and I saw someone – or perhaps some*thing* – against one of the tree trunks as the car came up the drive. It was very dark, and the headlights bleached everything they touched, so I can't say whether the fabric I thought I saw then was lavender or any other colour.

Little prickles of disquiet run through me. *A figment of my imagination, born of bad sleep and loneliness* – that's what I told myself at the time. If it had only happened that once, I could believe that, too. The mind plays tricks, and I know that better than anyone, me with my dreams that look and sound and feel so real that I wake up screaming. But I've seen those fluttering draperies too many times now for it to be pure imagination.

Say that someone is hanging around the house – a real, solid person, and not some trick of the eye. I can't think who that might be. Some local eccentric, who likes to walk around the countryside in an ankle-length gown? I frown. I could imagine that in the daytime – just about – but not late at night. A neighbour then, with a bone to pick? Someone who wanted to buy Barr Dubh House and saw it snatched from under their nose by the out-of-towners?

No, I think. *That doesn't make sense either. Nobody else even bid for it.*

I sip the tea, relishing the comforting, ordinary taste. These things are real, definite: the warmth in my hands, the sunshine, James in the other room, phoning London. Then I think about white porcelain flowers. I remember unpacking them myself and asking Belle to stow them in the sideboard. I had them in my hands; I felt the cool smooth surface of the petals. The ones I just saw at the

175

ruined chapel, grimy but otherwise identical – those were just as real.

I put the mug down on the worktop and head through to the dining room. The room is cool and the dark green walls make me think of forests, of quiet pine-smelling places where the shadows shift and blend. The highly polished oval of the dining table is a still pool. I think to myself that the white porcelain flower arrangement is a tangible thing; it can be compared with the one I saw at the chapel. Perhaps, after all, it will turn out that the two are not exactly alike, simply very similar examples of a particular convention. Perhaps they have no meaning other than coincidence. I squat in front of the sideboard and open the doors. The porcelain flowers are not there.

I push the doors right back on their hinges and duck my head so I can peer right to the back. I see the stack of gilt-edged plates and some glasses and decanters, and that hideous funereal inkstand. But there are no white porcelain flowers. There is a silver plated tray, an ugly thing with feet that would probably leave scratches on the table. I remember Belle putting the flower arrangement on top of that when she put it away. There's nothing on its tarnished surface now except a fine covering of dust.

I take the tray out of the sideboard and put it on the floor. I take the inkstand out too, though I still feel that odd reluctance to handle it. Then I take out a decanter and a couple of glasses. Even while I'm doing this, I know it's impossible that the flower arrangement is somehow being hidden by these things. I put a hand in and feel behind the stack of plates, in case the flowers have somehow been broken and the porcelain shards have fallen down the back of them. Nothing; my fingers touch bare wood.

I sit back on my heels and think about it for a moment. Has James been in here? I don't *think* he has. But why

176

would he move the flowers anyway? I start to unpack the rest of the things from the sideboard. It takes quite a long time, because there are a lot of things and many of them are fragile. Soon I am surrounded by plates and bottles and ornaments and a host of glittering glasses. If I tried to move from the spot, it would have catastrophic effects, like the legendary bull in a china shop. At last the sideboard is completely emptied. I have handled each item. There is definitely no porcelain flower arrangement.

While I am sitting and staring at the back of the empty sideboard, I hear footsteps outside, and then James comes into the room.

"Fen? You *are* in here. Laura says–" He pauses. "What are you up to?"

"I was... looking for something."

"Did you find it?"

"No," I say. I start putting things back into the sideboard, starting with a stack of plates. I have to move them a few at a time, because the whole stack is too heavy.

"Do you want a hand?"

But he can't get near me, because of all the glasses arranged haphazardly on the floor.

I slide the silver plated tray back into the sideboard, and put the inkstand on top of that, silently vowing to get rid of both of them as soon as I can. I don't know why I put the decision off. It's not that hard to make.

"I didn't even hear you come back into the house," James says. "Did you find the chapel?"

I pause and look up at him, an empty glass in each hand. "Yes, I did. That old guy wasn't kidding when he said it was 'the remains' of a chapel. It's a complete ruin."

James leans against the wall, arms comfortably folded for a conversation. "Picturesque Instagram ruined or hopelessly ruined?"

"Hopelessly. And there's no path or anything. You'd need to get bulldozers in. And anyway..." My voice trails off.

"And anyway...?" James prompts me.

"I didn't really like it," I say carefully. "It's full of..." I stop again. If I say it's full of gravestones, James will want to see it for certain. "...rubbish," I finish. "It's not a lovely romantic ruin. It's depressing."

"Shame."

"Yes. James, the thing I was looking for was a kind of decoration, made of white china flowers. Belle put it in here for me, when we were unpacking stuff, but now it's not there. You didn't move it, did you?"

James shakes his head. "Not guilty. I haven't even opened that cupboard since she was here."

I look at him for a moment. "I haven't taken it out either."

James shrugs. "Well, maybe it was some other cupboard you remember her putting it into."

"No, it was definitely this one."

"Perhaps Belle moved it," he suggests. "What did you say it was? China flowers? What did you want them for?"

"I just wanted to take another look at them," I say, as casually as I can. I look down, at the things spread out around me on the floor. "I mean, I should clear some of these things out. When are we ever going to use sherry glasses, or a gravy boat?"

"Never," agrees James cheerfully.

I put the glasses back into the sideboard and pick up others. "What did Laura say?" I ask him. I keep hoping he'll say, *She's pulled off this huge deal and now I know the money's coming in there's something I want to tell you.* But he doesn't say that.

"She's sold rights in Lithuania. No news on the film.

178

And she's nagging me about the new book."

"Well," I say lightly, "What are you standing around here for? Shouldn't you get back to work?"

"No rest for the wicked," says James. "I need coffee first. Do you want tea?"

I shake my head. "I've just had one."

After he's gone, I sit for a while on my heels. I think about what James didn't say, and I look into the sideboard, as though those white porcelain flowers are going to materialise in there if I just concentrate for long enough. I didn't move them. James says he didn't move them. But then who did? I have that feeling again, that there's something right in front of me, something I'm not grasping.

I think about the night I sleepwalked and woke up downstairs. Is it possible that I moved them when I was *asleep?* I don't *think* I did, but I hardly trust myself any more. When I dream, I see and hear and feel things that are not there. Objectively, whatever I heard and felt in the ruined chapel wasn't really there either. It occurs to me that perhaps the same is true of the white porcelain flowers. Maybe they were never there at all. Maybe I imagined them. I press a hand to my face. No. I didn't imagine them. I saw them and I know Belle did, too. She had them in her hands, for God's sake.

Later that day, when James has gone into the town for something, I video call Belle on my phone. I feel self conscious about doing this. We've messaged plenty of times since she visited, but we haven't *spoken.* I guess we were both thinking the same thing: least said, soonest mended.

When Belle appears, she isn't looking at me – she's looking at whatever else she's doing. I can see at first glance that her hair is no longer magenta; now it's turquoise.

"Go away, Brendan," Belle says to someone I can't see.

"I'm about to talk to my bestie." She pauses. "I mean it. Buzz off."

"Hi, Belle," I say.

"And shut the door," she adds, sternly. Then she says, "Fen. How are things in Brigadoon?"

"Sunny," I say evasively. "What about London? Streets paved with gold, as usual?"

"I wish."

We chat for a bit, about Belle's job and about work – "I literally cannot believe you said yes to that!" says Belle. I update her on the wedding plans, telling her about the chapel where James had to reverse away from the tractor. I don't mention the ruined chapel on our own land. Eventually, however, I get to the point.

"Belle, you remember when you were up here and we were emptying those removal boxes in the dining room?"

"Sure."

"Do you remember unpacking a kind of decoration made of white flowers?"

"Yeah, I remember that. Weird sort of table decoration or something."

"Can you remember what you did with it?"

"I put it in that cupboard in the dining room, like you told me to."

"Are you sure?"

"Sure I'm sure." Now Belle is looking directly at me, with her head on one side.

"And you didn't move them after?"

"Nope. What's the matter, Fen?"

"Nothing," I said, as lightly as I can. "I was just looking for them and they're not in there any more."

"Maybe James moved them."

He just told me he didn't.

"Yeah, that's probably it," I tell her. "It was just bugging me a bit. I hate losing track of things."

"That's what happens if you live in a huge country house," says Belle. "You probably left it in the East Wing or something." She leans towards the screen, peering at me. "Are you sure nothing's the matter?"

"Absolutely sure."

"You look a bit... I dunno, stressed."

"It's that thriller. You'd be stressed if you had to read 90,000 words of that."

"I did warn you," says Belle, rolling her eyes.

Not long after that, we ring off. The phone still in my hand, I sit and gaze out of the window, not really seeing anything.

It's just a stupid ornament, I say to myself. *Who cares what happened to it?* I rub my temples with the fingers of my free hand, squeezing my eyes tight shut.

Who cares?

Chapter Twenty-Five

First, I'm aware of a clock ticking. It sounds eerily loud, because there is no other sound in the room. A faint light is slanting through the window, outlining the dim shapes of heavy old-fashioned furniture. It is evening. The colour is fading from everything with the dying of the light; soon it will be altogether dark. I look down at my hands in my lap, and I see without surprise that I am wearing a long dress with voluminous skirts. The boned bodice is a cage against which my flesh is pressed almost painfully tightly. The colour is grey in the low light, but I know that it is really lavender – the colour of half-mourning. The ring on my right hand has a cluster of pearls on a black enamel ground, set into gold.

The clock begins to chime, a series of shrill notes that seem to shiver on the air, and then it strikes the hour. I count six, and each successive strike is a distinct and sharp pang. The hour of six has a terrible meaning for me.

I rise from my chair with a rustle of heavy fabric and move slowly across the room, threading my way between overstuffed chairs and fussy little occasional tables loaded with dusty ornaments. I am impelled to do this, drawn by some unseen undertow. My skirts sweep the floor; my shoes move over the soft nap of a rug and then resound crisply on polished wood. The door stands ajar, the unlit passageway beyond it a dark tunnel. I plunge into it, feeling my way along the wall with outstretched fingers.

I perceive all this as though through a series of transparent layers: there are the bare details of what I see, and there is myself, Fen, and there is something that is not-Fen, a thing whose actions I must perform and whose feelings seep into mine like a bitter stain. Pale fingers move along the dusty wallpaper, feeling its texture under the sensitive tips, and they are not my fingers but I feel them anyway.

Ahead of me I see twin columns of coloured light glowing softly in the darkness and I see that they are stained glass panels set into a door. I make my way haltingly towards them. My hands reach unerringly for the metal bolts; they know how to unfasten the door in the dark even if I, Fen, do not. I pull the bolts back and turn the handle, pulling the door towards me.

Cool evening air rushes in. I stand for a moment, still within the threshold of the house, framed in the doorway like a plover in the mouth of a crocodile. I know this view. This is what I see when I open the front door of Barr Dubh House. Oh, the sweep of the drive is different, and the trees that line the first part of it are smaller – younger. But the landscape is the same: the shape of the hills, the patches of forest.

The sun is setting behind me, behind the house. Every detail of the view is picked out with sharp contrast and all of it gives me the most exquisite pain. I know that there is an absence imprinted upon that view. There is a longed-for return that will never happen, not even if I stand here forever. The sun may rise and set again a thousand times or ten thousand times and I will never see that familiar figure at the gate again nor hear that firm tread on the path that leads up to the house.

I step out of the doorway and walk a dozen paces, turning my face up to the darkening sky. Grief is a great lump in my throat. I drop to my knees and even through the thick fabric of my skirts the sharp stones cut into my flesh. I put my face to the ground and it smells of cold damp earth, of things that were once alive, now disintegrating. I close my eyes and make the world dark.

"Fen?"

With a great effort I open my eyes, and find that I am lying in a broad stripe of golden light spilling out from the front door of Barr Dubh House. Everything else is dark. I am so cold and stiff that at first it is completely beyond me to move, to unfold myself from my huddled position on the ground.

James is crouched by me, his hands hovering over me as though he is afraid to touch me in case he breaks something. The light is behind him so I can't see his face, but I hear the panic in his voice.

"Christ, Fen. What happened? Say something!"

"James," I say. "I'm cold."

"Are you hurt?"

"No," I say. I have to drag the words out of myself. "Just cold."

It feels as though it would be easier to shut my eyes again and drift off into the numbing dark, but James is having none of it. He gets an arm around me and hauls me up onto my feet, and since those don't seem to be very steady he supports me as I stagger back into the house. The gravel nips at my feet. He puts me in the chair in his study, because the room is small enough to warm up quickly if he puts the heater on. He fetches the duvet from the guest room and covers me with that, and then he makes me a mug of tea. He pours himself something that smells suspiciously like Scotch. Then he pulls over the desk chair, sits down next to me and looks me in the eyes.

"Fen, what happened?"

My fingers and toes are burning as the life comes back into them.

"I don't know," I say, but I can see that won't be enough. Worry is etched into James's face. "I dreamed I went outside."

"You dreamed it? So you were sleepwalking?"

I look at him listlessly. "I suppose so."

"I woke up and you weren't there," he says. "I thought, oh, she's just gone for a glass of water or something, and I was going to go back to sleep. But it was taking me a while to drop off again and I started to wonder where you were. If I hadn't..."

He falls silent, not wanting to pursue that line, and takes a mouthful of the whisky. After a while, he says, "Have you ever sleepwalked before?"

I shake my head. "Not that I know of." Then I think of the night I woke up from a dream to find myself sitting in an armchair downstairs. I open my mouth to tell James about this but before I can speak he says, "Fen, are you happy here?"

"James..."

"Because you seem distracted a lot of the time. You've been like it since Belle came up. And then this..."

"I'm tired," I say. This is true. I feel as though I could just close my eyes and drop off, right here in the armchair. "I'm not sleeping very well. I keep having these weird dreams."

"That night after Belle went, when you woke up yelling,

you said it was like being dead. And now... you dream you're walking out of the house. I'm not a psychologist, but..." He grimaces. "It seems like you're not happy about something."

In spite of the cold exhaustion encasing me, this kindles a spark of alarm.

"I'm not unhappy, James." This is true: I am uneasy, and confused, and sometimes actually afraid, but I am not unhappy, not in the way he means. Not with him. I *can't* be. "I'm just... I don't know. Maybe I'm still getting used to sleeping in a new place. It's so different from the flat – it's so quiet here."

"I've been thinking about that," says James seriously. "Maybe it's *too* quiet. It's great for me – I've never been so productive. But you're used to having other people round you. When I'm shut in here with my laptop, you're on your own."

"I'm supposed to be working too," I point out.

James is silent for a little while. Then he says, "What's wrong, Fen?"

He says it as though he's bracing himself for bad news. I know with a sudden chilling certainty that now is the moment to tell him that I know about his debt. He's asking me for honesty.

I can't do it. I'm freezing cold and exhausted and afraid. Right now I just want James to hold me tight. I don't want to see the shock spilling across his face when he finds out what I've done, when his secret is out.

The silence stretches out until it feels like a barrier between us.

At last James says, "Fen, if it's not working out here, we could go back, you know." He puts out a hand and touches my wrist, his fingers warm against my cold skin. "We could rent this place out and go back to London for a while. Or permanently. Nothing's been done that can't be undone."

He means it, too. James is not afraid of making big decisions, nor of the myriad of logistical problems that follow them like a swarm of biting insects. I'm the one who thinks of the practicalities first: the things we have and haven't done to Barr Dubh House, the probability of finding a tenant or buyer, the difficulty of finding anywhere affordable in London. The cost of moving. Money. *Money.*

I make those kinds of decisions when I *have* to; when my back is against the wall. My mind skips back to that afternoon in my old university room: the way the flames leapt up from the stack of law books; the heat on my face. It was the same with getting out of London: I did it to escape. My old life was wearing me out. Barr Dubh is the fairytale castle I struck out across the freezing water for, and I am determined that this time the magic will be real.

I shake my head. "I don't want to go back to London. I want to stay here, at Barr Dubh."

"But Fen–"

"James," I say, as firmly as I can, "The things that are wrong were wrong before we came here. I still miss my brother. I'm never going to *stop* missing him. And I'm never going to sort things out with my parents. I don't even know how to think about them. I don't know if I should feel guilty or grateful or both or nothing. Sometimes I think about them and it hurts, but I think maybe it doesn't hurt *enough* and so I just try not to think about them. But if it weren't for them, we wouldn't be here at all. It's all mixed up in my head and..." I hesitate. "Maybe I just need more time."

Everything I tell him is true, although the things I *haven't* said hang over me. At any rate, I have convinced James, even if I haven't convinced myself. There's no more discussion about leaving that night. When the tea is finished, James gently takes the mug out of my hands and takes me upstairs, still wrapped in the duvet. We get back into bed, and he pulls me close so that the last of the chill is absorbed into the warmth of his body.

I lie with my face pressed into the side of his neck, listening to his breathing becoming slower and deeper as he descends into sleep. I think about the night he came home late from Spain, when I watched the car headlights coming up the lane, and I think about the dream of standing on the doorstep looking east for someone who would never come, and soon the two things are jumbled up in my head. I press myself close to James, as close as I can, and follow him down into sleep.

Chapter Twenty-Six

When I imagine it, it's always a bird's eye view. I am flying high above the landscape on invisible wings, rising and falling with the air currents. In the far distance, the horizon is a shimmering blur. Below me, the countryside is spread out like a rumpled green velvet cloth patched here and there with fields of yellow rape. It is bisected by a road that runs east to west, winding its way around natural features – a hillock, a bend in a river – like a stream finding its way amongst boulders. I hover above this road, facing east, looking for the flash of reflected sunlight from a windscreen that will tell me there is a car speeding towards me.

There. The light winks at me before the vehicle disappears briefly under the cover of some overhanging trees. The road has many features like this: canopies of vegetation throwing shade across the tarmac, sharp bends that swing the vehicles perilously far out, dips that conceal them altogether. It is a sly, deceitful road, not taking travellers directly and honestly from A to B in the open sunshine but leading them into any number of traps.

The car that is approaching is a dark grey saloon, a

souped-up model from an expensive manufacturer. The numbers on the clock do not even run into five figures yet: the car is very new. At the wheel of the car is Michael Haig, aged forty-two, salesman, golfer, connoisseur of malt whisky, father of one and recent participant in an extremely messy divorce. Mike is late for a meeting so he is speeding, grasping the wheel with one hand and holding his mobile phone to his ear with the other, trying to call the client to let them know he's on his way. He ought to be using hands-free but he hasn't set it up in the new car yet, a fact that will be commented upon later: the company should enforce it. Of course, he could pull over to make the call, but he's already running late. Mike's colleagues all agree that he is very conscientious; he would do anything to avoid being late for a client meeting. It's possible that they might privately agree that he is a bit of an arsehole: he has had several tickets for speeding already and if he gets another one it will probably mean a ban. But they won't be expressing this view in the future, not under the circumstances.

Mike knows the road pretty well, so he drives confidently – overconfidently, some might say, assuming that he will not encounter other vehicles in places where he has never encountered them before. He goes wide at the curves, the tyres of the expensive saloon crossing right over the white lines. After the next couple of bends there is a straight stretch, and he intends to put his foot to the floor and regain a few lost minutes.

A mile or so west, a car is travelling towards Mike from the other direction. This is also an expensive model of car, though older than Mike's. The bodywork is gleaming black, a sober, respectable choice of colour befitting the profession of the owner, who is a judge: my father. In the passenger seat is my mother, her handbag at her feet. The pair of them are travelling to see my mother's sister, my aunt. They are not without a sense of family, these two, even though they no longer really speak to their daughter. They visit my aunt every other month, and in the intervening months she comes to them.

My father and mother are *not* late, and my father never speeds, disapproving (as he naturally must) of law breaking of any kind. However, he takes the black car up to the speed limit, because he has driven this road many times before and knows all the dips and corners. The sun goes behind a heavy bank of cloud and suddenly the black car is obscured; it slips through the deep shade like a minnow darting underneath the shadow of a riverbank.

From my great height I see them racing towards each other: the dark grey car going west, the black one travelling east. Each of them follows bends and corners, heading towards the one straight piece of road that stretches between them like a garrote held between two fists. Seen from this distance, the road is small and narrow, and it seems impossible that two vehicles travelling that fast can miss each other. But in reality, there is plenty of space for them to pass each other safely. Except...

Halfway down the straight stretch there is a third car, a small red hatchback crawling along like a ladybird idling its way up a twig. It catches the eye because of its bright colour, and perhaps that is the reason for what happens next. Perhaps Michael Haig's attention is snagged by the splash of crimson, so that he fails to notice the black car sliding into the dip on the other side of the blind summit. Or perhaps he simply only has so much attention to give, and at least half of it is on the call he is trying to make on his mobile phone.

He is approaching the red car far too fast, perhaps cursing the driver for moving so slowly that nobody can possibly be expected to sit patiently behind it. With a jerk of the wheel Mike swings into the other lane, accelerating to overtake just as he crests the summit. A second later the gleaming dark bulk of the judge's car fills his vision as it races up to meet him. There is no time to react.

Mike Haig and my mother die instantly. My father dies a little later, at the scene. The driver of the little red car, who calls the accident in, has hysterics at the side of the road. After this, there is no more; my imagination soars away on its invisible wings, up into an empty sky.

Of all the terrible things I have dreamed, I have never dreamed any of this. It is reality, reconstructed in my mind's eye from the details at the inquest, and from visiting the spot where it happened. I went, not to lay flowers, but to look for answers. There are none.

Chapter Twenty-Seven

RESURGAM, it said on Euphemia Alexander's grave. I didn't know what that meant when I read it, but I've looked it up since. *I shall rise again.* I suppose we all think that, at some level: we can't quite believe our own death is going to be permanent.

My father left very specific instructions for his funeral, as if the careful execution of them would give him some personal satisfaction. I stood between James and Belle, listening to Pachelbel's *Canon in D* playing over the crematorium's sound system and feeling horrible. The situation seemed unreal: there was a flat, remote feeling to it, as though we were watching ourselves in a poorly-made film. I recall thinking that I never knew my father liked that piece of music and that I would have to ask him why he chose it when I next saw him, even though I had not spoken to him at all for a long time. Then I remembered that he was gone, *dead*, and it would be impossible to ask him or my mother anything again. I made a noise, not a sob or a groan but a noise of not understanding, and James took my hand in his, pressing my cold fingers with his warm ones. After the service, a lot of people came up and expressed their condolences, shaking my hand, but they might as well have been making obeisances in front of an Easter Island statue. I could not seem to respond or even smile.

After the funeral, there was a mountain of work to do, and it was impossible to put it off. The executors did most of the paperwork, but I had to make decisions about the house and all its contents. I could not live in it myself; I knew that the moment I slid the key into the front door lock and the widening gap as the door opened exhaled that familiar scent of furniture polish and disapproval. Nor could I simply leave it while I thought things over: a house that size does not run on nothing. I began the job of clearing it with the help of James and Belle but the task seemed too huge and heartless, which was why so much stuff ended up in remover's cartons, unsorted and unexamined. My aunt took some things, and what was left – mainly bulky pieces of furniture – was removed by professional house clearers. The house was sold, and suddenly the theatre in which our family dramas had run for so many years was someone else's exciting new renovation project. I suppose if I went down that street now, I would see the changes that have been made, but I have never been able to bring myself to do it. Supposing the new people have cut down the tree Stephen used to gaze up at, as he lay in the grass? No. It is better not to look, and to let the tree flourish in my memory.

As for the money, that felt as unreal as everything else did. I couldn't think why they left everything to me. They didn't understand anything I did, beginning with the fire in my room. Why should they? I didn't understand it myself, not in any way I could put into words. I just kept thinking about my brother, Stephen, lying on the floor of his room with the law books open on his desk and the blossoms on the tree outside his window, and there was nothing else I could do.

I remember the university authorities were much kinder than I expected them to be. There was no question of continuing with law, but they supported my transfer to a different course at another university, much further away from home. My parents did not understand that, either. At least, they did not understand why I wanted to waste my time studying English. They did understand, however, that I was escaping. The conversations we had were full of anger and disapproval. When I graduated, they didn't come to the ceremony; Belle came instead. When I landed a job in publishing they were not pleased. I suspect they were angry that I had not fallen into the failure and penury that my disobedience deserved. They never visited my flat in London. They never met James, not even once. By the time they drove along the stretch of country road where Michael Haig was to meet them so disastrously, we had not seen each other in person for over two years.

No matter how much I think about them, I cannot fathom it. I don't think they *hated* me, but I seemed to offend them. Whatever they wanted, I was not it. I didn't expect anything from them, any more than I expected them to be gone so suddenly, without warning, from one moment to the next.

There was no mistake about their intentions. The will that left me everything was a recent one. Sometimes I think they left it to me because that was what they had to give. Not patience when Stephen or I struggled with anything; not applause when we achieved something. Not even tears when Stephen died. Things. Money. A string of figures on a piece of paper.

After they died I felt – strange. I had seen them so rarely over the previous years that their absence was hard to take in. I went from not seeing them but knowing that they were there, to not seeing them and knowing that they were gone. The numbness I had felt at the funeral went on and on, seeping through each hour and day like a spreading stain. I suppose people thought I was "coping amazingly well" because I didn't break down at the office. Each passing day felt as though it was adding another layer of lacquer to my unnatural composure. I suppose it was bound to crack in the end.

James and I went out one Sunday afternoon, to walk along the side of a lake. The weather had been cool considering it was now summertime, but that day it was actually hot. The parkland around the edge of the lake was very lush and green; it had not yet reached that point in the late summer where everything starts to look parched and weary. Even in the middle of the park you could hear the distant roar of traffic along the main road, but there was enough calm and greenery to create a remembrance of wilder places. Perhaps that was why Scotland came into my mind.

We had been strolling for perhaps half an hour when we came to a spot at the water's edge where there was a crescent of sandy earth, like a tiny beach sloping into the shallows. There were people picnicking on the grass and just as we came up, one of the children, a girl of perhaps ten with blonde plaits, ran past us, heading for the lake's edge. She was wearing jelly shoes but otherwise she was dressed for the land, not water, in cropped trousers and a t-shirt. The purposeful way in which she was moving snagged my attention. I watched her run onto the sand, where she paused and looked round, to see whether her parents were watching. Then she stepped very deliberately into the lake, and waded out a little way, until the water was halfway up her thighs and her trousers were sticking to her legs in a way that looked uncomfortable. That was as far as she went, but I stopped walking and gazed at her, wondering whether she would go any further – whether she would try to swim.

I felt a tug on my hand. I had stopped walking, but James hadn't until he felt my resistance.

"Fen?"

I shook my head, and started walking again, this time more briskly, not wanting the child or her family to see my face. I made for an old beech tree, and when we were safely on the other side of it I let go of James's hand and leaned against the trunk.

"Fuck," I said. I put the heel of my hand to my eye and it came away wet. "Fuck. I'm sorry."

"For what?"

"It's just..." I shook my head again. "That girl in the water. I did that once, when I was a kid. Just walked into a loch in my clothes, and swam. I thought for a moment she was going to do that. It just made me think..."

James waited for me to say what it made me think, but I was struggling to put it into words. I remembered doing exactly that, striding into the water and feeling the chill of it soak right through to my skin. The drag of the water on my clothes, the taste of it on my lips. I remembered looking back and seeing Stephen standing on the bank, a tiny figure glimpsed across an alarming distance; feeling the terror and exhilaration of having swum so far out to get away from our parents. All of that was gone, that family structure that felt like a cage. My older brother was gone; I was older than he was now. Our parents were gone. I would never have to run away from them again, but nor would there ever be any peace between us. The day I walked into the loch and discovered that the fairy castle was just a ruin existed only in my head. No matter how

197

carefully I described it, I could never tell James exactly how it had been, and everyone else who had been there was dead.

At last I said, "It was years ago, when we were on holiday in Scotland. Stephen watched me do it. My parents were furious. And now all of them are gone – Mum, Dad and Stephen. The house has been cleared. There isn't even a place to go back to. I feel like I'm wandering around and all the landmarks have gone. I don't belong anywhere."

James put his arms around me and pulled me close to him. For a few moments he just held me without saying anything at all. Then he said, "Let's get married then."

It took a few seconds for this to sink in.

"What?" I said.

"Let's get married. Then you'll belong with me."

He said it in such an insouciant way that I could hardly believe my ears. I wondered if I'd misunderstood him somehow.

When I didn't reply, he added, "Unless you don't want to."

"Of course I do," I found myself saying. I felt slightly dazed; I hadn't expected this. "Yes," I remembered to say eventually.

James laughed a little at that, and I smiled, and when I smiled I saw something kindle in his eyes: he was happy because he had arrested my downward swoop into misery. Behind the cover of the beech tree he kissed me, and then we walked on.

I don't remember anything we talked about after that. My head was too full of what had just happened, a hazy feeling of unreality still hanging over it.

Sometimes I still feel it, that sense of faint disbelief. I feel as though with James I have been too lucky – that it cannot possibly last.

Chapter Twenty-Eight

I am sitting in the kitchen on a bar stool, with my laptop open in front of me. I still haven't done anything about a proper office space for me. It doesn't feel as though there's any particular hurry – I quite like working in the kitchen, which is mostly light and cheerful, except in the nastiest weather. It also means I get five minutes' chat whenever James comes through to get himself a coffee. I wonder if I'd see him otherwise? He's right about being productive here at Barr Dubh. Me – not so much.

I look down at the screen. The work is slow. The hero in this manuscript is infuriatingly smug and all the female characters have the sort of names you'd give to a small dog. I wouldn't be surprised if I turned the page and found the next one was called Fluffy. The one positive thing about wading my way through the diabolical prose is that the process feels familiar and ordinary. I've done this many times before. All the stuff that's been crowding in on me – things I can't change from the past, the dreams – seem less real. I even find myself worrying less about James's debt, because at least both of us are working. I feel as cheerful as any copyeditor can possibly feel when they have just read a sentence in which the protagonist is looking down someone's blouse for no apparent reason. My finger hovers over the touchpad as I debate whether to suggest he looks into her eyes instead. Then I imagine him catching her rolling her eyes, and I laugh out loud.

More tea, I think. A job like this can only be tackled when properly fuelled with a nice strong well-sugared mugful. So I slide off the bar stool and while I'm waiting for the kettle to boil I look wistfully out of the window. It's cool in here and I rub my hands together absent-mindedly, trying to bring a little more life into my fingers. I miss something. I'm not wearing my engagement ring. I know where it is – I took it off earlier before doing some chores. It's sitting in a little china dish on the windowsill. So I saunter over and I have my hand outstretched to pick it up when I stop and stare.

There are two rings in the dish. One of them is my engagement ring, a sparkling solitaire diamond set in white gold. The other – well, the other doesn't belong to me at all. I have nothing that heavy and gloomy-looking: a cluster of seed pearls on a black enamel ground, set round with gold.

I don't like the sight of the two rings nestling together in the dish: my bright silvery-looking diamond and that funereal-looking black and gold thing. I fish my ring out of the dish with my fingertips and hastily slide it onto my ring finger. Then I stand there looking at the other one.

Am I going mad? Is that what is actually happening?

I know that is not my ring. I don't have anything even remotely like it. I know I didn't put it there in the dish, either. But I recognise it. I remember looking down at myself in the dream and seeing the lavender silk of the dress I was wearing, and my hands clasped in my lap, that ring on one of my fingers.

200

How can this be? I struggle to think of an explanation. Is it possible that I dreamed about it because I'd seen it before, and that I've just forgotten doing that? I look at the thing doubtfully. It seems unlikely; it's such a distinctive design. And anyway, that wouldn't explain how it's suddenly appeared in the kitchen since I took off my own ring this morning. I hug myself, gazing down at it. Somehow I don't like to pick it up, so eventually I carry the whole dish over to the spot where I've been working, where I can sit down again and study it under the kitchen spotlights.

It's old, I conclude: the pearls are a little grey with age and the setting is worn-looking in places. An antique, then. It occurs to me to look for a hallmark. I rotate the dish, peering at the inside of the gold band. There's something stamped or inscribed in there. I squint at it, but I can't make it out. In the end there's nothing for it but to pick the ring up and hold it under the light, closer to my face. I tilt it, trying to reduce the reflective gleam of the polished gold. I read: E.A. C.R.

First I think the *R* might stand for "king" or "queen" – like a Victorian letter box with *VR* on it for *Victoria Regina*. But I can't think what the *C* would stand for in that case. *Charles?* I can't remember when the last King Charles was. And *E.A.?*

Euphemia Alexander. The name just pops into my head. All of a sudden I can't put the ring down fast enough. I drop it back into the dish, and without thinking about it I find myself wiping my hands on my skirt, as though the thing is contaminated.

Coincidence, I tell myself queasily. *And anyway, it doesn't just say E.A. What's C.R.?*

The idea's in my head now though. Supposing it's hers? And then I think: *whose?* Do I mean whoever is lying six feet under that lichenous slab in the overgrown remains of the kirkyard – or the person in the lavender dress, whom I inhabited in my dream?

Or both.

I was dreaming of Euphemia Alexander.

I grasp the edge of the worktop, steadying myself. *Get a grip, Fen,* I say to myself as sternly as I can. *There has to be some logical reason for this.* I force myself to think it through. Supposing the ring did belong to the Euphemia Alexander buried by the chapel, she could have lost it somewhere in the land around the old house. James could have picked it up outside and brought it in – left it in the dish and forgotten about it. Maybe I saw it lying about but didn't really take it in, and it just re-surfaced in my dream. I stare down at the ugly thing. It's the only explanation I can think of, given that I know *I* didn't bring it in, and nobody else has been inside the house since Belle left.

I chew my lip. I'm very tempted to get rid of the ring without saying anything at all to James. What if I ask him about it and he denies all knowledge – what then? Maybe it would be better not to ask, given that I've already worked out what must have happened – right? Anyway, it's just a ring.

And those porcelain flowers, those were just a decoration.

I ask myself again if I'm going mad. There was that inkstand too – we never got to the bottom of that. I keep staring at the ring lying in the dish. I know it's real – I had it in my hands a minute ago. All the same, I pick up a pen lying near my laptop and poke the ring with it. There is a tiny clatter as it moves. It's solid enough.

"Fen?"

I lift my gaze and see James standing in the doorway with a mug in his hand, looking at me quizzically.

"What've you got there – a beetle or something?"

I laugh uneasily. Too late to get rid of the ring without saying anything.

"A ring. James, did you put this here?"

He comes over to take a look, leaning so close that I get a distracting waft of aftershave.

"Nope. It's a mourning ring, isn't it? A bit Gothic for your taste, I'd have thought."

"It's not mine."

"Well," says James drily, "It's not mine either."

"Then how did it get here?"

There's a pause. A shrug. "Maybe Belle–"

"It wasn't Belle," I say, and then stop abruptly. It came out more snappily than I meant it to, because I'm feeling unaccountably anxious about this whole thing.

James looks at me.

"I'm sorry," I say. "I didn't mean to sound as crabby as that. It's just... it's creeped me out a bit."

"Chuck it out then."

Quite unconcerned, James leans over and plucks the ring out of the dish. Touching it doesn't seem to bother him at all. He turns it over and over in his fingers.

"It's old," he comments. "Sort of a shame to throw it out."

"I don't want it," I say quietly.

"You could eBay it or something," he suggests, putting it back into the dish.

Or throw it into the nearest river. I don't say that; instead I just say, "Maybe."

"Anyway," James says, "How's the book going?" He speaks casually, but his gaze is serious. I sense it's not really the book he's asking about.

"Awful," I tell him, keeping it light. "What about yours?"

"Really well," he says. "It's practically writing itself." He grins ruefully. "Sorry. I feel your pain. Honestly."

"You really don't," I tell him. "You have no idea." I slide off the bar stool again and pretty much into his arms. "I'm glad yours is going well though. At least one of us is having fun." I look up at him slyly. "Are you going to tell me what it's about yet?"

James never tells *anyone* what his work in progress is about, not even Laura – not in any detail, anyway.

"No," he says cheerfully. "Not until it's finished."

"Oh, go on. At least a clue."

"Well, it's pretty dark."

"All your books are, James. They're always about dead people."

He tries unsuccessfully to look put out. "There are some live ones too."

I keep looking at him, not letting him off the hook.

He says, "Well, it's set here."

"What, right here?"

But he won't be drawn. "Scotland."

I look at him beseechingly but he shakes his head.

"You're so annoying, James."

"And you're very tempting, but it won't work."

Shortly after that, he fetches himself another coffee and vanishes back into his study. I sit and look at my laptop, the screen now dark from neglect. Then I look at the dish with the black and gold ring still sitting in it. I could ignore it. It's just an old ring, after all.

I sigh and get down from the stool again. I carry the dish out of the kitchen and down the passage. In the room which may become my office and which is currently a repository for all the spare bits of furniture, there is an old bureau. I pull open the lid, put the dish into one of the cubbyholes inside, and close it again. Then I march out of the room and pull the door closed behind me.

Chapter Twenty-Nine

"Love you," is the last thing James says before he gets out of the car, right after: "Make sure the doors are locked, okay?"

I sit behind the wheel and watch him walk into the station. The windscreen is speckled with raindrops; I have to turn on the wipers before I pull away. It's not just the rain that's dismal. James is going to be away tonight. I shall be sleeping alone at Barr Dubh House for the first time since James's trip to Spain. That time, when he went off, I knew I'd miss him, but I wasn't *worried*, because that was before the first of the dreams. Now, I'm dreading it. Before, I thought I'd have a bit of me-time and relish being in our fabulous new home. Now, I think about dark passages and rooms and the blind black squares of windows looking out into an absolutely lightless night. I think of myself wandering around in my sleep, with no James to find me if I manage to make my way outdoors again. I chew my lip, thinking up preventative strategies in my head. *When I've locked all the outside doors I could hide the keys somewhere I can't easily get at them – I could lock the bedroom door –*

I follow the curve of the street and in the rear view mirror the station vanishes from view. A couple of minutes later, I pull into a small and crowded car park. There is one space left. After I've parked, I sit there for a few moments looking at the building in front of me, distorted by rivulets of rain running down the glass.

I told James I was going to look at another bridal shop. It's not actually a lie. I probably will – after I've finished here. I get out of the car, wincing at the rain driving into my face, and scurry towards the building. I pull my coat close around me. It's cold today – properly wintry. I hunch my shoulders, shivering as I skirt a puddle.

The building looks old from the outside, with a stone portico and big arched windows. It's a surprise to get through the lobby and find myself in a well-lit and very modern-looking library. It's instantly reassuring, too. Books have been my friends, my comforters, my advisers my whole life long. I hope that they will help me now.

I don't even have to ask where to start looking. Directly ahead of me is a staircase, and halfway up there is a notice reading *Local and family history*. I start up the stairs, unbuttoning my coat as I go.

Euphemia Alexander, I say to myself. *If you're here, I'll find you.*

A little of my confidence ebbs away when I get to the top of the stairs. There are a lot of different sections. Do I start with *Local history* or maybe *Biography* or perhaps the big banks of what seem to be actual card files, something I haven't seen in a very long time? There's also a glass door with *Archive* written on it in large letters. I suspect I'd have to speak to someone if I went in there, which might be awkward. I'd have to think how I'd explain a personal interest in Euphemia Alexander, died 1872, no relation.

Too late. A middle-aged woman with an armful of

books has seen me hesitating. "Can I help you?" she says.

"I'm looking for some information – historical information – about a particular... area."

"A parish?" she suggests.

"I guess so."

"In Perthshire?"

"Yes."

"How long ago?" She doesn't wait for a reply, but heads over to one of the bookshelves. She juggles the stack of books so that she has a hand free and points to a row of dry-looking volumes in identical cream dust jackets. "There's the *Old Statistical Account of Scotland*; that's 1791 to 1799. It has a description of each parish and its population, the crops that were grown, some local history and so on. If you want something a bit later, there's the *New Statistical Account*, which is over there." She's already walking off towards another bookcase so I trail after her again. When she reaches the shelves she turns to face me, her free hand resting on a book bound in red, with faded gilt letters on the spine. "The *New Statistical Account* is from 1834 to 1845."

New? I try and fail to do the exact calculation in my head, but 1845 is definitely over a hundred and fifty years ago.

"Is that the most recent one?"

"No, there's a *Third Statistical Account*," she says crisply. "We have that too. The Perthshire volume was published in 1979."

"I guess I'll look at the new one," I say. "Thanks."

After she's gone, I carry the volume over to a table and sit down. When I open it, I detect a faint musty smell of old book. It's hard to imagine this ancient tome telling me anything relevant to the here and now; it's like expecting the dead to speak. That particular thought is not encouraging. I turn the pages gingerly.

The contents pages run to two sides, beginning with *Aberdalgie and Dupplin* and ending with *Weem*. Barr Dubh House lies about halfway between two of the towns listed, so I start with those. It's hard going. The entry for each parish begins with its topography and natural history before moving on to civil history, population, industry and parochial economy, whatever that is. "There are few animals in the parish which can be called rare in Scotland," begins one of the sections.

The bits about civil history seem to include information about important families living in the parish, but there's nothing about anyone called Alexander. I drum my fingers on the desk, considering. Is there an index? I turn the book over and open it at the back. *Yes.* Quite by chance, I've opened it at *B*, so I glance down the page, looking for *Barr Dubh*. There's nothing. I remember the old man we spoke to saying that the spot wasn't always called that. Its real name, he said, was Barr Buidhe. I leaf back to the previous page and there it is: *Barr Buidhe.*

I check the page number and then I'm leafing through the book, eager to see what it says. It turns out it isn't in either of the parishes I've already tried. It belonged to one I've never heard of, one that no longer exists.

"Much of the land in the parish is in the possession of Miss Alexander of Barr Buidhe, the last scion of the Alexanders of Strathearn, all other family members being deceased. Miss Alexander is at the present time engaged to be married to Mr. Charles Robertson of Fortingal."

Mr.Charles Robertson. I think about the mourning ring that's still sitting in the old bureau at Barr Dubh House. E.A. C.R., that was the inscription. Euphemia Alexander and Charles Robertson. It has to be them. What are the chances of it belonging to anyone else with those exact same initials? Unease wells up, but I force it down.

I have to be objective; I have to *know*.

That's all there is. After that, the topic shifts to changes to the parish boundaries. I go back to the index and look up Fortingal, but after reading the entire section on that parish from end to end, I can find nothing about Charles Robertson. I go back to the entry about Miss Alexander of Barr Buidhe, wondering if I can glean anything from that.

"At the present time engaged" – but when was that? I flip through to the frontispiece, which helpfully has a date entirely in Roman numerals. After a little pondering, and some internet searching on my phone, I manage to work out that it says *1844*. The overgrown grave of Euphemia Alexander gave a death date of 1872, and an age of 60. That would mean that the woman buried there was born in 1812, so by 1844 she'd have been 32 years old.

I rub my forehead with my fingers. It's difficult to think straight. It has to be the same person. It can't be a sister or anything, not if there was only one member of the Alexander family living.

Something about that phrase "At the present time engaged" strikes me as a little strange too. Is it hinting at something – perhaps that the engagement is somehow impermanent? Then it occurs to me that for whatever reason, it didn't actually come off. Euphemia was still an Alexander when she died and there was no mention of a marriage on her tombstone. So either she broke up with Charles Robertson or something happened to him.

That last dream slides unbidden into my mind: standing at the door of Barr Dubh House, but an older Barr Dubh House than the one James and I inhabit, gazing east with anguish in my heart. I remember the keen pain of knowing that I was looking for the return of someone who would never come. The mourning ring was on my finger and when I crumpled to the ground I felt myself tangled in long skirts. I was seeing through the eyes of Euphemia Alexander. I don't know how this can even be possible, but I believe it. The time I saw was her time and the pain I felt was her pain. The person she was looking for was Charles – the man she was engaged to, but never married.

I put my elbows on the desk and my head in my hands. Unpleasant sensations move sluggishly in the pit of my stomach, like the flow of a poisoned river. I should pity Euphemia Alexander, or whatever faint echo of her persists. Imagine losing someone you love so much you've promised to marry them. Imagine if I lost James. The thought is so awful I feel as though I could choke on it. She must have felt that – I know she did, because I felt her agony in my dream. I should be crying for her and for all the years she endured alone. But I don't feel pity or sadness. I feel dread. I have this horrible feeling that in some way she is trying to get at me. There was the night James came home, when I saw a thin figure pressed against the trunk of a tree, and the time we walked back from the pub and I glimpsed it there, on the very doorstep of the house. There was that feeling when I was at the ruined chapel, that something unseen and ominous was sweeping towards me. There were the times I glimpsed a distant figure in lavender, too far away for me to make out the details. James has never experienced any of these things. It's me she's haunting, and I don't like it. What can she possibly want from me? I can't change anything that happened to her.

I have to know more – even though part of me doesn't want to know at all. It's like the impulse to gorge on something unhealthy. The more I get of it, the worse it makes me feel, but I can't seem to stop.

I get up, leaving the *New Statistical Account* and my bag on the desk, and scan the shelves. There's a section of local biographies, but I don't really expect to find anything there alongside the lives of poets and Duchesses, and sure enough I don't. The local history section seems to have histories of whole families: *The Oliphants of Gask* sits alongside *The Ruthven Family Papers*. But there is no history of the Alexander family. Well, who would write one? If Euphemia Alexander was the last of her family, and she died unmarried, there probably wasn't anyone to do it.

There is nothing to be found in either *Crieff: Its Traditions and Characters* or *Annals of Auchterarder and Memorials of Strathearn*. Time is slipping by. What concentration I had at the beginning is fading and I'm starting to think about going downstairs to the little café for a cup of tea when my fingers close on a slim blue volume called *Strathearn Folk*, published in 1872. The binding is leather, with the title stamped in gold on the spine, and the edges are worn-looking. I open it at the back, perusing the index without very much optimism, and there it is:

Alexander, Euphemia..........106

I turn to the page and read the title *The end of the Alexanders of Strathearn*.

I stare at the page for a moment, a strange cold feeling under my breastbone. The name *Euphemia Alexander*, further down the page, snags my eye, but I force myself to start at the beginning.

"There has been much sorrowful interest locally in the extinction of the old family of Alexander, who dwelt in the house and lands called Barr Buidhe in the old Gaelic tongue."

I blink at the old-fashioned language. It's hard to imagine this ever being a tourism bestseller.

"The place was named for the abundance of yellow gorse that grows there on the hillside. The house that was the home of the Alexander family for some generations also took its name from this. The last of this family was Miss Euphemia Alexander, who lately died at the age of sixty. Miss Alexander was well known in the parish and in the nearby towns, for she had lived there all her life, but also for the tragic circumstances of her earlier life.

"Past the first blossoming of youth, she had despaired of matrimony when at the age of thirty she became engaged to Mr. Charles Robertson of Fortingal–"

Despaired of matrimony?! At the ripe old age of thirty? It would be funny if the whole thing wasn't so creepy. I read on.

"Her happiness was of short duration. Shortly before the wedding was to have taken place, her intended husband was numbered amongst the victims of the Garside locomotive fire, to which so many lives were lost. Miss Alexander at first entirely refused to credit the news. Her incredulity was supported by the grisly circumstance of the victims' bodies being so badly burned and otherwise mutilated as to render identification impossible in many cases. She persisted in her hope that her betrothed would one day return, and it was her custom to stand outside the front door of Barr Buidhe House at sunset and look for him. While she persisted in believing that he would return, she would on no account consent to go into full mourning; however, with the passage of years she at last adopted the colours of half-mourning, which she wore to the end of her life.

"It was common to see her taking solitary walks about Barr Buidhe dressed all in lavender. The staff of the house and those rustics who lived nearby knew better than to approach or speak to her during these walks, because she looked at them so wildly and strangely. She rarely received visitors except for her lawyer and physician, and lived for several decades in seclusion, not even attending the parish church, but preferring instead to carry out her devotions at home.

"After Miss Alexander died at her house, it was found when her will was opened that she had desired to be buried in her wedding dress, and on the directions of her lawyer, this was done. It was further discovered that she had bequeathed her entire estate to Charles Robertson, then some twenty-seven years deceased, perhaps in some faint hope that he might still return and profit from it. There is at this time no other prospective heir, and the house stands empty."

I shut the book gently and slide it back into its place on the shelf with hands that tremble only slightly. Then I go back to the desk and pick up my coat and bag. I leave the *New Statistical Account* lying there closed and walk downstairs, across the lobby and out of the front door. The rain pelts me as I make my way to the car, gripping the front of my coat closed with white knuckles. I cannot imagine going shopping for wedding dresses right now. Instead, I get into the car and sit behind the wheel.

Buried in her wedding dress. The words go round and round my head.

It is a long time before I feel steady enough to drive home.

Chapter Thirty

I sit up that night, far later than I ought to. I find myself reluctant to lie down and close my eyes.

Perhaps, I think, *if I get too tired to dream...*

When I find myself falling asleep over my laptop, I have to go to bed. But first, I go around the house and make sure all the doors are locked, that the keys are removed from the locks so I cannot turn them in my sleep. I read a little from *Jane Eyre*, trying to fill my brain with something other than Euphemia Alexander's terrible history. I leave my phone within reach, reassuring myself I can reach James if I need to.

In spite of everything, it happens again. I wake to find myself in darkness, dressed in unfamiliar clothes that pinch and rustle. I explore the space around me with my hands and discover that I am confined. I push at the surface above me with the flats of my hands, then I hammer on it with my fists. My feet drum uselessly on the boards. The air that I draw into my lungs with each panicked breath becomes thinner and thinner, until I can't even scream any more.

At last I wake up, and in the dispassionate stripe of moonlight that lies across the bed I choke and cough and finally cry for a long time, hugging James's pillow for comfort. Then I get out of bed, because even if I could go back to sleep, I'd be afraid to. I go into the bathroom and splash water on my face, and a hag looks back at me from the mirror, dark circles under her eyes.

I put on my dressing gown and then I go downstairs, holding onto the bannister like an old woman. The clock on the front of the oven says *03:46*. I put on every single light and make myself a cup of very strong, very sweet tea.

I can't go on like this. That's the thought that keeps hammering through my head. I sip the tea and try to think objectively about what to do, but it's hard to think straight. The shiny black squares of still uncurtained windows make me uneasy. I imagine something looming out of the darkness out there like a drowned thing rising to the surface of inky water; I imagine hands like pallid starfish pressed to the glass. Watching the windows is unnerving but turning my back is just as bad. The back of my neck prickles as though I sense eyes on me. But why am I fearful of something getting in? In some way it's already inside. It's in my head. In my dreams.

There's the other thing, too – the thing I hardly dare think about. Euphemia Alexander was buried in her wedding dress. It was there in the book, in black and white. Was it possible that she wasn't really dead? I remember that little green glass bottle of laudanum – a dangerous opiate. Perhaps she overdosed accidentally; perhaps it was suicide. But instead of death, maybe it only brought the appearance of death. Did she literally wake up in her coffin?

I wonder if it's possible to know the answer to this question, after all this time. I imagine taking a shovel and a crowbar and going back to the ruined chapel to find out. Climbing through the wire fence, picking my way through the undergrowth. Levering up the weathered stone with RESURGAM carved into it, and breaking the hard earth with the edge of the shovel. Digging down, my

216

arms and shoulders aching, blisters forming on my hands, perspiration trickling down my back. Perhaps there is still something to find. The shovel might hit the splintering lid of a coffin. I could lever it off and look at what lies within, at the crumbling skeletal remains in the rags of a bridal dress, the lipless teeth grinning up at me under the discoloured headdress of wax flowers. The bones of fingers still wrapped in shreds of thin gloves. I shudder. No. I don't want to know.

I rub my face with my hands and glance at the clock on the oven. It now says *04.01*. Time is passing agonisingly slowly. It won't get light for another four hours. Black night presses against the windows. I feel horrible, hung over with shock and exhaustion, but grimly wakeful.

What am I going to do?

I'm so tired that it takes a while for me to form any coherent thoughts about that, but it's obvious, really. It's not, what am *I* going to do; it's what are *we* going to do? I have to tell James. I have to tell him all of it. I can't keep this walled up inside me any more. He'll probably ask all the things I asked myself: is this a figment of the imagination, a psychological message, a real person trespassing on the land around the house? But I have proof now. The things I dreamed of really happened. Someone lived and died right here where our house stands. She suffered a terrible tragedy and spent the rest of her life grieving over it. Even if it weren't for the dreams, that would be pretty fucking creepy.

I make more tea and wait for the sun to come up. At some point during that long, long night, something occurs to me: a thought I had not had before. If something has survived of Euphemia Alexander...

Stephen, I think.

I suppose something might survive of my parents too, but what would I say to them? They seemed so angry with

217

me all the time – so bitterly disappointed. It is impossible to imagine them as anything other than angry ghosts. But Stephen, poor Stephen...

He didn't mean to die, I think to myself. *He just pushed himself too hard.*

I think of him lying there on the floor between the bed and the desk covered with books; the curtains, opened or closed, I'll never know which, and the tree with its riot of blossom outside, seen or unseen.

You helped me escape, I say to him, and I am not sure whether I have said this aloud or not. I want to feel something – a presence, a sense of understanding, anything that will tell me that some part of my brother endures. But I feel nothing. Where Stephen ought to be, there is only emptiness.

When at last daylight comes, the world outside the window looks grey and damp. I look out and see what appears to be sleet coming down. At least it is getting light, though. Sort of.

I drag myself upstairs again and lie down on the bed. My eyes won't stay open any longer and it's daytime now anyway. I'm bargaining on the fact that I won't have one of those appalling nightmares during broad daylight, and I don't.

Chapter Thirty-One

I awake to the sound of my phone ringing on the bedside table. It rings half a dozen times, stops, and then a few seconds later it begins again. This time I manage to pick it up and press the green button before the call goes to voicemail.

"Fen?" There's an edge to James's tone. "Where are you?"

"I'm..." I hesitate, groggy with sleep. "Where are *you*?"

"At Perth station."

"At Perth..." I sit up, rubbing my face with my free hand. "Oh, shit."

There's a pause. "Does 'oh, shit' mean you forgot?" says James.

"I... not exactly," I say, sliding out of bed. "I was asleep."

"It's three o'clock in the afternoon."

"I know," I say, pulling open a drawer and rummaging with one hand for a clean t-shirt. "Look, I'll leave in the next five minutes. The next *two* minutes. I'm sorry, James."

"Forget it," he says. "I'll get a taxi."

"From Perth?" It must be twenty miles.

"Yes," he says, tersely. "See you later." And he rings off.

I sit on the bed, the t-shirt crumpled in my fist. "Fuck," I say to nobody in particular.

Forty-five minutes later, I hear the doorbell buzz and realise that I left the bolts across the door; James can't get in. It buzzes again twice while I am hurrying down the hall and drawing back the bolts. Then I open the door.

James looks as irritable as I have ever seen him, but when he sees me his expression changes.

"Fen, you look terrible." He steps inside, dropping his case on the floor. "What's happened? Are you ill?"

I shake my head. Where to start? "I had a really bad night, and then I slept in. I'm really sorry I forgot to meet you, James."

"Never mind that," he says. "Come on, Fen. What's up? Has something happened?"

"There's been some stuff," I say. "Stuff we need to talk about."

I see the shadow that passes over his face when I say that. "Should I be worried?" he asks.

"It's we," I tell him. "It's whether *we* should be worried."

"Okay," he says, after a pause. "But it's been a long day. Shall we pour ourselves a stiff drink first?"

We go into the kitchen and James puts his coat over one of the stools while I find two glasses and a bottle of Talisker. James takes a sip of his and then he puts the glass down, looks me in the eyes and says, "Spill the beans."

I take a deep breath, and then I tell him. I *try* to tell him. James is the magician with words, after all, not me, and in spite of – or perhaps because of – sleeping so long I'm so groggy that my brain feels scrambled. I start with the dreams, because he sort of knows about those. He was there the night the men came to nail down the coffin lid and I woke up screaming, and the night I let myself out of the house that hasn't stood here for over a hundred years, and he found me lying on the gravel. He doesn't know how often these things have been happening though. And he doesn't know how detailed, how *real* they are.

"I can see and hear and *feel* everything," I tell him. "I can feel the fabric of the clothes I'm wearing. When I touch the inside of the coffin I can feel the grain of the wood under my fingers. My lungs hurt when the air starts to run out, for God's sake."

"Fucking hell, Fen. Why didn't you tell me any of this before?"

It's the first time he asks me this and I struggle to reply. The truth is that when I had the very first dream, the night he was in Spain, I was afraid it was something from inside myself, something I did not want to face. If someone who was engaged to be married said that they had dreamed of being buried alive in their wedding dress, it wouldn't take Sigmund Freud to draw certain conclusions about that. And then when Belle had that dream about the house being *wrong* in some way I was upset for the same reason, thinking she was insinuating something. Finding out about the money James owes made it worse. I wanted things to be perfect. I still want them to be perfect. They *will* be. I am determined.

So I simply say, "I hoped it would stop." It's a lame explanation, but it's true.

"It could be some kind of weird sleep disturbance," James suggests. "Night terrors."

I'm already shaking my head. He hasn't got it. These experiences go beyond dreaming. I'm *there* – in the coffin, in the armchair, in the doorway of old Barr Dubh House.

"Maybe you should see the doc," he starts to say, and I say, "I've already seen her. She suggested keeping a sleep diary."

"You saw the doc? When?"

And then he says it again, "Why didn't you tell me any of this?"

I push my hands into my unkempt hair, grasping handfuls of it. I feel pushed into a corner. Because it wasn't just about my unconscious thoughts, was it? There was the letter I opened, with that shocking credit card statement inside it. After that, it wasn't just about subliminal doubts. It was about knowing for certain that he had kept something secret from me – something he is still keeping secret. But that is not something I want to talk about now.

"Look," I say at last, "It doesn't matter. It's not a sleep disturbance. It's the house."

"The house? This house?"

"Yes. No. I mean, sort of. The house that used to stand here, on this exact spot."

All of it comes spilling out then. The figure dressed in lavender – the unlucky colour, the colour of half-mourning – glimpsed first at the treeline and later, near the house. The gravestone of Euphemia Alexander, RESURGAM chiselled boldly across it. Her woeful history, pieced together from musty old books in the reference section of the library. The conviction that the dreams I have been having are not really dreams: they are the real experiences of someone who has been dead for over a hundred and forty years.

It takes a long time to explain all this. James asks questions – lots of questions – as anyone would. He wants me to describe the dreams down to the tiniest details: the clothing I find myself wearing, the contents of the rooms, the scraps of overheard conversation. He wants me to tell him exactly what happened the morning I went to explore the ruined chapel. I tell him about the feeling I had, of being watched by someone standing behind me and slightly to the left, and that sound like a long indrawn breath, as though the whole wood were breathing. Even as I am telling him about these things, I realise how insubstantial they sound. They could be the product of an overactive imagination. If someone else described these things, that's what I'd think. By the way James's brows are drawn together, I can see that he is perplexed and that he still cannot understand why I did not tell him any of this at the time.

When I explain how I pieced together Euphemia Alexander's unhappy story, he wants to follow every step: the websites I checked, the titles of the books I consulted.

"When was this?" he says, and then, "So you went to the library? I thought you were going wedding dress shopping."

I stare at him, biting back a defensive reply. I feel as though I have been detected in committing a string of little deceptions but I know it wasn't like that.

He stares back at me for a moment. Then he says, "Never mind. Look, let's think about this logically. Is it possible you'd heard this story before but forgotten about it? Unconscious memory, power of suggestion type of thing?"

I shake my head vigorously. "Absolutely not."

Both of us are silent for a little while after that and the atmosphere is heavy with unspoken words.

Then James says slowly, "Okay, we know for a fact that this Euphemia Alexander lived in the house that used to be here. But how do you know for sure that any of these dreams, or whatever they are, are about her?"

I think about that. "There was that ring – the mourning ring. The one you said I should throw out if it creeped me out that much. I was wearing that in one of the dreams. It had E.A. and C.R. engraved inside it. Euphemia Alexander and Charles Robertson. It can't be a coincidence, those initials."

"*Did* you throw it out?"

"No. I put it away in the old bureau in the room that's going to be my office."

I slide off the kitchen stool. "I'll go and get it and then you can see for yourself."

I leave James taking a swallow of the whisky and go down the hallway to the room where the bureau is stored. I open the lid and look at the cubbyholes. The little dish is there in one of them, where I left it. I slide it out. It's empty. I look at it for a moment and then very gingerly I slide my hand into the space and feel about for the ring. My fingertips touch the wooden surface at the back, but there is nothing in there. Squatting down, I peer into all the cubbyholes. In one of them there is an old till receipt, yellowing and curled up at the edges. There is nothing in any of the others. I pull open drawers, I run my hands across surfaces, finally I get down on my hands and knees and look on the floorboards underneath the bureau. No ring.

I go back to the kitchen. "It's not there."

"Are you sure that's where you put it?"

"Of course I'm sure," I say, a little more sharply than I meant to. I spread out my hands in a gesture of helplessness. "It's like that decoration with the white flowers. It's just gone."

James looks at me and I see a brief flicker of something in his expression: uncertainty, or disbelief. I can't blame him really because the whole thing sounds insane, but I feel frustration welling up.

"This is not my imagination," I say, folding my arms. "I didn't move those things, so unless you did..."

He shakes his head. "I don't know where you put the ring and I've never even seen the other thing, the decoration."

"You were looking at me like I'm nuts or something."

"I don't think you're nuts." James sounds perfectly sincere. He puts out his hands to pull me into a comforting embrace, and the warmth in the face I love so much gives me a sudden wave of tenderness.

"I just wish you'd told me before," he says.

I'm anxious and afraid and so exhausted that I can't think straight, and when he says for the umpteenth time that I should have told him before, I feel a tiny flash of anger.

"You're a fine–" I retort, and then I stop dead. I shut my mouth. I didn't mean to say that.

There's a pause.

"A fine one to talk?" says James slowly. "What do you mean by that?"

"I didn't mean anything," I say, hastily, but I can't quite meet his gaze.

"Fen." He says it flatly – not angrily, but gravely, as though he's trying to get my attention. That single word is the chisel that breaks through the armour of my silence.

It comes out in a rush, before I've had time to think. "I know you owe money, James."

"What?" He looks genuinely shocked.

"On your card. I didn't mean to look, I swear."

"You opened my *post*?"

"Not deliberately –"

"How else can you open someone's post?" There is an edge to his voice.

"The letters were wet. All the letters. We'd come in from the rain and dripped water all over them and I thought they'd just turn into papier mâché if I didn't open them and dry them out. You were on the phone for ages so I just opened yours as well as mine."

"And had a good look?"

"I couldn't not look, James." I can feel my own temper rising. I can't bear the familiar feeling of being unjustly accused. "You owe nearly twenty-two thousand pounds. It kind of stood out."

"Only because you were reading my post. Addressed to me."

"I'm sorry, James. I apologise for reading your post. But that's not the issue. The issue is that my fiancé owes nearly twenty-two thousand pounds and didn't think to mention it."

"That's *my* business." James looks as grim as I ever have seen him, but there is no turning back now.

"It's my business too! We're getting married, remember?"

"Of course I remember." James's voice is steely. "But we're not living in a sodding Jane Austen novel, where people have to prove they have an independent fortune before they get married."

"It's not about the money! It's about the fact that you didn't tell me." My voice is sliding up the scale towards a shout. "We could pay the whole lot off, you know that, if we cut back on the wedding plans and used our savings. But we have to plan that *together*. You just let me go on buying armchairs and looking at dresses and God knows what else and all the time you had that massive debt. It's practically *lying*, James."

"I'm not the only one," he snaps. "You knew about this and you didn't say anything. If you didn't mean to look, why didn't you own up right away?"

"Own up?" I am outraged. "I'm not the one in the wrong here."

"You're the one who snooped."

"I did *not* snoop!"

James picks up his tumbler of whisky from the counter and drains it in one. Then he turns away.

"Where are you going?"

"Upstairs," he says. "To change. I've been travelling half the day and then standing about at Perth station. I don't need any of this right now."

For one moment I am tempted to pick up my own glass and throw it. I fight the impulse down. Instead, I stand there in silence and watch him go, the bitter poison of anger circulating through my body. We have never fought like this before – never. I have no idea where we go from here.

Later, James comes downstairs again and goes straight into his study. I am calmer now, though still angry, and I go and stand outside the door, debating whether to go inside and have it out with him. Then I hear his voice through the panels and realise that he is phoning someone. Laura, probably. Always bloody Laura. I stalk away and leave him to it.

Barr Dubh House is big enough for two people to be in it without interacting at all. I don't see James all evening, although I hear him come out of the study and clatter about in the kitchen for a bit. He doesn't come to find me, and I don't seek him out either. Eventually he goes up to bed. I hear the boiler fire up as he takes a shower. When it goes off again and the bedroom door shuts, I am still downstairs in the living room. I have a book open on my lap but I haven't read more than a paragraph; I can't concentrate on it. All the same, I sit there for another half an hour, until the darkness outside the windows is beginning to play on my nerves and I shut the unread book.

I creep into bed beside James. He isn't lying on his back tonight, in his usual confident posture; he is on his side, his back to me. I turn my back to him, too. It takes a while for me to get to sleep, because I am still tense with anger and misery. And perhaps these bitter emotions have armoured me against whatever haunts Barr Dubh House, because when I finally do sleep, I don't dream of anything at all.

Chapter Thirty-Two

When I wake, it is light outside, and I am alone. James's side of the bed is empty. I lie there for a while, looking at the ceiling.

Soon, I will have to go downstairs. What do I want to happen when I get down there? I don't know. The hot anger I felt yesterday evening has cooled. I no longer feel like throwing glassware around. But I'm still sore about being accused of snooping. I *wasn't*. And then James seemed to think that my opening his credit card statement was worse than his concealing a huge debt... I am beginning to feel angry again. There's no way I'm going to be the one to apologise first. Or at all. I turn onto my side and glare at the wall.

Gradually, though, the bitter current of anger blends into the slow dragging sensation of misery. There is no satisfaction in believing that I am in the right. Not long ago, we were happy. Now I have no idea how to get back to that place. I don't even know how James will be when I finally go downstairs: angry, resentful, contrite, silent? This is the first real row we've had.

Eventually I get out of bed, put on my robe and go

downstairs, padding silently on bare feet. The kitchen is so still and quiet that for a moment I think I'm alone in there. Then I see James standing by the window, staring out. He doesn't turn round, even when I pick up the kettle and fill it from the tap. It's as though he hasn't noticed I'm there. It's not until I've finished making myself a cup of tea and laid the teaspoon carefully in the sink that he says, "Fen."

He does turn round then, and we look at each other. He looks tired, I notice.

"I didn't think I'd ever need to tell you," he says. He sighs. "I nearly didn't have to."

"But it's so much money," I say.

"I could have covered it. I've got some big advances coming in – I thought they'd be in by now, but it takes them ages to get round to paying, and then Laura sits on the money for twenty eight days. I phoned her last night and told her to sort it out or I'd find another agent."

"Oh, James." I am impressed with this, in spite of everything. "What did she say?"

"She said she'd sort it out."

"Wow." I shake my head. "But James, you could have told me. It's like you said, we're not living in a – what did you call it? – a sodding Jane Austen novel." I can't help it; my lips twitch at the memory of that.

"I know," he says. "But there was never a right time. Before we decided to get married, it was my problem, one I was going to sort out myself. And then you came into all that money. What was I going to do, say, oh, that's lucky, because I have twenty-two thousand pounds I need to pay off? I have *some* pride."

"You *are* living in a sodding Jane Austen novel," I observe.

"A George Eliot novel," he says, with the ghost of a smile. "The penniless but strangely alluring artist."

"James..." I hesitate. "How did you come to owe that much money to start with?"

"Gambling," he says, and then grins at my expression. "Not *that* sort of gambling. I gave up my last job to write my first book. I said to myself I'd give it a year, and if I couldn't write anything worth publishing in that time, I'd go back to work." He shrugs. "I know – it was risky."

"Very risky," I say severely. Hardly anyone lives on writing novels.

"Basically I lived on my overdraft and my credit card. I didn't run up the whole lot that first year. I finished the book and started sending it off to agents, and I got lucky. Laura was one of the first I sent it to and she loved it. But the first thing she wanted to know was whether I had anything else in the pipeline. So I thought: in for a penny. I didn't go back to work. I wrote *The Unrepentant Dead* instead. By the time I'd finished that, I was starting to think I'd have to give up full time writing because my card was maxed out. But then it won the prize and Laura started to get me foreign rights deals. I reckoned I could get by, and pay off the debts when the advances came in. And you know, I realised I loved writing and didn't want to give it up."

"Shame on you," I say reprovingly. "If you were a proper writer you'd say it was absolute agony pouring out your soul every day."

"It is," he says. "I'm just putting a brave face on it."

Now we're both grinning and I feel a great wave of relief. We are alright. Nothing is irreparably broken.

"I'm sorry I looked at your post," I tell him, and now I actually mean it. "I really didn't mean to snoop. I was trying to be helpful."

"I know," he says. "I guess I overreacted. I wasn't trying to lie about anything. I'd probably have told you anyway, now that I know the money's coming in, only..."

"Only...?"

"You haven't been yourself, and I didn't know why... because you didn't tell me." He says this without rancour.

"It just sounds so crazy," I say. And it does, at this time of day, when the bright sunshine is slanting in through the windows. "I mean, if someone else told me the stuff I told you yesterday, I'd think they were making it up, or else that they were delusional."

"But you're not."

"I don't think so. I mean, do I seem delusional to you?"

"Well, you're marrying me, for a start..." James shakes his head. "No, I don't think you're delusional. But I can't explain any of the stuff you told me."

"I can't explain it either. I mean, I can't explain *how* it's happening. But I think I'm genuinely dreaming about someone else's experiences. The details are so exact."

James rubs his face with his hand. "I'm not going to make any sense of this until I've had some coffee."

So he puts the coffee maker on, and I drink my first cup of tea and make myself another. Then we sit either side of the breakfast bar and look at each other.

"Look," says James, "I know I've already asked you this, and don't get mad, but is there any way at all that you could have heard the story of Euphemia Alexander before the dreams started? It's the obvious explanation."

I'm already shaking my head.

"You used to come up here on holiday when you were a kid, didn't you? You could have heard it then and forgotten it, at least consciously."

"I really didn't, James."

"What about all the research you've been doing, on the house and her life? Could that be influencing what you're dreaming about?"

"The dreams started before I did any of that." I think about it. "The very first dream was one about being buried

232

alive in a wedding dress. And I didn't even find out that Euphemia was buried in hers until three days ago, when I read it in that book in the library."

"It's fascinating," says James. "If you're really experiencing someone's past life."

"It's not," I say with feeling. "It's horrible."

"But *why* is it happening?"

"Does there have to be a *why*? Maybe I'm just seeing an echo of the past or something, if that's even possible."

"Perhaps that's the point. Perhaps she wants her story told."

I look down into my tea. "But I don't want to hear it. I can't stand it, James. That's the truth. I'm afraid to go to sleep at night in case it happens again."

"Maybe it won't," he says. "Maybe she's told you whatever she wanted to say – if that's what's happening."

Maybe. If. I can hear from these words that there is still doubt in James's mind. It makes me feel desperate. I don't think this is about something as simple as listening to Euphemia Alexander's story and I don't think she's going to leave me alone if I do. I think about the times I've seen that indistinct form dressed in lavender roaming the land around Barr Dubh House. It's me who sees her. James never does. Then I think about the things I have found – the grave decoration, the ring, the inkstand. Items from a phantom house that no longer exists. There is purpose in these things, though I don't know what it is. What can she possibly want?

I've been silent too long.

"Hey," says James. He puts out a hand and covers mine. "Next time I have to go away, come with me."

I nod, biting my lip. I don't think it will solve the problem, but I also don't think I ever want to spend the night on my own at Barr Dubh again.

Chapter Thirty-Three

I am in Perth on a grey weekday morning, making my way along pavements that are shiny with rain, heading for the solicitor's. It's one of those offices that advertises properties for sale and offers conveyancing as well. James knows I am here, and why. Not more secrets, that's the agreement. I pause before I go in, perusing the photographs in the window while the rain patters off my umbrella. We could buy a town house overlooking the park if we wanted. We'd have neighbours on both sides and a busy street outside. I can't imagine feeling haunted there.

I push the door open, folding the umbrella carefully. The woman sitting behind the desk is perhaps ten years older than I am and very precisely coiffed and made up. A name plate on the desk top proclaims her to be *Jean Murray*. She looks at me over the top of a chic pair of spectacles with a thin gold chain and I see from her expression that she recognises me immediately.

"Miss Munro," she says, rising to her feet. "Or is it Mrs. Sinclair already?"

'Still Miss Munro at the moment," I say. "I'm impressed you remembered."

She gives me a tigerish smile at this, but there is a hint of restraint in her manner. There is no reason for me to be back here so soon and she is wondering what I want.

"How are you finding the magnificent Barr Dubh House?" she asks me, and I suspect that she is daring me to contradict her statement of its magnificence.

"That's why I'm here," I say evasively. "This is an enquiry really, not an instruction – not at this stage." I sit across the desk from her and put the dripping umbrella on the carpet by my feet. "In your opinion, if we put Barr Dubh back on the market, would we get a lot of interest? Would it sell fairly quickly?"

"It's an unusual property," she says. "It would depend on a suitable buyer coming along at the right time."

Which tells me nothing at all.

"Are people looking at properties in this price range at the moment?" I persist.

She folds her hands in front of her on the desk and gives me a direct look, radiating sincerity for all she's worth.

"To be honest with you, Miss Munro, the run-up to Christmas is never a very good time to sell. Winter can be altogether a difficult time. It can be hard to show a property off at its best, especially in a rural location. If you were to put it on the market in the spring, however..."

She lets the sentence trail off invitingly.

"If we lowered the price?"

Jean Murray purses her lips at this; the very idea offends her commercial soul.

"Of course, anything will sell if you price it low enough. But Miss Munro, you and Mr. Sinclair paid a very reasonable price for Barr Dubh when you bought it. I couldn't recommend going any lower, certainly not as a starting point."

"What if we rented it out?"

"The same considerations would apply, I'm afraid. Winter is not the ideal time. But if you asked us to handle the rental – or sale – we would obviously do our very best to get things moving as quickly as possible."

She goes on for a while after that, describing the company's credentials and the wonders of their personal service. Mindful of my English accent, she reminds me that under the Scottish system we only need to accept an offer and then things will move very quickly. A matter of weeks.

I'm not really listening. I nod every so often, but all I can think is: *I can't get away from Barr Dubh, even if I want to.* Oh, she's probably right about the spring being a better time, but I have all the rest of the winter to get through first – the darkest days, when it's light for less than eight hours out of every twenty-four.

I rouse myself. "The house was empty for a while before we bought it, wasn't it?" I ask.

"Yes," she says, "But an agent went in regularly. It was well maintained."

That's not what I'm getting at. "There was no other interest?"

"As I say, it's an unusual property," she says smoothly. "You simply need the right buyer."

"At the right time," I say flatly, and get a tight smile in reply.

"Exactly," she says.

Perhaps unreasonably, I am starting to dislike Jean Murray quite a lot. I decide I don't really care what she thinks of my questions. I am going to get as much out of her as I can.

I pause for a moment, as though sunk in important deliberations.

"The house is less than three years old, isn't it?" I say.

"The people we bought it from were the ones who built it."

She nods.

"We've been in it six months, and it was empty for – what, eighteen months before that?"

"That's correct."

"So the first people can't have been living in it for any time at all. Less than a year."

"I suppose not," says Jean Murray.

"So why did they sell it?"

There is a silence after I ask this question, and I let it stretch out, resisting the temptation to suggest any reasons that Jean Murray might seize upon.

"I really can't say," she says eventually.

"Didn't they say anything at all?"

"I can't really comment on clients' individual circumstances."

"Can you give me their forwarding address?"

She shakes her head. "I could ask Mrs. Clarke, the solicitor, if she is prepared to forward a communication to either of them. But may I ask what this is about, Miss Munro? If you feel that there was something irregular in the house sale, we'd like to know about it first."

"I really can't say," I tell her. I pick up my umbrella and stand up to leave. "Thank you for your time."

"Do think of us if you do decide to sell," she says, maintaining the professional mask to the last.

I step outside into the rain and put up my umbrella.

To either of them, I repeat to myself as I dodge puddles, hurrying past windows decked out with red and green Christmas displays. Maybe Jean Murray has told me something after all. Those words imply they aren't together now. Maybe they sold because they were splitting up – that's the simplest explanation. We don't have their addresses, but their full names are on the house sale

237

contract. I might be able to track them down somehow. There are a lot of things I'd like to ask.

Chapter Thirty-Four

I have an email from work. It's chirpy and cajoling and full of little phrases like *it would be absolutely super if* and *I'm sure you must have* but underneath the sugar-coating I can read the real message loud and clear: *why haven't you finished the manuscript yet?* It's like looking into a pram lined with pink satin and lace and frills and seeing a toad in it.

It's terribly tempting to ignore it, the way I have been pushing work to the back of my mind over the last few days. It is just one voice in a chorus shouting at me: the dreams, the row with James, the impossibility of selling the house. And I'm tired, because although in all the months we've lived at Barr Dubh House I've had the dreams fewer than half a dozen times, the fear that it will happen again hangs over me every time I put my head on the pillow.

But I can't ignore the email. I'm supposed to be super efficient, a mistress of every tiny detail. And this book is important, after all, even if it's 90,000 words of crude action and mangled prose. The last book sold an unimaginable number of copies. If I let this one slide, it will probably be the last job they give me and I can't afford for that to happen. We have James's debt to clear, a wedding to pay for and – perhaps – a house to sell at a loss.

I compose an email in reply, and even though I'm not an author myself, I manage to confect something any creative writer ought to be proud of: reassuring, dedicated, confident. Then I press *send*, make myself an enormous mug of tea and get straight down to work. I open the file and scroll down through thickets of red comments, until I find the place where I last left off: a toe-curlingly cocky monologue from the book's action hero. It's something of a mystery that the villain of the piece, who appears to be bristling with every kind of weaponry known to man, has the patience to stand there and listen to the whole thing without opening fire. In spite of myself, I'm soon engrossed in the task. My fingers fly over the keyboard as comments and amendments sprout all over the page.

I keep going until I find myself having to read sentences twice to make sense of them; then I know it's time for a break. I save the file and click onto the web browser instead.

The names of the people who sold us Barr Dubh are Craig and Susan Loughty. I try Craig first and get an entry on a directory of businesses: Craig Loughty Building Services. The address given is Barr Dubh House. The entry is out of date. There's a mobile number and I try that, but get a "number not recognised" message. There's a profile on a social media site too – luckily, Loughty isn't a common name, otherwise it would be hopeless trying to find him. I click onto it and there are all his photos. There are dozens of Barr Dubh.

It's fascinating, because the Loughtys built the house. The most recent photo is of Craig Loughty in the middle of putting up the fence that separates the future garden from the fields. He's posing heroically. *Fencing champion*, it says above the image. Underneath that one, there are a lot of snaps of Barr Dubh immediately after the house was finished. There's one of Craig and Susan raising glasses of champagne, with the house in the background, and others showing the building from every conceivable angle. You can see it's a new build, because there are piles of rich brown earth visible in some of them, or stacks of leftover materials.

I keep scrolling down, going further back in time, and there are pictures of the house when it was half built, when there were only foundations, and finally, when there was nothing but the bare plot. There's nothing much to see on that bare plot. No sinister-looking ruins from the old house, just scrubland with a few tumbled stones that might be anything. Before that, there are no photos of Barr Dubh. It's all personal pics and the occasional post about a sports result or a local appeal.

I feel like a stalker, looking at the personal photos, but I'm curious about Craig and Susan Loughty. We never met them when we came to look at the house. They'd already moved out and all queries were directed through the solicitor. I can't think why we never asked the agent who showed us round about their reasons for selling. I suppose I assumed they'd built it as an investment and never really intended to stay there themselves. It's funny, though; the house has never felt like a commercial project. It's designed so carefully, with so many charming features – it really feels like someone's dream home. That's why we bought it, after all. Now I wonder whether the Loughtys *knew* they were selling something other than a beautiful dream.

Can you tell what someone is like as a person from looking at their photograph? I doubt it, but it's all I've got. Craig Loughty looks about forty years old, with a broad, weatherbeaten face and blunt features. He has close-cropped red-brown hair and grey eyes with crow's feet at the corners, as though he spends a lot of time squinting into the sun. His build is robust, muscular even, as you would expect from someone who's spent a lot of time heaving building materials around. He looks practical, tough, uncompromising.

Susan Loughty is younger than he is, with blue eyes and blonde hair and a tan that was definitely not acquired from Perthshire summers. There is no photo in which she is not giving a dazzling smile to the camera and looking the photographer in the eyes. A warm, sociable extrovert. That's the impression she gives.

These are the two people who sold us Barr Dubh House. Did they *know* what they were selling us?

I think about the length of time they had the house – less than a year before they moved out and put it up for sale. If they'd been perfectly happy here, why didn't they stay until it was sold?

On the other hand, perhaps it's *me* who has the problem. James has lived at Barr Dubh for months without experiencing anything strange, after all. He has never seen anyone or anything untoward. Maybe the Loughtys didn't, either.

I scroll back up to the top and look at the last picture again, the one of Craig Loughty being the fencing champion. The date shows that it was posted nearly three years ago. There's been nothing since then – not unless he upped the privacy on his account at that point, and hid everything else.

I click on his profile details. There's no secrecy here. His birthdate is here, and his age (he's 42). There's the name of his secondary school and the name of his business, Craig Loughty Building Services. And there's his relationship status: *don't ask.* It's a strange option to go for if you're married. It also means there's no link to Susan Loughty's account, if she has one.

A search for Susan Loughty's name brings up nothing, on this site or any other. I sit back, drumming my fingers on the worktop. If *don't ask* actually means *in the middle of an acrimonious divorce,* she might have reverted to her maiden name. I have absolutely no idea what that is. I go back to Craig Loughty's account and look to see if he has any friends called Susan with any other surnames, and he doesn't. Come to that, he doesn't have all that many friends. I guess he's not a heavy social media user. It doesn't take long to click on a few at random, to see whether anyone is connected to a Susan. There are no Susan Loughtys anywhere, but I find a Sue Gardener, connected through a female friend of Craig's. There is a rather bad photograph of her, but I honestly can't tell if it's Susan Loughty or not – if it is, she's changed quite a bit, because this Sue is pasty-faced, scowling from under mousy hair with bleached ends.

The obvious answer to this is that the Loughtys have split up. They've sold the house because it's too lonely for one person or perhaps because they need to split the proceeds. Susan has reverted to her old name and probably posts under that. Craig doesn't post anything, or hides what he posts, on the advice of his lawyer, because too many snaps of the wrong thing might sink his chances of claiming straitened circumstances.

Fen, I tell myself, *your imagination is running away with you.* I take a sip of cold tea and grimace.

There is one obvious course of action here. I decide to message Craig Loughty and ask him about the house. It's no use being too direct, of course. If I sail straight in with *did you ever suspect there was something horribly wrong with Barr Dubh House?* he'll be straight on the defensive. Or he'll think I'm deluded.

In the end, I conclude that simplicity is best – and not too much detail. *Hi Mr. Loughty, it's Fen Munro here. We (James and I) bought Barr Dubh House from you! I'm doing some local history research and wondered if I could ask you something?*

I think for a bit and then I send the message, just as it is. I hope it's struck the right note of being friendly and non-accusing. Of course, he may not reply, so I decide to send one to Sue Gardener too. It's difficult to know what to say to her, because if there *has* been an acrimonious divorce, she won't be pleased to be asked if she's Susan Loughty. In the end I go for, *Hi – is it you we bought the house from? Sorry if not. Hoping to ask a question!*

After that, I make more tea and get back to work.

Chapter Thirty-Five

I'll never forget the first time I saw Barr Dubh House. It was in the springtime, though actual spring comes late in Perthshire; there were daffodils out in London when we left, but we arrived to bare trees with tight buds like tiny fists.

I was glad to get away from London for a few days. The atmosphere in the office had become – well, not exactly *strained* but a little less cosy than it had been, ever since word had got around that I was engaged to James. When we first started seeing each other, I didn't say anything about it at work. I wanted to hug the information to myself without handing it around for everyone else to cluck over, plus I thought it would be grisly if it didn't work out. Delia would be intolerable. Then we got engaged, which was different, and which we couldn't have concealed anyway, because all those eagle eyes would undoubtedly have spotted the ring. So I announced it in the office and was deluged with shrieks and hugs and congratulations, until I began to feel like one of the guests at the feast of Heliogabalus, who were suffocated with a ton of rose petals. Even Delia joined in, though I could see the expression in her eyes and the eyes of half a dozen other people: *jammy cow*, they were thinking. On the whole, it was a relief to take a break.

We were still deciding what we wanted to do; it takes time to shed the skin of an old life. So we made up our minds we'd go up to Scotland for a week and *look*, as though we were measuring the distance before making a leap. I booked us into what turned out to be the shabbiest hotel in the area. We spent the nights rolling towards each other in the saggiest double bed I'd ever slept on, and the days driving around trying to imagine ourselves living here. For the first two days it rained heavily, and it was difficult to see much of the landscape through the incessant grey drizzle. We looked at an oldish house on the outskirts of a village; it had views over the countryside (so far as we could tell through the downpour) but it smelled the same as my parents' house had, of furniture polish and disapproval. I hardly wanted to finish looking round it. Then on the third day, the sun came out, and we went to see Barr Dubh.

James talked to the woman who showed us over the house and I walked on ahead of them, through rooms which echoed to my footsteps and revealed nothing of the previous owners' lives except the colours they had chosen as a backdrop. It was a cold day, but clear and dry, and the sunshine streamed in. I went into the living room and looked out through the huge plate glass windows, at the expanse of rough grass and the distant trees, and beyond them the hill. A bird of prey was hovering high above the trees, but otherwise in all of that view I could see nothing moving. There was no wind; even the grass and the weeds were still. It was quiet here, too; the only sounds I could hear were the muffled voices of James chatting to the agent two rooms away.

I knew then that this was the place I wanted to be. This perfect peace was the lake I wanted to swim out into, leaving the fractious ghosts of the past ranting on the shore. I thought that here, their voices would fade away altogether.

When James came into the room, he saw immediately from my face that I had decided. He came up and put an arm around my shoulders, squeezing me gently. We didn't rave about the house to each other, not then, not in front of the agent, because it was more than we had wanted to pay; it had simply sounded interesting, and worth looking at. In the event, we didn't have to bargain very hard. The price was dropped. We didn't ask why. It was the lawyer's job to check that there were no land disputes, no plans to build a road through the site. The house was already empty, so of course it was in everyone's interests for new occupants to move in as soon as possible.

If someone had said to me then: *Barr Dubh House is haunted*, I wouldn't have believed them; it would have sounded laughable.

Now I think: *What does she want?*

I have to know. I can't go on, never knowing whether I'll wake up inside that coffin again, or whether I'll wander in my sleep through the rooms and corridors of a house that no longer exists. I'll break down under the strain of it, or else one night I will go outside to wait for someone who is never going to return and James won't wake up and find me.

We could leave – eventually, if we can find someone to take the house off our hands. But I fell in love with Barr Dubh, the very first time we visited it. It's rare to know what you want that much, that quickly. I'm not prepared to give it up without a fight.

Chapter Thirty-Six

I am in that room again, the one papered in a design of intertwined vegetation in shades of green and brown. There is that same musty odour; there are the same motes of dust drifting lazily in the sunlight that slants through the windows. Opposite me is the white marble fireplace with the tiled grate. There is no fire burning. Above the fireplace is the mirror in its ornate gilded frame, the glass freckled with dark spots. I see the armchairs, their overstuffed upholstery studded with buttons, and the spindle-legged side table. I can see the bottom part of the oil painting in its heavy gilded frame, but I am destined never to know what the whole picture shows, because just as before, I cannot lift my head nor raise my eyes.

Inside, I scream. Outside, I sit, motionless. Time stretches out with deadly slowness. The sun sinks outside, and darkness creeps in. I hear the soft bump of the moth on the outside of the window. My thoughts seem to congeal in a sickly mass of horror and tedium.

The hours seem interminably long, but at last the dawn breaks, grey and dismal. The contours of the room become visible again. The servant girl comes in to sweep out the grate and fails to notice me at first, sitting silent and rigid in the chair. When she does, she drops the dustpan and there is a soft *whump* as the ashes spill out. She screams at what she sees propped here with fixed eyes and gaping mouth. She runs from the room and a distant door bangs. Two of them come back to look at me, the young girl and the older woman. The older one sends the girl off to fetch a mirror; she takes the green glass laudanum bottle from my hand and hides it in her pocket, telling me that there is no need for anyone else to see it. Hiding the stigma of suicide.

The girl returns with the silver-backed mirror and they hold it to my lips, trying to see whether the slightest breath will mist the glass. They tilt it this way and that, and for a moment they hold it so that I can see myself in it.

I see, not the older woman I saw before, with her finely-lined faced and grey-streaked hair, but myself, Fen Munro, my skin still smooth, my hair dark, my eyes staring. Myself, starkly dead.

The terror that explodes in me has nowhere to go. My dead heart won't race; my dead lungs won't inflate. I cannot force the slightest sound from my frozen lips, nor turn my eyes in their sockets. My hands are cold lumps of meat in my lap, the fingers held a little apart where the laudanum bottle was prised from between them. Inside this dead shell, my consciousness, the inner Fen, is rampaging.

Wake up! Wake up!

If I don't, I know what will happen. They will dress me up in wedding finery like a great doll; they will lift me all unresisting into an oak coffin; the men will come and peer into the coffin, noting with curiosity my unclosed eyes, and then they will nail the lid down. Perhaps I will hear the first spadefuls of earth rattling onto the wood. Then I will lie there in the dark, silently screaming.

I burst back into wakefulness like a swimmer erupting from deep black water into the blessed air – coughing, sobbing, shivering. I touch my face, my hair. I hug myself, feeling the goosebumps on my bare arms. As my eyes adjust to the dark, I find that I am crouching in the wing-backed chair in the spare room again. The furniture, the boxes, are outlined by the pale moonlight seeping in. My limbs are cramped, as though I have been here for some time. When I unfold myself and try to stand up, I stagger a little and have to grasp the back of the chair to steady myself. The sensation of the brocade upholstery under my fingers is marvellously real. I cry a little, from sheer relief.

I make my way to the door, stretching out my arms in the dark for fear of running into something. At the threshold I pause for a moment, listening. The house is dead quiet. James has not woken up and noticed that I have gone, or I would hear him looking for me; there would be lights on. Please God, he would have found me and shaken me awake.

My throat is painfully dry. I fumble my way into the tiny downstairs bathroom one door down, thinking that I will drink straight from the cold tap. There is no window in here, so the darkness is absolute. I feel for the switch and turn the light on, narrowing my eyes against the sudden brilliance. Then I turn on the tap and bend low over it, greedily scooping up water in my cupped hands. I drink, then run a little more and drink again, thankfully.

What is it that first tells me something is wrong? Not a movement, a *non* movement. Behind the sink there is a huge mirror that takes up most of the wall; we put it there on purpose to make the small windowless room feel bigger and lighter. I am not looking at the mirror, I am looking down, at my cupped hands positioned carefully under the running water. At the edge of my vision I am aware of my reflection, and as I stoop, my hands moving rapidly to bring the water to my lips, I am aware of an absence, a stillness where there should be movement. I remain for a moment in that pose, bowing low over the porcelain basin, the water running over my fingers. Then I look up.

It's not me in the mirror, it's *her*. Euphemia.

I take her in in a heartstopping instant: the lavender silk dress, tight-fitting in the high-necked bodice and sleeves, voluminous in the skirts; the white face, in which the eyes blaze with furious intensity. Her mouth is a hard line, the lips leaden.

I cannot breathe. I stare at her and she stares back at me, and the only sound is the water splattering into the sink.

Then she is gone. I blink, and there is only me and my own reflection in the glass, two Fens in matching thin nightdresses, our hair dishevelled, shuddering with cold and shock.

I reach out and turn off the tap. There is a drip and then silence. For half a minute, a minute, I stare into the mirror, daring it to show me something other than my own self, but nothing untoward happens. Then I back out of the room. I leave the light on inside.

I creep up the stairs, into the bedroom where James is sleeping. His breathing is soft and even. The curtains are not quite closed and with the moonlight coming in, I don't need to turn on a light. I can see and feel well enough to lock the door from the inside and remove the key. I put it in my jewellery box and close the lid. Then I get into bed.

It is a long time before I can get back to sleep.

Chapter Thirty-Seven

Craig Loughty has blocked me. I check I've entered his name correctly in the search box. I have. His account profile just isn't there any more.

I sit back in my chair and stare at the screen. All sorts of unflattering epithets for the owner of Craig Loughty Building Services flit through my head, but there's no-one to fling them at. He's gone, with no way to know why. Perhaps he's simply one of those people who instinctively avoids anything that might be vaguely troublesome. Or perhaps he knows very well what I want to ask him about. Either way, he doesn't want to talk.

Then I try Sue Gardener. She's gone too. I can't help it; I give a squawk of frustration. I'm pretty sure she *is* (or was) Susan Loughty – why block me otherwise? Why not just drop me a line to say, *I'm not the Sue you're after?*

I put my head in my hands. Whatever *don't ask* means, whether they've split or not, those two really don't want to be reached.

What about you, Fen? If the house went back on the market, would you tell people?

I think about that for a long time. In the end, all I can

really decide is that I wish I could speak to the Loughtys. I want to know whether other people living here have been troubled.

Then it occurs to me that even if the living won't speak to me, perhaps the dead will. The Loughtys were the first to live on this plot since the old house was demolished, but someone might have lived here after Euphemia Alexander died.

My work is waiting for me. The file thumbnail is lurking at the bottom of the screen like an ominous prophecy of clichés to come. Instead, I click back onto the search engine and look for that database of historical sites.

It doesn't take long to find the entry for Barr Buidhe, as it is listed. There is the engraving of the house, with the sundial and the tiny figures of a man and woman in front of it. Another click brings me to the notes on the site. There is not much to read. There are some details of the design of the house for the Alexander family by an Edinburgh architect whose name I don't recognise. I scroll down a little and there is a dry summary of alterations made in the early 1800s. At the end of the entry, I read: *Demolished in 1890.*

That's it. No other details. But that means the house stood for eighteen years after Euphemia died.

Lavender lady, lavender lady...

Fragments of song unfurl in my head. Something must have happened in those eighteen years for the superstitions to have started. But how do I find out what?

Twenty minutes later, I'm in the car, driving east. James didn't want to come; he's at some critical point in his book. So it's just me, with nothing but my phone for company. Once or twice it has chirruped, indicating that an email has come in. I ignore it. I don't need reminding that I ought to be working.

It's a miserably dark day, the sky a mass of dense low cloud. As the days shorten and the solstice approaches, it sometimes seems as though it barely gets light at all. I never noticed this when I lived in London; there were lights everywhere, even if I came home after midnight. Here, the darkness has a suffocating weight. If we drive between Barr Dubh and the town after dark, or between other villages, we can go miles without seeing any lights other than our own headlights, miserable grey beams that hardly penetrate the blackness before dissolving into it. Overhanging trees loom up, briefly bleached by our lights, then subsiding into the gloom. Once, we saw an owl flit across in front of us. It is no wonder that strange stories abound in a place where the night still closes in much as it did in the days when there were only candles to keep it away.

I drive into the city centre and park outside the library I visited before, the day I dropped James at the station. As I walk through the lobby, I mute my phone and then I go upstairs to the reference section.

The middle-aged woman I spoke to last time isn't anywhere in sight. Instead, there's a man about my age manning the information desk. I explain what I want to him. He listens carefully, without any signs of surprise.

"So you want to know who lived in your house in the years following 1872?"

"Not our house. There was one that stood on the same site, up until 1890."

"Well, it may still be possible to identify it. There will be census records for 1871 – is that too early?"

"I know who lived there then," I tell him.

"1881 then. There's also the census of 1891."

"It was demolished before then."

"So there's probably only one set of census records

for the period you're interested in. You could also look at valuation rolls. Those were done annually. But those will only tell you who owned the property, and the main occupant or tenant. It won't list everyone who lived in the house."

"But the census will?"

"The census will tell you the names of everyone who was in the property when the census was done. So if someone was away from home, they won't be in it, and if someone was visiting the house, they will."

"Can I look at both?"

"Of course you can." He smiles at me. "They're on microfilm. Have you used a microfilm reader before? No? No problem, I'll show you."

He goes off to find the microfilm and as he goes, he glances back at me. The expression on his face is – puzzled? Amused? I suspect I look tense – oddly tense for someone who is researching old property records.

They may not tell me anything, I remind myself. Maybe some tenant farmer lived there quite happily for the whole eighteen years and never noticed anything odd at all. And finding names is only the start. Once I have those, I have to hope that there's other information available about them and I have no idea how to go about doing that.

The man is back. "This is the one," he says, flourishing a little reel of film. He leads me to a desk with a computer and a film reader. It takes a couple of minutes for him to thread the film into the machine and to show me how to go backwards and forwards through the records.

"It could take a while," he says. "The pages you want are near the end." Then he leaves me to it. An elderly couple have approached the desk and are looking in our direction with grim reproachfulness. He goes off to see to them and I start going through the census records.

255

It takes a long time to search. I have to keep zooming in to read the handwritten entries. I find some properties in the tiny hamlet which is our nearest neighbour, but nothing under either Barr Dubh or Barr Buidhe. I backtrack, then I forward the film again. Nothing.

The old couple take up a lot of time with the man on the desk, because they do not seem able to get to grips with computerised records at all, but finally they are finished. I stand up and go over to him.

"I can't find anything at all."

He glances at his watch. "It's sort of lunchtime but–"

"I'm sorry–"

"No, don't worry. Let's have a look."

But he can't find anything either. He sits back, grimacing. "You're sure it was in that parish?"

"Yes."

"Well, it's possible the place wasn't inhabited in 1881. We could look at the previous census, the 1871 one. If you know who lived there at that time, and we can find the entry, we'll know we were looking in the right place."

"Thank you–"

But he's already on his feet, off to find the other reel of film: a man on a mission.

Once the new reel is loaded, I start the weary task of scanning through it – forwarding, pausing, zooming in, zooming out again. Just as I start to think I'm not going to find anything again, or else that I've got too tired and missed the entry, I see it. It's written in a neat cursive handwriting: *Barr Buidhe House*.

Found you, I think, with a cold frisson. It shouldn't bother me, since I know perfectly well who was living in the house in 1871, but I still feel uneasy looking at that name carefully written out: *Miss Euphemia Alexander*. She is listed as the head of family, and as unmarried.

Underneath that are some other names, listed as "domestic servant" or in one case, "gardener." The servants include Jane Dinnie, aged 47, and Catherine Stalker, aged 19. I think of Euphemia Alexander sitting dead in her chair and the two women holding a silver-backed mirror to her lips to look for breath. The memory of it is very vivid. I find myself breathing hard, as though I am still struggling to move, to scream.

The man at the desk is looking at me again, a quizzical expression on his face. I do my best to smile at him, but I can feel how stiff and unnatural it is.

I look back at the entry on the screen. I rewind a little way and then forward a little way. I remember seeing some of the same properties listed in the 1881 census. Barr Buidhe wasn't among them. So in 1881 there wasn't anyone living there. The census records can't tell me anything else, so I rewind carefully to the beginning of the reel, then go over to the desk and ask to see the valuation rolls.

For those, I have to go into the archive. There are several people already working in there – a man with a beard, a severe-looking older woman. Pencils (the only writing implements allowed) whisper over paper, and the woman sighs at my intrusion. I sit at the table, in front of the volumes the archivist lays out for me.

This time, I think I'll start with Euphemia's time in the house. I leaf through the volume marked 1871 in gold letters on the spine. It doesn't take me long to find Barr Buidhe. The proprietor is listed as *Miss Euphemia Alexander* and the tenant as *Said Miss Euphemia Alexander*. The yearly rent or value is given as *£80 00 00*, which I take to mean eighty pounds, zero shillings and zero pence – probably a lot back then.

I close the book and open the one marked 1873. Barr Buidhe is again listed, but under "proprietor" it says *Heirs of Miss Euphemia Alexander.* I don't know who that would be, given that she was supposedly the last of her family. Under "tenant" it says only *unlet.*

There are a lot of other volumes. It's possible, I suppose, that every single entry for Barr Buidhe will read *unlet,* right up until 1890 when the house was demolished. Still, I might as well plough through a few more.

I open the volume for 1874. I feel I'm getting the hang of it now; it doesn't take me as long to leaf through the book to the right district. I run my finger down the page and there it is again: Barr Buidhe.

The proprietor and occupier are the same person: Mr. Charles Robertson, of Fortingal.

Chapter Thirty-Eight

The man with the beard looks up at the odd little strangled noise I make. I drop my gaze to the page again.

Yes; it's there in black and white. *Mr. Charles Robertson, of Fortingal.* I look at the spine of the book again. *1874.* Then I go back to the title page, leafing through with trembling fingers, because I think I must have got this wrong somehow, but that says *1874* too.

Charles Robertson was *dead* in 1874. He'd been dead for the greater part of three decades. I remember reading about his death in *Strathearn Folk*, a little blue volume that is probably sitting out there on the shelf in the main reference library at this very moment.

I leave my stuff spread out on the table in the archive and go out into the library. It doesn't take long to find the book – I guess people aren't falling over themselves to lay hands on *Strathearn Folk*, published in 1872.

"Shortly before the wedding was to have taken place, her intended husband was numbered amongst the victims of the Garside locomotive fire," it says, and then: "Miss Alexander at first entirely refused to credit the news. Her incredulity was supported by the grisly circumstance of

259

the victims' bodies being so badly burned and otherwise mutilated as to render identification impossible in many cases. She persisted in her hope that her betrothed would one day return..."

And I guess he did, I say to myself. I read the lines again, but that's all there is. Eventually I slide the book back into its place on the shelf and go back to the archive. For a while I just sit and look at the entry in the valuation rolls. Is there any way this could be someone else? I don't think so. Even if Charles were the same age as Euphemia, he would have been around sixty by 1874. So this probably isn't his father. His son? That doesn't seem very likely either. He died unmarried, after all – assuming he *did* die.

I stare and stare at the page, but the fact is, I can't know what happened without more information than either the census or the valuation rolls can give me. I take a quick snap of the page and then I shut the book.

Back at the information desk, the long suffering librarian is back in residence – or else he still hasn't had his lunch. He looks up at me cheerfully.

"Did you find what you needed?"

"Sort of," I tell him. "I found something I wasn't really expecting." I hesitate for a moment. "The house passed into the hands of... well, it wasn't the person I thought it would be."

"Intriguing."

I laugh, a little uneasily. "I guess so. What I'm wondering is... how can I find out about this person?"

"Well, you could try Births, Death and Marriages – but you'll have to go to the Registrar for that. Or you can get them online."

"You don't have them here?"

"No. You could also look at the estate papers, if there are any. What was the name of the property?"

"Barr Buidhe." I spell it for him. "It came to be called Barr Dubh later on."

His fingers rattle across the keyboard. "Buidhe, you said?"

"Yes."

He shakes his head. "Nope. What was the family name?"

"Alexander, up until 1872. And then Robertson."

"Hmmm. Nothing." He thinks about it, and then tries something else. "There's something in *Strathearn Folk–*"

"I've read that. It's about a year too early."

"Well, you could try the local newspapers, I suppose, if you know when you'd be looking. We've got all of those here, on microfilm." He glances at me and I suppose he can see the look on my face at the prospect of going through pages and pages of microfilm, because he adds, "Your nearest library has physical copies, if you'd rather."

"Thanks," I tell him. "You've been really helpful."

I walk downstairs and out to my car, where I sit behind the wheel for some time wondering what happened all those years ago. Euphemia died by her own hand, either accidentally or deliberately. And then seemingly Charles came back. None of it makes any sense. Maybe Charles didn't die in the railway disaster; that seems the most logical conclusion. But if he didn't, why did she spend all those years yearning for him?

I start the car and drive slowly back through the outskirts of the city and the lonely miles of open countryside, thinking. My unfinished copyedit is waiting for me, back at Barr Dubh House. I ought to go back and get on with that. It's going to pay the bills, after all, and furthermore, I don't want another of those emails enquiring how it's going. I know all of this and yet when I get to the town I don't turn onto the road leading to Barr Dubh. Instead, I take the one that leads to the library.

This isn't a big, old-fashioned library. It's a modern one, shared with the high school. There are computers, most of which seem to be occupied by teenagers in school uniform, and a coffee corner with a hot drinks machine. It doesn't feel like the sort of place you'd go to ask about the key events of 1874. I'm about to turn around and walk out again but then I think about the archive and its grisly microfilm machine. It has to be worth asking whether there's anything better here.

It turns out that there is. Right at the back of the room, behind the racks of crime thrillers and the tables crowded with schoolkids, there is a local history section. All the local newspapers, dating back as far as they go, are collected in hardbacked volumes so big that they can't be put onto normal shelves; instead they are laid out in stacks. Some of them, the ones nobody has looked at for years, are wrapped in paper with the dates scrawled on the spines. The earliest ones seem to be from the 1850s.

While I'm looking for the 1870s, a bell rings somewhere, and most of the schoolkids file out. Now there's space for me to examine the volumes in peace. I decide to start with the death of Euphemia Alexander, which should be mentioned in 1872, if at all. She died on 14th February, so I try Saturday 17th February. Nothing; the four deaths mentioned are all other people. I try the following Saturday, 24th, and there she is: ALEXANDER, Miss Euphemia, aged 60 years, of Barr Buidhe House.

Two weeks further on, I find the first notice posted by Euphemia's lawyers, trying to find her heirs. It seems from this that everyone assumed that Charles Robertson was dead – which stacks up with what I read in *Strathearn Folk*, about the house standing empty while the lawyers looked for prospective heirs. I keep going, turning the crisp and yellowed pages carefully with my fingertips.

I don't really know what I'm looking for. Perhaps there won't be anything; not everything gets reported in local newspapers. What *does* get reported seems to be distinctly random: weird snippets from around the world mixed in with very dull local stories about crops and game. The front page is always a mass of advertisements, for writing paper, bonnets, boots and shoes, piano music.

I look at the top of the page. I've only got as far as May 1872. The whole thing seems hopeless. All the same, I keep turning pages, taking great care because the paper is so thin and brittle. Perhaps the answer is in here somewhere. If it isn't, I don't know where else to look.

In the event, I nearly miss it. *A CASE OF AMNESIA*, the article is titled. *Lawyers for Miss Euphemia Alexander, recently deceased, of Barr Buidhe House, have advertised for Miss Alexander's heirs, believing the named beneficiary of her will, Mr. Charles Robertson, to be deceased following a railway accident. However, in circumstances that might have been taken straight from the chapters of a sensation novel, Mr. Robertson has contacted Messrs. McRae & Son to advise them that he is alive and well, and had been suffering from amnesia.*

I have to read that again – twice. *Amnesia?* That doesn't even seem possible. For twenty-seven years?

The article continues: *Mr. Robertson was a survivor of the Garside railway disaster which captured the public imagination nearly three decades ago, many of the dead having been so badly burned as to render identification impossible. At the time, he was engaged to be married to Miss Alexander of Barr Buidhe, a lady some years older than himself. Following the accident, Mr. Robertson fell victim to an amnesia so complete that he was unable to recollect anything about his fiancée or his previous life.*

I sit back and stare at the page. I don't believe this.

I suspect the writer didn't either, from the reference to sensation novels. Charles got cold feet, is my opinion. The accident was a convenient way to get out of an unwanted entanglement.

Seeing the advertisements for heirs to the estate, Mr. Robertson miraculously recovered his memory.

I bet he did, I think. It's hard to believe the brass neck of the man.

Having contacted the lawyers and established his identity, he now finds himself master of the Barr Buidhe estate.

That's pretty astounding, but the last line is the kicker.

Mr. and Mrs. Robertson are believed to have toured the house and land, with a view to carrying out some work prior to moving in.

Mr. and Mrs. Robertson. So Charles had got married to someone else, while he was off supposedly suffering with amnesia. All those years Euphemia waited for him, standing on the threshold of Barr Buidhe House at twilight, staring dismally into the distance – and he was courting someone else. The years she wore lavender, mourning for someone she hoped would return, but who never did. And then she died...

With a little help, I think, remembering the green glass laudanum bottle.

She died, and was laid to rest in the wedding dress she never got to wear in life. I hope – I hope so much – that she was really dead. If not, she woke to the dark and the enclosed space and the stale air, and screamed herself to oblivion.

And then, Charles came back. Not on his own, but with a wife by his side. And he inherited *everything*. The house and land that Euphemia had looked forward to sharing with him. The money. The future.

I sit and think about that. After a while, I resume my laborious trawl through the pages of the newspaper, thinking that there may be something more. I get right into the middle of the following year and there is nothing. It seems that Mr. and Mrs. Robertson got their happy ending, while out by the chapel the remains of Euphemia Alexander crumbled away into the earth, unloved and forgotten. It's sad, and horrible.

I keep turning the crackling yellow leaves, scanning local headlines that have long been meaningless. It's getting late, so I suppose I should give this up. I've probably found out everything there is to know. Then I turn one last page, and there it is.

MURDERED IN BED reads the headline. *Mr. Charles Robertson of Barr Buidhe House may be remembered by the readers of this newspaper as the inheritor of the estate of the late Miss Euphemia Alexander. His return to the area caused much interest because he had long been suffering from amnesia following a railway accident. Alas! Mr. Robertson enjoyed his inheritance for all too short a time. Yesterday morning, his manservant discovered him in bed with – horrible to relate! – a kitchen knife through his heart. His assailant has not yet been discovered. His wife, Mrs. Clara Robertson, is too prostrated with grief to be interviewed.*

I sit for a while and look at this page.

It was all for nothing, I think. *The disappearance. The lies. Deserting Euphemia and marrying another woman. All for nothing. How long did he enjoy his ill-gotten gains? A year? By 1875 Charles was dead. And in 1890 they demolished the house.*

At last I close the volume with care, and slide it back into its place on the shelves. It feels like sliding a coffin into a mausoleum. How long will it be before anyone looks at those pages again? Maybe they never will.

I leave the library without looking back.

Chapter Thirty-Nine

James is still shut up in his study when I get back to Barr Dubh House, and I'm not sorry. I want to think about what I've found out. I stand at the window, gazing towards the place at the treeline where I've seen someone dressed all in lavender, her skirts billowing in the breeze. There is no-one there now. It is twilight and a cold wind is bending the naked branches of the trees.

Do I feel sorry for Euphemia? Yes. I'm afraid to close my eyes at night in case I find myself imprisoned in her coffin again – but I do feel sorry. I feel her fear and anger and loneliness. All of it for nothing. Charles wasn't worth it. Did he ever care for her at all, or just for her money?

I feel a stab of something uncomfortable at that thought and push it away. James loves me, and I love him. There is no chink in that armour for doubt to worm its way in.

So why? I think. *Why did she show me these things? Is it possible that she just wants someone to know?*

I think about the Loughtys. They were the first people to live here in over a hundred years and they hardly lasted any time at all. I don't know *why* they left, though. *Don't ask,* says his social media account. Maybe they split up for the same reasons anyone does. Maybe the dream home was just the glue that was supposed to stick a broken relationship back together again. *Maybe.* Or perhaps Susan Loughty started having dreams like the ones I've been having – dreams of being confined in a coffin, of hearing the lid being nailed into place. She may have wanted to leave – she may have insisted on it – and Craig Loughty would have been angry or upset because of all the work that had gone into the place. Or perhaps he didn't believe her. There are so many ways it might have gone wrong. Ways which I am not going to find out about, because the pair of them have made themselves untraceable.

Can't blame them for that, I think, biting my lip. *If we'd spoken to them about the house and they'd told us all this stuff, I'd have thought they were both barking mad.*

Outside, darkness is falling. We are fast approaching the darkest part of the year. It doesn't get light until well past eight in the morning, and night falls around four o'clock. I go around switching lights on, warding off the dark. I remember what I saw in the mirror the last time I awoke from one of those dreams, and even though it's only early evening and I am wide awake, my heart thumps at the thought of seeing it again. But the shapes that loom up in the darkened windows only coalesce into myself.

I go into the dining room, now completely green, meaning to shut the curtains. There is the sideboard, its doors carefully closed. On impulse, I go over and open them. The inkstand has gone. All the other things I expected to see are there: the stacked plates, the glasses. But there is no sign of the inkstand. I will ask James about it, whether he has moved it, but I am fairly sure I know the answer already. He hasn't touched it and nobody else has been in the house since Belle left. It has just gone.

I wonder if it is possible that it is finished. Nobody else

followed this trail so far, but I have pursued Euphemia's story to the end; there is nothing more to know. Perhaps she can rest now.

Please, I think.

I think of Stephen again, too. I still feel nothing in the place where Stephen should be. There are so many things I would like to say to him, but can't. But I suppose I should be happy, knowing that there is something afterwards – even if I don't know why some people come back to speak to us, and others stay silent forever.

I go back to the kitchen and a little while later James comes out of his study to join me. He looks tired and he's carrying five empty coffee cups, but he looks cheerful.

He says, "How did it go at the library?"

And I say, "You won't believe what I found."

Chapter Forty

THE END

I never thought I'd get there. But here we are, at the final page, which like the others is covered in red comments. The hero has defeated the villain (unsurprisingly, since the villain kept stopping what he was doing to deliver long exposés of his motivations), and is quaffing cocktails with the heroine. With *one* of the heroines. And they're drinking strawberry daiquiris, of all things.

I save the file and then I compose an email to send with it. It's probably the most euphemistic email ever composed, larded with words like *interesting* and *success*. I can't bring myself to say that the book is amazing, because that would actually be lying. It is with a great sense of satisfaction – not to mention relief – that I send the thing off. I expect it will ping back into my inbox after Christmas, with another round of checks to be done, but it won't be as bad as this time, and anyway, that's in the future.

James is in a good mood, too. I can hear him singing in the kitchen, while he makes lunch. I expect that means the conversation with Laura went well.

I decide to give Belle a call and tell her the thriller is finished. The first thing I notice when she appears on the screen is that her hair is no longer turquoise. Now it's purple.

"Fen!"

"Hi, Belle."

"What's up?"

"You know that thriller? I've just finished it."

"Oh my *God*! That must be *such* a relief."

"It really is."

She peers at the screen. "You look... well, you look thinner but kind of... better. Was it that awful?"

"No. Well, I mean, yes, it was that awful, but if I look better, it's not because of that."

Belle squints at me. "What was it, then?"

"Is anyone in the office with you?"

Belle looks around. "No."

"Because this will sound crazy."

"Intriguing," she says. "Go on, spill."

"It's the house. I mean, it *was* the house. You were right about something being off. I didn't tell you before, when you came up, because I thought maybe I was the one going nuts."

Then I tell her the whole thing. About the horrible dreams. About finding out that there really was an older house on the same site as ours. About the long and winding road that led me to the truth about Euphemia Alexander – and Charles Robertson.

"Fuck," says Belle, succinctly.

"Indeed," I say. "And I'm sorry. For reacting the way I did."

"So now what? Are you going to sell up and move out? I mean, that's some weapons-grade creepy, right there. I wouldn't want to stay somewhere where that had happened."

I shrug. "No. You're going to think this is even weirder, but since I found out about Charles, I've just felt... better."

"You have?" says Belle, dubiously.

"Yes. Honestly, I have. It took a long time to get to the bottom of the story, but now I have... I feel as though someone just had to hear it. Euphemia, she spent nearly half her life waiting for Charles to come home and he never did, not until after she was gone. And he'd married someone else."

"Arsehole," says Belle. "But what about Euphemia? Do you think she was genuinely buried alive?"

"I don't know. I hope not."

Belle shakes her purple-dyed head. "I wouldn't want to stay there, after finding all this out. No offence, but..."

"None taken," I say lightly. "It's really alright, though. I haven't had any more dreams, not since I found this out."

"How long has it been?"

"A few days. I don't know, nearly a week."

"Did you have that many dreams, before?"

"It's not that. I just feel different. Like a shadow has lifted. I don't think the dreams are going to come back."

"And James? What does James think about all this?"

"James is happy as long as I'm happy."

"Hmm."

"Seriously," I say.

"Okay."

There's a pause.

"And what about the wedding?"

"How long have you got?"

"Ages," says Belle.

So I tell her about a couple of places I've visited, thinking they might make good wedding venues, and about possible wedding colours (not lavender; I'm never going to fancy that ever again), and about flowers and music and a hundred other things. I'm smiling when I finish the call and I'm still smiling when I wander into the kitchen, where James is putting out plates. He's also put out a bottle of Prosecco.

"Celebrating?" I ask him.

"Yep. The first chunk of my US advance is in."

"Wow." I hop onto one of the bar stools. "So now you're a single man in possession of a good fortune, which means..."

"I must be in want of a wife, yes," he says, grinning.

We have far too much of the Prosecco considering it's the middle of the day. I have to put off my plan to go into the town and see Seonaid, because I'm in no state to drive. But as soon as I get a moment, I'm going to drop into McBryde's, look at some more fabric samples, and tell Seonaid the whole story. I reckon she'll be amazed to hear exactly *why* lavender is supposed to be so unlucky – and what that song is all about.

Lavender lady, lavender lady... she'll put ye on like a suit of clothes...

I find myself humming it around the house. It doesn't feel sinister any more. Sad, yes, but not frightening. It's true what I told Belle: it feels as though a shadow has lifted. I feel happy, and unsuspicious, and safe. Tomorrow is the solstice, the shortest day and longest night of the year; after that, the days will start to become longer and brighter. I feel as though I have been through winter. Soon, it will be spring.

Chapter Forty-One

How long have I been standing here, staring down? My head feels foggy. I think I have been here for a long time. It's like waking from a dream – there is that sense of having been thinking very hard about something, something elusive that has slipped away with the coming of consciousness.

I know this room. There is oak panelling, gleaming in the soft light of a candle. There are polished wood bookcases, full of carefully lined-up hardbacked volumes, the titles picked out in black or gold. There is a desk standing in front of the velvet-curtained windows. It is a large desk, with pigeonholes, a desk from which the entire work of the house can be organised. On it is an ebony inkstand.

I look at that inkstand for a long while, and the slow anger burns its way through my veins and sinews. I sat here once, and wrote a last will and testament with that ink, with that quill. I had it signed by my housekeeper, and the maid. Everything that I owned was left to Charles Robertson: the house, the land, the money. I kept the faith. He did not. He married someone else and now the two of them will enjoy everything that I owned in the world. That, at any rate, is what they believe. They have no idea of the anger that can build up – an anger that is so strong that it can transcend anything. Even death.

What was he doing, Charles, when I was discovered in my room, with the fire burnt down and a laudanum bottle in my lifeless hand? When they hammered the lid down and carried me to my last resting place? Was he sitting opposite *her*, laughing and smiling? The thought makes me fiery with anger – I am drunk with it. They cannot be allowed to get away with this. I will not allow it.

I take up the candlestick and turn away from the desk and the inkstand. My bare feet whisper over carpet, and then wooden boards. I go into the hallway. It is silent here, and dark. Even the servants have gone to bed, in their attic rooms far removed from here. There is no danger of them hearing me moving about. Even if they did, what would they see? I pause before a print of the house that hangs on the wall here, seeing my own reflection dimly in the glass. They would see the new mistress of the house, Mrs. Clara Robertson, in her long white nightdress, her hair down, her feet bare.

Softly, softly, I move down the hallway, towards the back of the house. The kitchen is here. I wait for a moment behind the door, listening, and when I am sure there really is no-one inside, I push it open and go in.

It is warm in here, even though it is nighttime. The servants have banked up the range. In the light of the candle flame I can see rows of gleaming copper pans hanging on the walls. In the centre of the room is a scrubbed deal table with things set out for the morning: a teapot, cups and saucers. There is a set of scales, and a row of earthenware pots. In the silence, the ticking of the kitchen clock is very loud.

I look at the pots and pans. These are not what I am

looking for. The kitchen is strange territory to me; the mistress of a house rarely has cause to come here. I open a cupboard and find myself looking at stacks of plates. No. I slide open a drawer, very carefully, not wishing to make a sound, and find rows of dinner knives and forks and spoons. I touch one of the knives, thoughtfully. Then I slide the drawer closed and move on.

The next drawer that I try is a little stiff. I pull gently, then a little harder, and it slides open with a small clash of the contents that makes me freeze and listen. The house is still and silent. I look into the drawer and see knives: long, gleaming, wickedly sharp. I put the candle down on the table and take out one of the knives. I heft it in my hand, testing the weight, the feel of the handle. It feels *good*. This is a knife that can wreak vengeance. A knife that can stab to the heart.

I do not bother to close the drawer. I take up the candle again, and creep to the door, knife in hand. I open it carefully; there is nobody outside. I make my way silently down the passage. When I get to the bottom of the stairs, I stand for a few moments and listen again. Then I put my foot on the bottom tread and shift my weight gently onto it. I have walked up and down these stairs for many years, and I know every one of them – their creaks, their groans. I mount slowly, very slowly, knowing that I cannot eliminate sound altogether, but I can prevent it from being rhythmic. I step cautiously, and wait, and then move up again. At the turn of the stairs I pause, but everything is absolutely silent.

At last I reach the top of the flight, and the hall stretches out in front of me. I know exactly which door I want. There is no light coming from inside, although it stands slightly ajar. The occupant is deeply asleep. I stand there for a moment, savouring what is to come. Then I set down the candlestick on the floor, and slip inside, the knife in my fist.

A four-poster bed stands in the middle of the room. It is mounded up with pillows and covered with layers of blankets, the top one a brocade. Amongst the pillows, Charles Robertson lies on his back, snoring like a hog. Hate and fury blast through me like a hurricane. The knife twitches in my hand, longing to sheath itself in his flesh.

I tiptoe to the side of the bed and look down at him. It is dark in the room, but the flickering light of the candle I set down by the door, and the glowing embers of the fire, show me enough. This is a face I used to love. It has grown older and fatter and coarser, and the whiskers are streaked with grey, but I would have known him anywhere. I am so angry I think I must explode with it. I lift the knife, high above my head, poising it to strike him to the heart.

And then a voice says: *Fen.*

I pause.

Wake up, Fen, it says. *Wake up.*

I know this voice. I look at Charles sprawled out in front of me, defenceless in sleep. The knife trembles in my hand.

Wake up, Fen.

It is the voice of someone I know. It is the voice of my brother, Stephen. But Stephen–

Wake up, the voice tells me, and I do.

I open my eyes and I am standing by the bed in our own room in Barr Dubh House. I am wearing my nightdress; my feet are bare. The lights are all out, but moonlight seeps through the gap in the curtains. It is enough for me to see. I am so close to the bed that my knees are touching it. In the bed, James is sleeping deeply, his breathing slow and regular. He lies on his back, confidently, exposing his chest to the world. My right hand is raised above my head, and grasped in my fist there is the longest, sharpest knife from the kitchen block.

Chapter Forty-Two

I have the presence of mind not to drop the knife. That is all. I back away from the bed, one step at a time. I am overwhelmed with the terror that I might somehow carry through the action I have started, the raising of the arm to strike – that the blade might slice down and into James's unprotected flesh. One step, two, three. I lower the knife, my whole arm and hand trembling. The shaking is a contagion; soon my entire body is flinching from what I so very nearly did. I keep backing up, until my shoulder blades touch the bedroom wall. My chest is rising and falling and my mouth opens and closes, but no sound comes out.

I cannot stay here. If I fall asleep again, what will happen? I close my eyes for an instant. The terror of it is too awful. I nearly stabbed James. I nearly *killed* him. If I fall asleep again, if Euphemia possesses me again... *She'll put ye on like a suit of clothes.* Then I know what will happen. I won't wake up in time. I – she – will kill him.

I open my eyes again and force myself to move. The door stands ajar, so I walk slowly to it, like a very old woman, a woman of a hundred years. I go outside, into the corridor, and pull the door closed behind me. Then I lean on the wall. The knife is still in my hand. I don't know what else to do with it.

After a while I get moving again. I have to. I go down the stairs, holding tight to the bannister with my free hand and wincing at every tiny sound. Then I go into the kitchen, put on the light and carefully re-insert the knife into the block. It takes me a couple of attempts; my hands are still trembling like crazy, and the point of the knife dances all over the slot. At last, though, it slides home.

There is a drying rack in the corner of the kitchen, and I help myself to clean things from that, because there is no way I am going back into the bedroom tonight. A bra and pants, a t-shirt, a pair of jeans. There are no socks but I don't care. I put the things on and leave the nightdress lying on the floor. The t-shirt is still slightly damp but I don't care about that, either. All I can think about is putting as much space as possible between myself and the thing that nearly happened.

My phone is sitting on the work surface, so I slip it into my handbag, alongside my wallet.

Keys, I think. Those are probably on the table in the hallway. I go through, and yes, that's where they are. I put on a jacket from the row of pegs in the hall, and a pair of boots. The boots feel strange without socks. Too bad. I have to go. I have to go *now.*

I go out of the front door and close it carefully behind me. The light from the hallway is abruptly cut off, but there is a moon tonight. I can see enough to get into the car. I start the engine. It sounds appallingly loud in the cold quiet night air. I move slowly down the driveway and turn out onto the lane that leads away from the house. I start driving towards the town, but after about five minutes I have to pull over because I am crying so hard that I cannot see where I am going. I sit in a muddy layby and sob my heart out.

I nearly killed James.

I keep thinking about it, about the knife raised in my fist, about James sleeping so quietly and trustingly. If I hadn't woken up, right then...

After a while I stop crying and start driving again. It is shortly after midnight and there is nobody else on the roads. When I get to the town, I see McBryde's, the front window still illuminated to show off a simple satin gown. I pause for a moment, but it is no use trying to knock on Seonaid's door. I don't even know if she lives in the flat over the shop. Instead, I turn onto the road that leads out of the town.

I drive out of the town, into the countryside, and keep going until the road eventually meets a dual carriageway and then a motorway. I am heading south, with no other thought in my head than to put as much space as possible between myself and Barr Dubh House. What else can I do? I can't imagine waking James and telling him what I almost did. I can't imagine going back to sleep in that house, not for one last night, not for one single moment.

Shortly after three in the morning, I pull into a motorway services. I don't know where I am; somewhere in the north of England, I suppose. Tiredness is rolling over me in waves; if I keep going I will fall asleep at the wheel. I lock all the doors, wrap my jacket around me and lean my head against the window.

For a while, the darkness enfolds me completely. It's utterly dreamless. Now that I am far away from Barr Dubh House, nothing can get at me. I can't sleep for long, though. An unheated car in December is not a comfortable place. Even with the jacket pulled close around me, I wake up shivering. So I get out of the car and stagger into the services in search of caffeine.

With a very large cup of tea in my hands, I start to feel more human. Outside, it is still dark. It won't get light for at least another four hours. I am miles from anyone I know. James is three hours behind me; Belle is many hours ahead. I sip the tea and try to think logically about what to do.

Barr Dubh House is dangerous to me: that's clear. Every moment I spend under its roof is a risk. But what is James going to think, when he wakes up and finds I'm not there beside him? I consider that. He will probably think, at first, that I have gone downstairs. When he goes down himself and discovers that I'm not there, he'll be surprised, and then alarmed. At some point he will look outside and find that my car has gone. What will he think then?

I should phone him. But I don't know what I will say. *I woke up and I was standing over you with a carving knife, and that's why I left?* I rub at my temple, trying to organise my thoughts. Can I tell him what I nearly did? How can I explain why I left, if I don't? Round and round go the thoughts, and I'm exhausted and don't know what to do.

I have to call him, though. Now that the first panic is over, now that I have put so many miles between me and Barr Dubh House, I have started to wonder whether my leaving was enough. Whether Euphemia's vengeful ghost will be satisfied with my flight. I do not think she will. She wants James dead, the same way she wanted Charles dead. Do I really think she has nothing left to try? Am I prepared to take the risk?

At last I think: *Just call him. Tell him something. Tell him whatever comes into your head.*

I haul out my phone. 1% charge. *Damn.* It dies in my hands while I'm looking at it. No problem. There's a payphone across the corridor from where I'm sitting. I put down my empty tea cup and go over to call James on that. I'm pretty sure his phone was on the nightstand, next to the bed. I dial, shivering a bit. The phone rings three times and then James answers it.

"Hello?" he says, his voice slurred with sleep. It's a little after 4.30 a.m., after all.

"James, it's me."

There is a long pause. "What do you mean, me?" he says.

The question throws me for an instant, but of course he's just been woken up. He's still groggy, half-asleep.

"It's me, Fen."

"Fen?"

"Yes–"

"Is this some kind of joke?" he says. "Because it's not funny, whoever you are. It's four thirty in the bloody morning."

"No, really, James. It's me, Fenella."

"The hell it is."

"James, listen. *Please*. I'm at a service station somewhere. I don't even know exactly where–"

"This is bullshit," he says, and I can tell he's about to hang up. "It's four thirty a.m. and you are one hundred per cent *not* Fenella."

"But–" I gape at the phone, before rallying. "Why not?" I say.

"Because Fenella is right here, next to me."

For a moment I am struck dumb by the horror of it. In my mind's eye I can see James, roused from sleep, half-sitting up on his side of the bed, the phone in his hand. What is lying next to him?

"James," I whisper hoarsely, "That's not me, it's not Fenella."

"Of course it is. Who is this? This isn't–"

"Look at her, James," I say. "Look at her properly."

There is a pause. He doesn't reply to me, but down the phone line I hear him say something indistinct, rousing the thing that is lying next to him. Perhaps it turns over;

perhaps it sits up in the bed, and then – then he sees it for what it really is. I cannot see what happens, only hear it. I hear a cry – a terrible, choking cry – and then the phone goes dead.

I stare at the receiver in my hand. Then I call the number again, my fingers shaking. The phone goes straight to the automated answering service. I put the receiver back on the hook and run out to the car.

Chapter Forty-Three

I am fully awake now. It doesn't matter that I've only had a few hours, broken fragments of sleep. There's a charger in the car – stupid, I should have thought of it before – so I plug my phone into that. As soon as it gets enough charge, I'll call again.

I have to force myself not to drive like a maniac. The important thing is to get there in one piece, I remind myself as I floor the accelerator. The car screams out of the services' parking area, along a service road and back onto the northbound carriageway. My heart is thudding.

Fenella is right here, next to me.

I know what was next to him, and it wasn't me. My knuckles are white on the wheel. I think of the knife-point, poised over James's heart. I think of something sitting up in bed next to him, something which has revealed itself for what it really is. I drive faster, pushing the car as hard as I dare to.

The motorway seems interminable. I stop briefly at another services for fuel and now I have enough charge, so I try calling James again, but I still can't get through. I want to scream, to cry, but I dare not waste any time. I drive on through the darkness, my face grim.

At last the motorway becomes a dual carriageaway and that becomes an A road, and I am swinging around the bends as fast as I can, haring towards Barr Dubh. It is closer to morning now and I pass a few cars going the other way, their headlights looming up out of the darkness. I get to the town and there are actually one or two people about, trudging through the wintry morning air with their heads down. They look up as I go past, driving too fast for a town centre.

The road to Barr Dubh is winding. I take the curves on the wrong side of the road and pray I won't meet anything coming the other way. It must be nearly three hours now since I spoke to James on the phone. Every second counts.

At the turning, I have to slow down a bit; the track is so full of potholes that the car would be shaken to pieces otherwise. But I keep moving, as fast as I safely can. I turn in at the gate and drive up to the gravelled area outside the house, stones flying up under my tyres. Then I kill the engine and get out of the car.

In half an hour, the sun will be up, and already it is dimly light enough for me to see the whole silent bulk of Barr Dubh House. The house is entirely dark. I left some of the downstairs lights on – I know I did. Now they are all off. For one moment, I stare at the house, my heart failing me. But I must go inside. I must know what has happened.

I unlock the door and the sound of the keys jangling is very loud in the silence.

"James?" I call out, as I step over the threshold. "James?"

There is no reply. I reach for the light switch and press it, but nothing happens. No power. The house feels cold, too. I put down the keys and my bag on the hall table.

"James!" I shout it as loudly as I can, in case he is still

asleep upstairs, *praying* he is still asleep upstairs. Then I listen, but there is absolute silence. I walk down the hallway and my footsteps sound unnaturally loud. I get to the foot of the stairs.

He is lying there, at the bottom of the flight, face down. He has a t-shirt and shorts on, sleepwear for cold nights. He must have leapt out of bed like that and run blindly in the dark. Panicking, disoriented. Desperate to get away. The top of the staircase a black pit, invisible in the dark. A precipitous fall down the whole flight. He is dreadfully, horribly still.

"James," I say, and as I go over to him and kneel on the floor, "James, James."

There is no reply. His face is turned away from me, but I can see the small pool of blood that has run from his head and congealed on the parquet floor. I am crying now and my hands are hovering over him, as though I don't know where to put them.

"Please wake up, James. Please, please."

I put my hands on his bare arm, and he is cold.

Chapter Forty-Four

I gaze at the newly-turned earth where all my hopes lie buried. The soil is dark and heavy and wet. No grass will grow here until the spring. I want to fall on the grave, screaming, crying, trying to claw my way down to James. But it is no use. However hard I scream, he cannot hear me. I turn away, my heart dead.

Back at the house, it is absolutely silent. Even the clock whose ticking normally pervades the hallway has stopped: a battery has run down, a mechanism has broken. Motes of dust hang on the air. I walk through my house, alone, grieving. But of all the things I have feared, and do fear, the return of Euphemia Alexander is not one of them. She has got what she wanted. She has taken James. He is hers.

It will be dark soon. The days are so short at this time of year. I go into the big empty kitchen and think about making food but I do nothing. I'm not hungry. I don't care if I starve. I drink some water, but even that tastes of dust and ashes.

Eventually I go upstairs, to the room James and I shared. His things are scattered around the room. I pick up a t-shirt from the floor and sit with it in my hands for a while. I think about what I did wrong.

When I woke up and found that I was standing over James with a knife, I shouldn't have run. I should have woken him too. I should have said: *Barr Dubh House is trying to kill you. We need to leave, now.* I should have overruled all his objections, about sleeping until morning and then thinking about it again. I should have made him get up and leave with me. We could have made it to that motorway services together and sat there, cradling a hot drink each, while the sun came up. The whole thing would have seemed insane when we were far away from Barr Dubh. Perhaps – evil thought – we could have persuaded ourselves that it was a mental aberration. We could have put the house back on the market and walked away, like Craig and Susan Loughty undoubtedly did.

But I didn't do that. I simply ran. I left James alone with something infinitely cold and vengeful. I left him to die.

I put down the t-shirt, and go into the bathroom. There is a ghost in the mirror, thin and haggard. I ignore it as I brush my teeth half-heartedly. When I've finished in there, I change into a nightdress. Then I climb into bed, and turn out the light. A little moonlight seeps in between the curtains as I lie there, trying to sleep.

After a long time, I hear a sound downstairs. A gentle thump. I think: *someone at the door.* But I do not think there can be anyone there, not at this time of night. Not out here, miles from the nearest town. I must have imagined it, or else it was a bird flying into a door or window. I turn over in bed, putting out a hand before remembering that there is nobody else there.

Then I hear a very definite click. I know that sound. It is the sound of the front door closing.

I think: *Did I lock it?*

I can't remember. I think I did, but things escape me in my shell of grief. I roll onto my back again and listen, staring up into the dark.

For a while there is silence. I start to think that I imagined the sound of the front door closing. Then I hear them: footsteps, slow and deliberate. I ought to spring out of bed, to grab my phone, barricade myself in the bathroom, in case it's a burglar. Instead, I lie there listening. They have come from the hallway, those footsteps, and now they have started on the slow climb up the stairs. Sometimes they pause and the seconds stretch out until I think that there will be nothing more, until there is another soft impact. The person climbing the stairs may be trying to be quiet, to go undetected. Or perhaps they are slow, lacking co-ordination.

I could not move now, even if I wanted to. I hear that soft tread on the landing. The person out there is bare-footed. The door is ajar, and for the first time I think I detect a hint of something on the air: a faintly earthy smell, like damp soil. I look towards the door, my eyes straining in the darkness. The light switch is only an arm's length away but I don't want to use it. Someone is there, just outside the door – someone slow and silent. There is no sound of breathing. They stand there, unmoving.

"James?" I say, and my voice is so hoarse, so soft that I cannot believe anyone could hear it.

Another silence and then the door creaks gently as someone pushes it open. He stands there in the doorway, another shadow in the deep darkness, and the air between us blooms with the scent of corruption. I half sit up. My throat is very dry.

I know what this means. Euphemia Alexander thought that she could claim him, that she could drag him down into death with herself. But James does not want Euphemia. He wants me. Even now, he wants *me*.

His feet move over the floorboards like a whisper. He approaches the bed, and all I can see is his silhouette. In the gloom of night it is impossible to make out his face, his features. I swallow. Then I throw back the covers on his side of the bed.

The mattress sags under his weight as he climbs in. The cold scent of earth and decay is in my nostrils. I want to say his name, but I cannot force the single word from my lips. He turns to me, slowly, a person without any human reflexes. When he touches me, his fingers, his hands, his arms are cold. So cold. He pulls me into his embrace, leaching the warmth from my live body into his freezing one. He is heavy, so heavy.

Chapter Forty-Five

I wake from the dream breathing hard, and realise that the scream was only in my mind. The world slowly coalesces about me. The cold grey light of morning is seeping through the thin curtains. Outside, I can hear traffic – engines running, the occasional irritable honk of a horn – and voices. London is already awake.

I roll onto my side and look at James sleeping. He still has a visible scar on the side of his forehead. I suppose it might fade with time. I remember finding him at the bottom of the staircase in Barr Dubh House and thinking that he was dead. He was so still and so dreadfully cold. He had been lying there for several hours in nothing but a t-shirt and shorts, while the house, devoid of power, cooled down around him. If I hadn't come back, or if I'd left it a day or two, I think he might have died of exposure. It was December, after all, and Scotland. Euphemia might have got him in the end.

But he didn't die. I called an ambulance, sobbing down the phone as I begged them to come and help us. They came and took us both away. Since that moment, I have never spent a single night under the roof of Barr Dubh House. I have never even been inside it after dark. James has recovered, although he can't remember much about the accident. He has even started working on his book again – and I have resumed working too, because now we can't afford not to.

We had to move back to London, of course. This flat was the best we could get. The windows don't fit very well. When a heavy vehicle passes, they rattle. Cold air circulates, and warmth bleeds out. It is not very much better than my old place. It's bigger, that's true, and there aren't any maniacal partygoers on the ground floor, but it's shabby, and noisy, and cold. I expect in the summer it will be too hot. This is something that has to be lived with, until something is done about Barr Dubh House, and at this moment I have no idea what that might be. It *might* be a safe place for new people to live in. Perhaps whatever game Euphemia Alexander's ghost was playing has been played out. But somehow I do not think so. I think that our beautiful dream home, with its extensive land and its very own ruined chapel, is as dangerous as a shark pool, or quicksand. The house could be pulled down and the land sold, although a lot of money would be lost if that happened. And then there are all our possessions – far too many things to fit into a tiny London flat. Too many questions – too many decisions to make.

Although I do not intend to return to Scotland, I have kept in touch with Seonaid. I asked her to do something for me: to go to the library, to look through the yellowing pages of the local newspaper for 1874 and afterwards, and see if she can find out what happened to Mrs. Robertson. I was not surprised by her reply. Clara never recovered from her "prostration with grief". She died in a lunatic asylum. To the end, she claimed that "the lavender lady" killed her

293

husband. No-one was officially tried for the murder and her words passed into local folklore.

Stephen has never spoken to me again. Sometimes, in quiet moments, I try to listen for him, but as before, there is always a space. A nothingness, where Stephen should be. I thank him, though, for saving me from something too terrible to think about, and I hope for his rest.

I think about all these things and I watch James, the way his chest rises and falls as he sleeps, the tiny movements of his lips and eyelids. I feel his warmth, the subtle shifts of his body next to mine. Our plans for the future have been derailed, but we still have each other. I put out a hand, to touch him, to know that he is really there, and then I close my eyes and driftly slowly back to sleep, which, at last, is dreamless.

Acknowledgements

This book was inspired by the part of Scotland that I and my family call home.

I would like to thank Clare Cain and Fledgling Press for publishing Fen's story, and I would also like to thank Graeme Clarke for the wonderful cover design.

Thanks are due to Clare Wallace of the Darley Anderson Agency, who represents me.

In addition, I would like to mention the staff of the A.K.Bell Library in Perth and the Strathearn Community Library in Crieff who pointed me in the right direction when I was researching this book.

A big thank you to Steve Duffy for suggesting the quotation by Sir Walter Scott which is the title of this book.

Finally, as ever, thanks to Gordon.